Sonia surveyed her bottom in the mirror. The cheeks were rosy red.

'Look what you've done to my bum,' she cried.

Bart knelt behind her and began to stroke the burning skin.

'Your hands are too rough,' she said. 'Kiss it better.'

She was surprised how horny she felt. The sweet touch of his lips and the long lick of his tongue on the hot flesh of her buttocks heightened her randiness. She'd never been spanked by a man before, had never permitted it. She knew of a woman who loved it, who said it made her feel like a bitch on heat, but Sonia had never thought it was for her.

Now she realised she'd been wrong . . .

Under the Whip

Nick Aymes

HEADLINE
DELTA

First published in 1995
by HEADLINE BOOK PUBLISHING

A HEADLINE DELTA paperback

10 9 8 7 6 5 4 3 2 1

ISBN 0 7472 4635 1

Printed and bound in Great Britain by
Cox & Wyman Ltd, Reading, Berks

HEADLINE BOOK PUBLISHING
A division of Hodder Headline PLC
338 Euston Road,
London NW1 3BH

Under the Whip

Chapter 1

The party was in full swing. The piano was tinkling the haunting melody of Hoagy Carmichael's 'The Nearness of You'. The black American pianist was good, damned good, but nobody appeared to be listening; the hubbub of background noise drowned out the music. Sonia wondered why the pianist had been engaged. All they deserved was a screaming rock group to go with the raucous laughter and high-pitched voices. She sat balanced on the arm of a chair, cradling her umpteenth glass of champagne.

It had been an exciting day. The stable had won the St Leger and they'd been celebrating ever since. It certainly wasn't every day that the stable had a Classic winner. In fact, the last had been the Derby ten years ago, which was long before Sonia's time. Winning the St Leger wasn't exactly unexpected for the horse had been the favourite and after the race they'd celebrated at the course. The owner's box had been packed full of revellers and, later, everybody had been invited to a party at his luxurious home

1

near Warminster. It had been a hair-raising drive down from Doncaster and it was a wonder that the long procession of Rolls and Mercedes hadn't been stopped by the police. The party had been well under way by the time Sonia had arrived.

She glanced at Bart, who smiled back bleary-eyed through a haze of cigar smoke. Bart trained over a hundred thoroughbreds at Collyer's End, and she'd been his assistant for the past three years. His assistant and his mistress, too, but that was another tale. Suddenly she wanted to go home.

'We should go, Bart.'

'Why? Aren't you enjoying yourself?'

'Yes, but it's late. It'll be dawn in a couple of hours.'

He grinned. 'Then I shan't bother to change. I'll ride out as I am!'

'Don't be silly. What would the stable lads think?'

'You take life too seriously, Sonia. We've had a Classic winner. That's something to celebrate. Or would you rather be celebrating in bed?'

She blushed. He was nearer the truth than he realised. 'Don't be daft,' she murmured.

He leaned forward towards her, resting one hand familiarly on her knee. 'Don't worry, I'll see to you later, you sexy little trollop!'

She knew he wouldn't. He was far too drunk. She brushed his hand away and looked around the room. *God*, she needed a fuck. It was as if somebody had fed her half a pint of Spanish fly. She crossed her legs three times in as many seconds giving anyone who cared to look a glimpse of bare thigh above her sheer nylon stocking tops.

The only person looking was Daphne the dyke and she was positively leering. Daphne managed a Stud, and fancied Sonia rotten. Sonia saw her raise a quizzical eyebrow and she smiled back. Well, why not? If she couldn't get a nice hot cock she'd have to settle for the next best thing. She stood up and walked deliberately from the room knowing Daphne would be close behind her. It was when they were alone and Daphne's hand had suggestively touched her bare skin that she suddenly wondered what the hell she was doing.

It was too late to stop now. She'd made her bed, she'd have to lie in it. Daphne opened a side door and pushed Sonia through it into a small darkened room. She felt her back jammed up against the wall as the other woman trapped her with her large soft body. Sonia wasn't, and never had been, a lesbian — though she'd had one or two experiences when she was young. She struggled to free herself, but Daphne was the bigger woman and determined to have her way.

'Let me go, Daphne. I didn't mean . . .'

'Yes, you did.'

'I didn't,' she half sobbed, 'I had no idea you'd follow me.'

She felt the woman's hands grab at her breasts and force her head back against the wall. Hot lustful breaths scorched her face and Daphne's voice growled in her ear.

'You're a fucking tease, you little tramp. You're not going to tease me.'

'I've never teased you. I don't go with women. Leave me alone.'

She struggled, wriggling her body to break free, but Daphne proved the stronger. Sonia couldn't scream. To be found with Daphne would forever brand her a dyke. She stopped struggling and let her body go limp.

'Go on then. Have your way with me.'

Daphne chuckled. She realised she'd won. 'You silly sod. You sound like a B-movie.'

'What should I have said?' she asked cynically. 'Please rape me?'

The woman's hands were cupping her face; caressing her cheeks gently, urgently.

'You're not going to be raped, little girl. I'm going to love you, love you to death.'

Her tongue slid between Sonia's lips, flickering like a serpent into her warm wet mouth. Sonia relaxed, allowing herself to be engulfed by the deep French kiss. It filled her mouth and half her throat with a searching tongue that grew more and more demanding. Finally she was overcome. Her inhibitions came tumbling down and she began to return the lascivious kiss with pressure from her own mouth. Tongue caressed tongue, each sucking the sweet moist saliva of the other as if it was the nectar from some exotic fruit. It was Daphne who broke away first: 'I'm going to undress you, darling girl,' she whispered in Sonia's ear.

Sonia felt eager fingers slip the straps of her dress from her shoulders; it peeled from her body like a second skin. Instantly, her gorgeous breasts were bared and, when they kissed again, busy female hands fondled those tender orbs while dexterous fingers pulled at her nipples, firming them to pink-tipped points. Tense with lust, Daphne pulled away from her.

'I want to look at you. I must see your body. Let me turn on the light.'

She fumbled with the switch, but Sonia grabbed her hand. 'No, no. We'll be discovered.'

'Let them find us. I don't care.'

Sonia panicked. 'They'll stop us. You'll never have me.'

Daphne buried her face between Sonia's aching breasts. 'True, my love, True.'

As Daphne licked her tits Sonia realised that she was back in control of herself. In fact, she was now controlling the whole situation. Daphne had sunk into a bog of sexual craving and was putty in her hands. She cupped Daphne's face between her hands and eased her away from her bosom.

'*Feel* me, Daphne. I want you to take down my knickers and feel me.'

'Yes, my darling. I'll fuck you with my fingers if that's what you want.'

She scarcely felt her flimsy wet panties slip down her thighs, not until Daphne was urging her to step out of them did she realise that they were around her ankles. With her back still jammed against the wall, she spread her legs. A small shiver of anticipation tickled her spine as she eagerly awaited Daphne's gentle touch upon her sensitive pussy. When it came Sonia trembled. Daphne's long fingernails rasped along the whole length of her expectant quim, bringing an intense heat to her lusting loins. Simultaneously, she felt the woman's face slide down her belly towards the jewel between her legs. But she didn't want to be sucked there, she wanted the hard touch of Daphne's fingers. She wanted to be squeezed, pinched, *sullied*. She grasped Daphne's hand and held it tight against her belly.

'No. Finger-fuck me.'

Daphne wasn't used to being instructed. She wasn't sure she liked this young bitch telling her what to do. She slid her fingers between the thick outer lips of Sonia's moist vulva and opened it up, making it bloom like some exotic flower. The fingertips of her other hand swiftly located the small shaft of her clitoris and, with the expert touch of a woman who'd masturbated all her life, she fingered Sonia's most sensitive spot until she could have whooped with joy as the juice ran out from her like honey from the comb. But Daphne wasn't finished. The thought of being dominated by Sonia rankled. No man – or woman – was allowed that privilege. A streak of cruel carnal lust bit into her as she clenched her fist and positioned it at the opening of Sonia's saturated cunt. Gently, but firmly, she thrust the fist into her. Sonia flinched, then shook.

'No! No, you're not to fist me. Take your hand out.'

'You wanted fucking. Now you're going to get it.'

'No, please, Daphne. You'll damage me.'

'Keep still, woman, and you won't be hurt.'

Sonia's fright quickly disappeared. She knew she had to relax. If she stayed tense she wouldn't enjoy it. Christ, what was she thinking of? How could she equate enjoyment with a woman's hand stuck up her fanny. She breathed regularly and deeply, relaxing her quivering vagina. She was conscious of the fist beginning to move inside her, stimulating the walls of her vaginal tunnel, but it no longer excited her. She didn't want it to. It was like submitting to an internal examination. When it was over she silently pulled down her dress.

'What's the matter, darling. Wasn't my fist big enough for you?' drawled Daphne sarcastically.

She left without a word.

'Goodbye, darling,' Daphne called after her. 'Next time remind me to bring a bull's prick for you!'

Although she'd never have passed a breathalyser test, Sonia felt sober when she drove back to Collyer's End. Bart urged her to put her foot down but she drove slowly and carefully. The last thing she wanted was a drunk-drive charge. She thought about the three years she'd been with Bart. There was no doubt he was a first-class trainer and she'd learnt a great deal at his yard. Now she was ready to branch out on her own. All she needed was the cash, but that was easier said than done.

Most people would have thought that Sonia had no need of money with her sort of beauty. The gods had certainly been kind when they moulded her. Her body was perfectly shaped and her face as sweet and angelic as a novice nun's. Her magnificent mane of thick chestnut-coloured hair dazzled men and women alike and the rich colour was complimented by the sparkling green of her ever-dancing eyes.

When she was young her father, whom she adored, had affectionately called her his little Rita Hayworth and she'd watched all of the great star's films, wishing she could dance as gracefully. But her first love had always been horses. Her mother was a show-jumper who, before she'd married, had been a promising eventer. Thus Sonia had been brought up amongst horses and had had her own pony at five. Her mother had hoped she would follow in her footsteps but Sonia had been bitten by the racing bug early in her life. She and her cousin used to sneak off to Thirsk racecourse at every opportunity and, as they grew older, ventured further afield, to York, Wetherby and Ripon.

All that had finished when her parents were killed in a car crash. She was fifteen at the time and her grandfather had packed her off to boarding school.

Although it was a girls' school it was there that she learnt about sex and how easily she could manipulate men. Ever since, she'd never hesitated to use her body to obtain what she wanted. When she was eighteen she was swept off her feet by an older man, not so much by the man as by his lifestyle. A month before her nineteenth birthday she'd married him, and at that tender age became the step-mother of his two young daughters. The marriage had lasted three years, which was long enough to give her the taste for the good life and a disdain for her husband. Thus she was glad when he begged for a divorce so he could marry a member of the aristocracy. She naïvely agreed to be the guilty party, demanded nothing from him and left the country.

In the USA she returned to her first love by getting a job as a stablegirl in California. There she worked quite happily until Immigration caught up with her and she was deported back to Britain. By now racing was her life so she went to France to work in a stable in Chantilly. It was there she met Bart. She'd been leading a horse around the parade ring at Longchamp, dressed in a close-fitting waistcoat and skin-tight jeans when he first saw her. Not since he'd been a boy had a fully dressed woman given him such an obvious erection, and in public. As he stood watching her he knew he had to have her. During the meeting he'd wangled an invitation from her guv'nor to visit his yard. There he managed to corner her. He was surprised to learn she was British, and a well-educated young woman. The fact that she'd been brought up with horses, and had spent the last three years working in racing stables, enabled him to offer her a job as his assistant. Sonia jumped at the offer, even when she was told there were strings. Bart was a bachelor and she had to agree to be his live-in mistress if she wanted the post of assistant trainer.

That was three years ago, Sonia hadn't regretted a second of it. Bart had played fair, giving her her own flat in the huge house at Collyer's End, and had taught her all he knew about training racehorses. In return she'd granted him every conceivable kind of sexual favour and made him the envy of the racing set. As they approached the yard he awoke with a start. She was silhouetted in the driving seat against the backdrop of moonlight. For the hundredth time he thought how beautiful she was. His friends had advised him over and over again to marry her before she flew away, but he couldn't face marriage. It was too permanent. Besides, he didn't love her. She just wasn't the sort of woman you loved, more the type you climbed into bed with at every opportunity. He began to feel randy and surreptitiously slipped his hand beneath her short skirt. She didn't push him away. She never did. She tolerated her thigh being squeezed and fondled until she pulled up the car and climbed out. He got out unsteadily and followed her into the house. The yard was silent, the horses safely stabled for the night.

'Coming to bed, Sonia?'

'It's nearly four o'clock.'

'Never mind that.'

'Work starts in two hours. You've got the first lot to supervise.'

'I'll be there, you see.'

And he would. Sonia had seen him in worse states and he'd always been up in the morning.

'It's been a lovely day,' he wheedled, 'don't spoil it.'

'I'm not spoiling anything. I'm just going to my own bed to sleep.'

He grabbed her hand. 'Come on, Sonia. I'm horny.'

'You're drunk.'

'Okay, so I've had a couple, but I could still screw your arse off.'

She chuckled. 'You couldn't screw the top off a sauce bottle!'

He stood swaying unsteadily at the foot of the stairs. 'Try me.'

'You forget, I've tried you before in this condition.'

'You're frigid. *That's* what's wrong with you.'

She laughed. 'I need my beauty sleep.'

He clutched at one last straw. 'We can sleep in. I'll leave a note telling Barney to take out the first lot.'

She was silent. She'd been waiting for the opportunity to get out on the gallops without him. This could be the time.

'All right, you win.'

He grinned. 'You're a sport, Sonia. Always good for a roll in the hay.'

She grinned. 'Go on up. I'll write the note.'

She left him to stagger up the stairs, but had no intention of leaving any note. She would take first lot herself and that would give her the opportunity to make the first move in the scheme she'd formulated. Her burning ambition was to be a trainer in her own right. She hoped this was the first step in that direction.

She undressed and washed in the big bathroom adjoining Bart's bedroom. Through the open doorway she could see him sitting on the edge of the bed, struggling to get his trousers off. She grinned. She had to make certain the bastard slept soundly until well into the morning. She'd make sure he did, even if it meant shagging his balls off. She took a small bottle of scented oil from a cabinet and, spreading her legs, smoothed a few drops into her firm thighs. He was a sucker for perfume. She smiled. Perhaps if she sat on his face it would act like an anaesthetic. When she finally walked from the bathroom he was naked and stretched out on his back on the bed. As she padded silently across the thick carpet towards him, she saw his eyes were shut. With a bit of luck he might already be in a drunken sleep.

'Do I smell some exotic perfume of an Arabian brothel?'

'No, you don't,' she replied indignantly. 'It's Chanel!'

'Well, whatever, it's sexy.'

She climbed onto the bed and knelt over him, her

legs either side of his face. Immediately, his hands came up to grab the well-rounded cheeks of her bum. She quickly lowered herself onto him, supporting her body with her forearms, one either side of his thighs. She was now crouched over him in the classic soixante-neuf position, and could hear his deep breathing as he drank in the heady perfume between her legs. It aroused him and he pulled her down roughly onto his mouth and began to eat her out voraciously. Soon her groin was sticky with saliva and quim juice, and as he ate her so the syrupy wetness spread through her mat of curly hairs until her bush was soaking. His tongue slid along the fleshy folds of her streaming labia before dipping into the gluey hole of her cunt. He repeated that time and time again, and each time his searching tongue seemed to go deeper and deeper inside her. When he'd stimulated her ripe honey pot to the point where she was continuously leaking nectar, he began to suck her. His mouth covered her hot, slippery crack and as if to suck her dry. She groaned. What she'd thought would be a quick fuck was turning into a sex marathon. Drunk or not, he was loving her rosebud as if they were honeymooners.

She'd been happily bathing in his cunnilingus for what seemed hours when suddenly a small tingle of excitement began to run the length of her spine. It signalled her build up to orgasm. She began to feel deliriously randy. She opened her eyes to see his cock still lying half-limp on his belly. It didn't surprise her when she thought of the alcohol he'd consumed. What did surprise her was the voracity with which he worked between her thighs. Was he enflamed by the perfume and the taste of her cunt? Or was he just showing her he hadn't taken her to bed for nothing? She caressed his slumbering pego, fondling it between her fingers until a sign of life began to pulse through the heavy shaft. Swiftly her mouth swooped down to swallow his genitals into her warm wet orifice. Her red lips ringed the swelling shaft insistently, sucking it until he was as stiff as a poker. Then she sank down even further onto him until the blunt tip of that rampant weapon was nudging the back of her throat. She heard him gasp aloud as she licked and pulled with her soft wet lips until his throbbing organ was swollen and fully tumescent.

'Sonia, please. Fuck me,' he gasped, 'take me inside you.'

She quickly altered her position by swinging her legs high over his thighs. His words had triggered a need in her – she wanted to have him fill her. She was facing him now as she sat astride his loins; an Amazon ready for battle. His hands came up to grasp her swinging tits, and her nipples swelled to the size of plum stones at the touch of his rough fingers. She raised her buttocks until her cunt hovered above his upstanding pole, like some big wet fig. The swollen lips of her saturated pussy hung open, and she was certain she must be dripping her juices onto him, making him as wet as her. With mounting excitement she positioned herself for entry and with one long low groan impaled her body on his thick penis.

'Is this what you wanted of me?'

He grunted.

'To be swallowed up inside my body?'

He pinched her nipples in reply and she plunged herself down upon him yet further.

'Now I'm going to fuck you silly,' she whispered.

She commenced working above him; allowing his big shaft to go in and out of her like a great piston. Tension gripped her belly, and an extraordinary sensation of tingling pain swept through her loins as she was carried away on the tide of her orgasm. She squealed. The spasms juddered through her as she grasped his quivering prong tight in the velvet glove of her vagina, screaming as she climaxed. And as she quietly moaned in its aftermath she realised that he was still stiff within her – because of the alcohol he was still far from ejaculation. She began to work herself towards a second orgasm, the insides of her thighs lubricated with her own cream, sliding up and down his pole like a well-oiled piston ring. Soon she felt the pleasure stir and build within her again as she rose above him to ride his hot cock like a rodeo cowgirl. She clicked her head from side to side, moaning quietly, as she exhorted herself to another climax.

The stiff pole of his organ jabbed her gaping hole

as, consumed with lust, she spasmed with sudden convulsive jerks to a second magnificent orgasm, losing herself in a blur of pain and pleasure. When it had passed, and she was quiet again, his prick was *still* hard within her.

She looked down at him. His eyes were closed. She wondered whether he was asleep, in a drunken stupor, perhaps. She was conscious of a shiver of lust seeping through her tired loins as she realised she could treat herself to yet another orgasm on that unyielding prick. He was like a human dildo on which she could satisfy herself. She began to move her arse. She wondered how long it would be before the alcohol wore off. Would he finally ejaculate, or turn to jelly inside her? It would be enjoyable finding out. . .

A few hours later, Sonia lay half dozing in her own bed, her body pleasurably tired, thinking of her plan to become a trainer. She had listened to Bart snoring for some time before leaving him. It would be hours before he woke. She liked the man and she didn't want to hurt him, but she had to achieve her ambition.

She heard footsteps in the yard below as the head lad arrived to start the day's work. It was five-thirty. She tumbled out of bed and pulled on her jodhpurs and sweater. By six o'clock the yard was fully awake and bustling with activity. She could hear the horses moving in their boxes and the impatient chuckling sounds as they waited for their first feed. The lads were mucking out and watering the horses which weren't going out on first lot. Those going up to the gallops were being tacked up ready for their exercise. By the time she made her appearance the string was winding its way out of the stables in the early morning light on their way to the gallops. The lass holding her hack smiled at her.

'Morning, Mrs Beechly.'

'Morning, Betty. How's the horse?'

'Fine. He'll be fit to race again soon.'

The girl gave her a leg up and she slid into the saddle.

'Let's hope so. It's a long time since he earned his corn.'

The horse she rode was a six-year-old gelding which had broken down two years ago. Up till then it had had quite a successful racing career. Man Samson had been originally purchased as a yearling by Bart for a syndicate which had since wound up. Bart liked the horse and had bought it himself to sell on, but it had broken down and had been left on his hands. The vet had been over-optimistic saying it would race again the next season, but two years had passed and it still hadn't seen a racecourse. Recently Sonia had been using it for a hack, but there were signs of the horse returning to fitness.

A thin drizzle made the cool autumn morning miserable and the gallops were shrouded in a light mist. The riders sat hunched in their saddles wearing a colourful variety of clothing and cursing the rain which drove into their faces and made the leather reins slippery in their hands. It was a work day and, after they'd all trotted and cantered, Sonia divided them into pairs to gallop distances between three and six furlongs. The pairs competed against each other so the trainer could assess one against the other. It was a hit-and-miss business. A uniform pacemaker would be worth a fortune to a trainer but life wasn't as easy as that. She watched the pairs thunder up the gallops; the noise of the hoofs and the heavy breathing echoing over the quiet country-side. She watched the clouds of steam billow from their nostrils and the sweat flick from their muscled bodies. It never ceased to move her. She loved early mornings on the gallops.

There were only two work mornings in a week when the horses galloped. The rest of the time was spent at gentle exercise. Racehorses couldn't be overworked; many a race had been lost on the gal-lops. This morning she'd been desperate to supervise first lot because she wanted to gallop Man Samson against another horse. Recently the gelding had given her the feel that he was nearly ready to race again, and last week Bart had given him a pipe-opener over four furlongs. It was then that Sonia had been certain he was on the way back. Man Samson had felt alive under her like a powerful machine ready to take off. She'd said nothing to Bart, for the seeds of her plan were beginning to germinate. Today she wanted to test her theory. The horses who had already galloped were quietly cropping grass, their riders holding them on a long rein. Horses and riders looked relaxed, but it could be a dangerous time. Should a horse spook, the lad would have little control, and catching a loose horse was a bastard of a job.

Sonia chose a good handicapper to work against. Barney, one of the three head lads, was on board. He didn't usually ride out, but the horse's lass was injured.

'Come on, Barney. We'll go over five.'

He looked a bit surprised. 'Okay, Mrs Beechly.'

He kicked his mount forward, and Man Samson didn't take any urging to follow. He was ready, even eager, to race. When Barney's mount shot forward he followed without a pause. For four furlongs Sonia kept him tucked in behind. The pace they were going at was exhilarating. Sonia was no race rider: she'd never ridden on a proper racecourse under rules. The powerful horse snorted and stretched under her as she crouched forward over its neck. The rain, quite persistent now, drove into her face and she was glad of the gloves she wore to stop her reins slipping. The feeling of travelling at over 30 mph was one that never failed to excite her, or frighten her. She knew she'd never make a good jockey. They were cool, with nerves of steel. However, she knew enough about race riding to be aware that Man Samson was going easily under her. He was racing well within himself as she eased him out to take on Barney. Immediately the gelding saw daylight he wanted to race. Sonia could feel him impatiently pulling away beneath her. She daren't let him go. She knew he'd fly past Barney like a scalded cat and she'd have a hell of a time pulling him up. The horse tugged itself to the leader's withers as Sonia let him inch up until they were neck and neck, but Barney could see she was still holding him tightly. They pulled up snorting and panting.

Barney looked angry. 'What was all that?'

'All what?'

'You know what I mean.'

'I've no idea, Barney. What do you mean?'

'You could have pulled away whenever you liked.'

'But I didn't, did I?'

'You were holding him hard.'

She laughed half-heartedly. 'Of course I wasn't.'

'God, woman,' he exploded, 'I know when a horse is being pulled.'

'Don't talk to me like that, Barney,' she said sharply.

It didn't put him off. 'Then tell me why?'

She urged Man Samson to join the rest of the string. 'Not now. I'll speak to you later.'

She instructed first lot to return to the yard where they'd be cleaned down, fed and watered. It had stopped raining, but both horses and riders looked wet, bedraggled and muddy. Sonia could see Barney was still restless as he fell in beside her at the rear of the string.

She decided she'd have to let him in on her plan. She needed somebody else from the stables so it might as well be him. He was a reliable man of about fifty who'd spent a lifetime around horses. A rough and ready type, he was known for his quick temper and his fairness. All the stable lads and lasses respected him. He was tops at his job, and seemed to know everything about thoroughbreds without ever being bigheaded. He liked a pint and was generous to a fault. However, he wouldn't tolerate slack or slipshod work, and was quick to jump on miscreants. It was widely known he'd box a stableboy's ear, or slap a girl's backside, at the drop of a hat. None had ever complained. A stocky nine and a half stone, he'd been the stableboys' boxing champion many years ago, and had even turned pro for a few fights before he began to miss life with his beloved horses.

'You're right, Barney. Man Samson could have pulled right away quite easily.'

'Why didn't you let him?'

'I didn't want to give him his head.'

'You'll teach him bad habits. Racehorses are made to race.'

'I know, but I had to prove something.'

'That the horse is coming back?'

'Yes.'

'You're up to something, aren't you?'

'What would I be up to?'

'Mrs Beechly, please. I've been in racing a long time.'

She hesitated. 'Okay, I'm planning something.'

'A coup?'

'If you like.'

He grinned. 'I do like. Am I in?'

'You may not like it.'

'Lady, I'm a sucker for 'em,' he grinned enthusiastically, 'an' I've been involved in a few in my time.'

'How many have been pulled off successfully?'

He chuckled. 'One or two!'

She paused. 'I need this to be a big one.'

'Does the guv'nor know?'

'No.'

'That makes it dicey.'

'I want to win enough to set up my own stables.'

He looked at her steadily without speaking.

'I need money for that,' she continued, 'and this is the only way I'll get enough.'

'Okay, but if we pull it off I want to be your head lad.'

She knew Barney had never held that post. He'd been a head lad in a big stable where there were more than one, but never the top dog. Trainers fought shy of him because of his straightforward manner and quick temper. They liked someone between him and them. Someone senior to him to screen them from his strong personality. But Sonia thought she'd be able to handle him and, anyway, she needed him.

'You're on, Barney.'

He grinned. 'Right, my lady. When's the big gamble on Man Samson?'

'You guessed?'

'What other reason would you have for trying to hide that he's back to fitness and ready to race?'

They clattered back into the yard where most of the string were already unsaddled.

'Give it some thought, Barney. We'll talk later.'

Man Samson had won twice as a two-year-old, and at three had developed into a decent handicapper. He won twice over a mile at Salisbury and Bath, but it was when he was stepped up to ten furlongs that he excelled. He won two 0–100 handicaps at Kempton and Newmarket before getting up in a hot 0–115 race at York. It was after that the handicapper caught up with him, and the weights he was allotted for the remainder of the season made it impossible for him to win again. Bart gave him a chance in a Listed race where he finished third to several good animals. Then the following season he ran twice humping a big weight before he broke down.

Now he was back in training it was a great chance to grab a small race before the bookies realised he was a danger. Bart's plan was to bring him back slowly, to race him a couple of times before having a punt at a big 'un. Sonia had other ideas. She wanted to win with him first time out when there was a chance of getting a good price. But for that to happen she first had to find a race that he was sure to win, and she had to persuade the bookies that the horse wasn't really in with a chance.

Sonia arranged to meet Barney later in the saloon
bar of the Dog and Duck, a pub in a neighbouring
village not frequented by racing folk. She found him
sitting by the bar chatting up a buxom barmaid who
looked big enough to suffocate him. She was surprised at his smart appearance for he was dressed in
tweed jacket and cords like some huntin' an' shootin'
type. She'd never seen him out of riding breeches
and wished she'd put on a skirt instead of her old
jeans. He greeted her familiarly.

'Hello, Sonia. What are you drinking?'

'Gin and tonic, please.'

She sat at a small window table and he joined her.
He stank of beer so she guessed he'd been there some
time. She knew he didn't have a car so his old bike
would be thrown down somewhere nearby.

'Have you given my plan any thought, Barney?'

'I have that, my lady. I have that.'

'Tell me what you think. Then we can discuss it.'

'We have to find a race he can win and get him
entered. You'll have to do that.'

'I think I can find a race he can win, but getting
him entered may be difficult. The guv'nor does that
himself.'

'After that you'll have to persuade the guv'nor to
actually run him.'

She sighed. 'I know. It certainly won't be easy.
Bart's got his own ideas where and when his horses
run. You know that, Barney.'

'I do, Miss. But we can't make a killing unless the
horse runs, so it's up to you.'

'I know.'

They ceased their conversation when a couple of men entered. For a moment they feared they were racehorse owners, but they began to talk golf.

'The second thing, Miss, is to get the horse cherry ripe without anybody knowing, and finally we have to make certain the bookies don't smell out he's there to win.'

'A few more gallops will see him sharp enough,' Sonia mused 'but promising gallops are seen by the lads and watched by touts. Information like that will soon be transported onto the bookies' grapevine.'

'Not if we slow the horse down.'

'How?'

'We'll make sure I'm on him, and I'll weigh my waistcoat down with lead.'

'Great idea,' she agreed, 'two stone of lead will slow him down!'

'He won't beat his galloping companion with two stone overweight and those watching will never suspect his improvement.'

'Okay, now say we've got him entered in the right race what do we have to look at on the course?'

'Ideally we need two stable runners in the same race with our retained jock on the other horse. It would also help if the guv'nor wasn't at the races.'

'Why?'

'The bookies will take his absence as a sign that he isn't expecting too much from his runners.'

'They'll know Man Samson's past form. It's there for all to see.'

'Maybe, but he'll be having his first race for two years and he'll look like the stable second string. With the trainer absent, it will appear that there's no real stable interest in the race.'

'You make it all sound so simple. Here, let me buy you another beer.'

She ordered their drinks. The men around the bar all eyed her up, probably wondering what such a high-class woman was doing with the beat-up, pug-ugly little guy. When she'd plonked down the drinks Barney looked at her seriously.

'If we pull this off, you agree to employ me as your head lad with complete authority under you. Is that correct?'

'Yes, we agreed that. You'll make a good head lad.'

'I have another condition.'

She looked at him sharply. 'What's that?'

'The coup may not come off.'

'That's possible.'

'I'll be left with nothing and might even lose my job.'

She looked dubious. 'I suppose that's possible, too.'

'So I want something up front.'

'What?'

He stared her straight in the eye. 'Your arse, m'lady!' he murmured.

If she was shocked she didn't show it. She remained silent for a long moment. She'd heard he was a randy sod, but this was a bit over the top. Yet she couldn't suppress a little smile.

'You've got a nerve,' she said coldly.

'I know.'

'If I agree it will be a one-off. It certainly won't become a habit.'

'I wasn't expecting . . .'

She interrupted him. 'That's just as well.'

He grinned insolently. 'I've fancied you ever since you came to the yard.'

'And that makes it okay, does it?'

'All's fair in love and war!'

They left after another drink and he threw his old bike in the back of her hatchback when she offered to give him a lift home. It was a chilly night, but a full moon in a cloudless sky made it appear nearly daylight. The rain earlier in the day had blown over, but the last of it hung around in puddles by the sides of the narrow country lane.

'Don't mind me asking, but have you sufficient cash to stake a big win?'

'I hope to beg, borrow or steal enough, but a lot depends on the odds.'

'You should get 10–1.'

'Think so?'

'If Man Samson is definitely seen as the stable second string you may get more.'

'Let's hope so.'

As she drove she could feel him staring at her. She knew he wanted her. That look was packed full of desire for her body. The thought that she was his for the asking probably excited him beyond belief. She knew it wouldn't be long before he demanded his part of the bargain.

'You can stop here. I can cycle the rest of the way. We don't want any tongues wagging.'

She pulled up by the verge and sprung the boot for him to remove his bike. He bounced it out unceremoniously and let it freewheel into the nearest tree. She smiled and was about to pull down the hatch when she felt her hand grabbed. The man couldn't wait to get into her knickers. He urged her forward so that she was bent double with her head and shoulders inside the back of the car. She fell forward onto the palms of her hands and there she balanced with her feet planted firmly on the grass behind the car and her behind jutting out provocatively. His hands stroked her curved haunches above the blue denim of her jeans as his fingers deftly explored her waistband gently urging the fly-zip apart.

Her long red hair cascaded to the floor of the hatch and hid her eyes. She brushed it aside as she felt him struggling to jerk her tightly fitting jeans down over her ample hips. She smiled as he tugged at the tight material until he finally managed to work them over her rounded arse and they slipped down her long legs to her ankles. He didn't attempt to take them off so she planted her feet as far apart as the rumpled jeans would allow. The night air made her realise that her brief white knickers had slipped down inside them: her buttocks were quite bare. By peering under her body she could see him, impatiently zipping down his fly and taking out his penis inch by inch. Then, as if he'd just thought of it, he jerked down his cords before rubbing his party-sized prick between the cheeks of her bum. She was conscious of a spasm of pleasure as he stood for an intense moment with his smooth pego resting silently against the fleshy folds of her quim. After what seemed like an age he began to rub the monster between her thighs so that the blunt helmet buried itself in the soft nest of her curly muff.

Her shoulders heaved as she sighed softly. It appeared to spur him into action. He fell to his knees behind her, insinuating two, then three, fingers into her vagina; and she was soon soaking in her own juices. He patiently parted her cunt lips and began to suck at her clitoris, relishing her sweetness like some rare delicacy. She revelled in the erotic thrill of his lips as his tongue slithered over her open vulva while he sucked her.

Finally, when she was hot and ready to be entered, he stood up behind her. She braced her knees for penetration: and as his cock thrust into her slippery tunnel of love so she came to realise just how thick he was. His tool wasn't very long, but the circumference was enormous. It was like being plugged with a short fat pipe and she was consumed with a deep lust. She could feel the urgent passion that rose in his groin, and she commenced to writhe her arse so violently that he was forced to grab her hips to stay within her. When she orgasmed it was with a sudden convulsive jerk. Afterwards he stayed patiently within her until her breathing quietened. It was then, when she thought it was all over, that he crudely buggered her.

She was completely taken by surprise as he withdrew his saturated member from her steaming hot twat and plunged it, without warning, into her tight, puckered anus. Her high-pitched squeal rent the silence of the night, echoing like the screech of some great bird.

'Christ, man,' she gasped, 'you certainly want your pound of flesh.'

'I told you I wanted your arse.'

She winced. 'I didn't think you meant it literally!'

He thrust into her. 'Well, now you know.'

'My God, I do. I do.'

Because she hadn't expected to be sodomised, and because there was no warning of her impending fate, her sphincter had been nice and relaxed. Thus his unexpected invasion had met with no resistance. His thick wedge slowly and surely infiltrated her rectum until she was well and truly corked. She groaned a long low animal-like moan and, with a convulsive shake of her head, bent her knees and pushed back onto him. Aroused by her response, he began shafting her anal passage, stretching it with long slow thrusts until, allowing his passion full reign, he ejaculated violently into her most intimate depths.

'Jesus, I've never ridden such a filly,' he gasped.

'Nor will you again!'

'Don't tell me you didn't enjoy it, m'lady.'

She pulled her knickers up her legs and wriggled her wet bum into them. Her jeans were still around her ankles.

'No, I won't say that. I'm an honest woman. I hope you are a trustworthy man.'

He smiled. 'You'll find I am, Mrs Beechly, boss-lady.'

The clock was striking 11 pm when Sonia put her key in the front door, although it seemed to her that she'd been out screwing half the night. Bart was waiting for her.

'Is that you, Sonia?'

'Who else.'

He came out into the corridor. 'Fancy a drink?'

'No, thanks. I'm dead tired.'

'I've been looking for you everywhere.'

'Anything special?'

'About that gelding you've been using for a hack.'

'Man Samson?'

'Yes.'

'What about him?'

'We had a meeting about future entries.'

She looked anxious. 'I'm sorry I missed it. Anything I should know?'

'I've entered the gelding in two races. We'll choose where to run him nearer the date.'

'What sort of races?'

She held her breath for his reply.

'Both 0–100 handicaps. I don't want him carrying too much weight for his comeback race. It will only be a warm up.'

She cursed under her breath. The gelding would never be a certainty in that class, however fit he was. She'd wanted one of poorer quality.

'Wouldn't a lesser race at a small track have been better?'

'No, I want a true run race to bring him to his peak.'

'Okay, you're the boss. Goodnight.'

She set her alarm for 3 am, and when it rang crept silently down the stairs to the office. Spread out on the desk was the paperwork they'd used for the entries. She shuffled through it looking for the pencilled notes she knew so well. Somewhere Bart would have left a sheet with a list of entries to fax to Wetherbys. She found the pencilled notes on top of the cabinet. Six races had been outlined under the name of Man Samson, and red ink ticks had been marked by two of them. She knew this meant that Tom, his entry clerk, had selected six possible races and that Bart had chosen two for definite entry. When his secretary arrived in the morning she'd fax the names of the horses and the races ticked to the Entries section at Wetherbys.

Sonia scribbled down the names of the four races Bart had rejected and settled down with the fixture lists. After going through all the details and conditions of the races she found one of them was ideal for her purpose. It was a 0–90 handicap at Sandown on the same card as one of the races Bart had selected. Man Samson would carry more weight, but the conditions were perfect to give him a great chance of winning. She found the red ink pen Bart had used and put a tick beside the race on the entries sheet. Now she'd done her part of the job. The next bit was up to Barney.

Chapter 2

Two young women tumbled through the impressive front gates of The Dame Edna Wallis Academy for Young Ladies. Both were giggling and out of breath having run past the trees which bordered the vast ornamental lawns. Dressed in tight leather skirts and jackets they looked more like rock and rollers than pupils of a finishing school. Hidden around the corner in a leafy lane was a powerful Japanese sports car which roared into life when the driver spotted them. It stopped just long enough for them to swing open the door and tumble inside. The driver was a young man impatiently dragging on a cigarette.

'You're late. I nearly went without you.'

'Sorry. It was difficult getting away.'

'You said it'd be simple,' he snapped.

'Keep your hair on. We're here now.'

'I'll have to put my foot down.'

'Where are we going?'

'You'll see.'

They were the last to arrive at the isolated house on the coast road between Girvan and Ayr. A crowd was assembled in the big entrance hallway and the air was full of high-pitched banter. A tall, languid young man, who exuded aristocratic poise, beckoned them all to silence.

'Okay, boys and girls. We're all here now, so we'll make a start.'

The two girls glanced at the crowd around them. They were all young people. Young, but not adolescent. Jilly, the prettier of the pair, thought the average age of the men would be about twenty-four and the women about twenty. She was just under nineteen herself and a peach of a girl. Her straight honey-blonde hair hung to the middle of her back and her twinkling blue eyes were so innocent that the most cynical old roué would have believed her if she had said she was a virgin. Jilly certainly wasn't anything of the sort. She'd discovered sex when she was fifteen, and had blossomed on it. Afterwards, her body had grown even more softly rounded and feminine until, at eighteen, she could have won any beauty contest she'd cared to enter. However, Jilly's zest for life was way beyond beauty contests. Bunty, her friend, was a quieter, more serious girl who followed Jilly slavishly and landed herself in trouble because of it. She was pretty enough in her own way, but Jilly was beautiful.

'For the benefit of any of you girls who are new here,' continued the spokesman, 'we welcome you to the Jollity Club.'

Jilly looked round. She counted a dozen men, each with a partner. The men were all of a type, public school, hooray-Henrys. The girls were a mixture. Several Sloanes looking suitably bored, a few college students, one or two office girls and a couple of blatant harlots.

'Today is our second anniversary and we are here to celebrate it. Tonight we meet at the Blue Dolphin country restaurant to dine, and return here afterwards to party. This afternoon we go our separate ways to shock the good citizens of Ayrshire.'

Jilly cocked up her ears. That sounded like fun. She was a great one for a giggle and most of her giggles landed her in trouble.

'You will pair off and take a card from the silver platter as you go into the drawing room. On it you'll find your instructions for this afternoon. You'll honour them to the letter.'

Jilly found that her partner was the young man who'd met her and Bunty at the front gates. She knew his name was Paul, that he shagged like a rattlesnake – but little else. She'd met him at Lady Angela's twenty-first birthday party during a game of sardines and he'd had her knickers down almost before she'd closed the wardrobe door. She watched him select a card at random while a smile curled the corners of his mouth.

'Come on,' she urged impatiently, 'what does it say? What have we got to do?'

'Go to Ayr races.'

She laughed. 'Hey, that sounds fun!'

'Certainly does. I like a bit of a gamble on the gee-gees.'

'What's the catch?'

He grinned sheepishly. 'It's how we have to dress.'

'Go on. Tell me the worst.'

'I go as Colonel Blimp and you as Lady Godiva!'

'Pull the other one. I can't go parading about naked. They'd toss me in jail.'

'Seriously, I have to wear the military uniform they've laid out and apparently there's a dress for you, too.'

'What sort of dress?'

'It doesn't say. What it does say is that you aren't allowed to wear any knickers!'

'What! You're joshin' again.'

'I'm not.'

'Cripes,' she chuckled, 'I hope it's a long dress!'

The uniform was like a music-hall soldier's, and the dress was a mini. She changed her favourite leather gear for the flimsy silk floral thing which flared from the waist and was so short that when she leant forward her bum cheeks showed. She swivelled before the mirror and the light flimsy skirt circled her waist to display her all to the world and his wife.

'Great heaven,' she groaned, 'I'll catch my death of cold.'

'You'll catch every bloke's eye on the racecourse!'

She looked at him. 'And you look as if you've just come out of a Christmas cracker.'

The uniform was beautifully cut, but it was the

array of medals and braid which would catch the eye of non-military men, and prompt the questions of military men.

She grinned. 'What regiment are you supposed to be?'

'Lord knows.'

'What are you going to tell them when you're asked?'

'I'm hoping they'll all be too busy eyeing your bare arse to bother about me!'

She hit him playfully. 'Bastard!'

A light wind blew across Ayr racecourse. A wind naughty enough to tease a young lady's skirt until it billowed around her thighs, giving glimpses of those feminine charms which should be hidden. Jilly found she was soon gathering a following of young gallants who raised quizzical eyebrows at her very obvious lack of underwear. And louts who nudged each other and jeered at the slut with no knickers. Paul had forced her to climb to the top of the grandstand and she'd been ever-conscious of that monstrous regiment of young men gazing up her skirt. Her initial embarrassment soon faded to be replaced by a kind of inner excitement that only a born exhibitionist can know. The more men peered up her skirt, the more excited she became until she was tempted to part her legs wide in a blatant show of vulgarity.

Paul's troubles were different, and he soon tired of

the snide remarks and glib repartee. He'd gone into Tattersalls rather than the Member's enclosure to avoid the number of ex-officers who he knew would be lurking there. However, he realised he'd have to chance that as the hostility of young drunks was getting to him. On transfer to the Members, Jilly tried to avoid flashing all she had to the much staider audience. She succeeded by keeping a hand on her skirt and a eye on the wind, but Paul's troubles continued.

'What the hell are you supposed to be?' growled an irritable old gent sporting a military tie.

'Indian army, sir,' he replied glibly. 'Thirty-first Bengal Lancers.'

'Bengal Lancers, my arse,' thundered the old boy, 'I served beside the Lancers in Thirty-three. You're impersonating an officer. God, I've a good mind to call the police.'

'Sorry, sir. It's only a joke.'

'Joke? Joke, man? Do you realise what medal ribbons you're wearing?'

'No, sir, No idea.'

'The Victoria cross and the Military cross to start with. Bit of a slur on the chaps who won 'em, don't you think?'

'Yes, sir. I'm sorry, sir.'

He grabbed Jilly's arm, and they beat a quick retreat before the gathering crowd could lynch them.

'My God, I'd rather be wearing a kilt with nothing underneath.'

She chuckled. 'Trying to steal my thunder, are you?'

They walked towards the paddock and watched the horses just leaving for the third race. The crowd was beginning to move away from the parade ring back to the stands. Inside the ring was a figure who looked familiar.

'I'm going back to the car. I know it's cheating, but I've had enough,' grunted Paul.

Jilly stood mesmerised, staring at the woman in the ring.

'Okay,' she muttered. 'I'll meet you in the park.'

She walked forward as if in a dream, still unsure if the woman was who she thought she was. The eye-catching red hair and long slender legs had triggered her memory, but it wasn't until she turned that Jilly was certain. She ran forward blindly, breaking into a canter as the woman began to move away.

'Mum,' she cried out. 'Sonia . . . it's me.'

Sonia Beechly turned to see her eldest stepdaughter cantering towards her like a young filly. It was seven years since she'd seen her, but she'd have recognised her anywhere. She'd blossomed from a gawky adolescent into a beautiful young woman. The silken blonde hair, which she'd always worn short, had been allowed to grow; her body had developed too, into that of a Page Three girl. Maybe it takes one to know one, but Sonia instinctively knew that her stepdaughter was as sexy a young woman as you'd meet on a day's march. The one thing strangely out of place was that ridiculous dress she wore.

'Why, Jilly,' she said, 'where did you spring from?'

Jilly flung her arms around her stepmother and hugged her tight. She genuinely loved her. As a child she'd been afraid of her own mother. When she died, and her father had married Sonia, she'd got on with her like a house on fire. When her father had divorced Sonia, she'd cried for a week and had been determined to hate her new stepmother.

'I'm at a finishing school not far from here.'

Sonia smiled. 'A finishing school for young ladies? I can't imagine you there.'

She blushed. 'Daddy insisted.'

'You're much too lively.'

'I know. I'm always in trouble.'

'I'm not surprised.'

'What are you doing here? Do you own a racehorse?'

Sonia laughed. 'No, I'm a trainer. An assistant trainer to be exact.'

'Cripes, you train thoroughbreds?'

'I try.'

'Of course, I remember. You had your own when you were married to Daddy.'

'And you used to adore them.'

'I still do.'

'Good. I'm glad.'

'Tell me what happened to you after you left. You never wrote.'

'I thought a clean break was best.'

'Where did you go?'

'America.'

'What did you do there?'

'I worked in a racing stable as a stablegirl.'

'My God, you've got guts.'

'I had to learn.'

'After that?'

'I worked in France and now I'm an assistant trainer. I hope to have my own yard . . .'

She stopped abruptly. She could have bitten her tongue.

'Hey, that's great.'

'I'm only hoping. It probably won't happen.'

Jilly looked excited. 'It will, Mum. I'm sure it will. You deserve it.'

She wondered why Jilly called her Mum, while her younger sister never had. It seemed strange to hear it, especially coming from such a grown-up young woman.

'I don't know about that. I'm not certain I could make a success of it.'

'You will. You were always so good with horses.'

She never remembered Jilly being so loving to her when she was a child. She remembered her as rather an awkward little sod.

'If I remember you used to love horses, Jilly?'

'I still do. I ride at school and at home, although Daddy hasn't many horses now.'

'Doesn't your new stepmother ride?'

'She hunts, and nags Daddy to join her, but he won't.'

Sonia grinned. 'He was never much of a horseman.'

'Why did you leave him?'

'I didn't. He wanted to marry Lady Elizabeth, so I just disappeared.'

Jilly looked puzzled. 'He never told us that,' she said slowly.

'I was too young to stay where I wasn't wanted.'

'Didn't he give you any money?'

'What makes you ask?'

'Well, you said you had to work as a stablegirl.'

'That was my choice, dear.'

'Then you should catch him now. Make him pay for your new stables.'

Sonia laughed. 'It's too late for that.'

'I don't see that it is, Sonia.'

There was an awkward pause before Sonia spoke again. 'Tell me about you? What are you going to do when you leave this posh school?'

'God knows. Something will turn up.'

'You're a beautiful young woman. The world is yours to enjoy. Perhaps you'll marry a prince!'

She blushed. 'Don't be silly. I wouldn't want a prince anyway.'

'And you'd never get one dressed like that, girl.'

'This isn't mine,' she said quickly. 'I've been dared to wear it. I'm at a celebration, a sort of party.'

Sonia laughed merrily. 'Well, as long as it's not your own choice!'

They kissed goodbye. Jilly watched her stride languidly away towards the stables and wondered why her father had ever given her up for that aristocratic bitch who was now her stepmother. She was delighted she'd met her after all this time, and now she knew where to find her perhaps she'd look her up in the future.

What she couldn't know was that she'd planted the seeds of an idea in Sonia's head. At that moment Jilly's former stepmother was wondering whether she might approach her ex-husband to 'help' her towards her ambition.

Jilly found Paul in the car park and he drove her to the country restaurant. They were the last to arrive. Apparently none of the others had stayed at their afternoon's tasks for very long. Bunty came bounding over dressed in a dazzling blue-striped sweater several sizes too small, and a tight pencil skirt split to the thigh. Her short black hair had been plastered down like a boy's and her make-up was slapped on with a trowel. She looked a sight, as did her partner who was dressed as a 1950s spiv.

'Guess what we had to do, Jilly?' she trilled.

'Dressed like that? Heaven knows.'

'We've been selling little toy ducks out of a suitcase.'

'Any luck?' drawled Paul.

'We were nearly arrested twice.'

Over the meal they all swapped their afternoon's experiences and Jilly felt more relaxed. The food was good and the wine flowed freely. Afterwards, coffee was served with liqueurs and a small ornate silver snuffbox did the rounds. It contained coke. Jilly passed it on quickly. She wasn't into drugs, but she noticed most of the men and more than half of the women snorted. By the time the MC stood up she was sufficiently merry to be looking forward to the party time to follow. And she'd absolutely no illusions as to the kind of party it would be.

'Ladies and gentlemen,' the MC called, 'the time has come to party. We'll meet at Jollity's HQ, but to start the ball rolling we'll swap partners.'

There was a buzz of anticipation around the table.

'If the men will toss their car keys into the bowl as they leave for the park, the ladies can choose one and find which car it belongs to.'

Jilly found hers belonged to one of the older men. He drove a Jag. The man smiled blandly at her as he took an inflatable rubber ring from the boot. It was U-shaped like a toilet seat with the front cut away. He placed it carefully on the driver's seat.

'Would you care to drive?' he asked.

Jilly was surprised. 'You trust a girl with your Jag?'

He grinned. 'Just this once.'

She jumped behind the wheel. Her body balanced on the rubber ring he'd placed on the seat for her to sit on. She found it raised her quite high from the seat and gave her a more suitable driving position. Yet somehow she couldn't believe that was the purpose of it. She started the powerful engine.

'Why do I have to sit on this rubber ring?' she asked.

'You think there's some ulterior motive?'

'To be honest. Yes!'

She felt him lean towards her.

'And you'd be right.'

The next moment made everything clear as his hand slid beneath her short silken dress to rub the warm flesh of her naked thigh. She wriggled in embarrassment.

'Stop wriggling about, and keep your eyes on the road.'

'Then stop it. You'll have us in the ditch.'

'Not if you concentrate on your driving, woman.'

'How can I with your paws all over me?'

'Quite easily. You just do your job and I'll do mine.'

'And what's yours? Feeling me up?'

He laughed. 'If that's what you like to call it.'

His hand had already infiltrated down between her legs and his fingertips were stroking her curly bush, smoothing and parting it like long grass. She sighed and allowed her thighs to spread a little. She might as well enjoy it. She was already quite excited. She closed her legs, squeezing his hand against her slit playfully.

'Now you're trapped, big boy,' she chuckled.

She heard him laugh as his hand prised her legs apart and his fingers located the jewel which lay hidden amongst her soft fur. She couldn't contain herself and she gasped audibly. It encouraged him and she felt his fingers slide furtively between the fleshy outer folds of her pulsing quim. She eased her backside forward to enable those searching fingers to slip more easily into her; but instead they moved up between her pussy lips to rest upon her hooded clitoris. She moaned a little as his two fingers urged open the hood and gently pinched her tiny clit. She slowed the car. She found she had to concentrate on her driving just to keep on the road such was the sexual arousal in her. She was conscious of two inquisitive fingers moving inside her, pushing up into her moist hole until they reached their limit. She'd certainly never been finger-fucked while driving a car, and had always fought shy of wanking a bloke in the driver's seat. From the corner of her eye she could see he was holding something in his hand. As he bent across she saw it was a large plastic vibrator. She knew exactly where it was heading. She was going to get it up her cunt.

'No, you're not to. It's dangerous.'

'A simple vibrator is dangerous?'

'You know what I mean. I'm driving.'

'I'm not going to blindfold you.'

'I shall stop the car if you do.'

'And then we'll be late for the party, Cinderella.'

'You seem to be having a party here,' she muttered.

'Then open your legs and enjoy yourself'

Oh, what the hell, she thought. She'd sneaked out

of school to enjoy herself. She relaxed her thighs and felt the tip of the vibrator nudge against her crack. Without further ado he thrust it into her body and she felt it ride up into her slippery tube, bucking inside her, fucking her insistently. She gasped as its huge coldness filled her, stretching the elastic walls of her impatient vagina. Then he switched it on. It whirred into life and vibrated inside her like a thousand jumping devils. She jammed her foot down on the throttle and clung to the wheel. The erotic tingle in her groin had spread throughout her body. She was strangely exhilarated, even a little crazy. The tyres screeched as she took a corner too fast.

'Steady on,' he yelled, 'you'll kill us both.'

Now it was his turn to be nervous.

Back at the mysterious country house HQ of Jollity, a society she knew nothing of and cared less about, the party was beginning to swing. A grand selection of booze was laid out on a long table and the small silver snuff box was again in evidence. They all changed back into their own clothes and Jilly was glad to be wearing knickers again, although she guessed it wouldn't be for too long. The loud music and strong booze soon had everybody in a party mood and cheers rang out when the MC rose.

'Ladies. The time has come for you all to entertain. We command that each of you does a turn.'

He threw three plump cushions onto the floor in

the middle of the room and pointed at random towards three women.

'Kneel on the cushions, girls. You are to be first on the bill.'

The three women knelt obediently on the cushions and each was blindfolded with a wide strip of thick velvet. Not a word was spoken as the twelve men lined up before the three blindfolded women. Jilly realised that they'd done it before, and wasn't surprised when the front three reached inside their trousers to produce their throbbing ramrods. The three women could only guess what was happening until the blunt end of a thick penis was bounced against their nose. The high and indignant shrieks of the three victims could barely be heard above the laughter of the other women.

'Now let us commence,' called the MC, 'we have here a relay race. Our members have generously agreed to be fellated by you three young ladies. Each of you has four impatient organs to play a tune on, and to add a little competition the first girl to finish will win a valuable prize. The last one will get her bottom birched!'

To the oohs and aahs of the enthusiastic audience the three women grabbed at the batons waving under their noses.

'Oh, no! No hands to be used by either side.'

The minutes that followed were filled with drunken sexual merriment which bordered on hysteria. The blindfolded women snapped with open mouths at the knobs which they knew were there, but couldn't see. Some of the men co-operated by guiding their lances towards the lips that waited to gobble up their spunk. Others teased by swinging their cocks just out of reach of the searching mouths. When their mouths finally closed over their quarries the women sucked as if their lives depended on it. None was aiming to win the prize, but each desperately wanted to avoid the twigs of a birch rod flaying her bare arse. Whether the threat was for real they knew not, but none wished to chance it. Soon spunk was flying like sea spray as the girls frantically sucked in their cheeks to drag out orgasm after orgasm. The female audience grew silent as they watched the scene with unbelieving fascination. It was like some weird erotic dream. The girl who finished first whipped off her blindfold. She'd swallowed every ejaculation, but the other two had withdrawn their mouths at the vital moments to finish spattered with thick globs of cream. The last to finish looked close to tears.

'We've mislaid the birch, lovely lady, so your pretty bottom's safe for the moment!'

Several minutes, several drinks and a snort of coke later the MC cleared his throat again.

'Can we have the next three ladies, please?'

He pointed to another three at random. Bunty was amongst them. They took their place in the middle of the floor, standing beside the cushions, and watched a tea trolley being wheeled towards them. On the trolley was a platter and on the platter were three condoms packed with crushed ice. They'd been well filled before the party to a healthy width and a length of some eight inches.

'Now girls. You're all pretty enough to melt a man's heart, but can you melt an iced prick?'

He handed an iced dildo to each of the girls who took it gingerly between two fingers. They hung down like huge pornographic icicles.

'Are you ready, girls? All you have to do is melt the ice to water. The winner gets a prize to warm her heart, the loser the birch to warm her bottom.'

The three women stood nervously, unsure of what to do.

'Sit on it, Bunty,' called Jilly.

'Put it under your armpit,' advised another voice.

'Stick it up your jacksy,' growled a young man.

The women went into action spurred on by the thought of the mislaid birch. It could so easily be found again. Jilly knew Bunty was full of competitive spirit, but was surprised to see she was the first to strip off her panties. One of the other girls had opened her blouse to place the icicle in her armpit, but withdrew it quickly when it froze her to the marrow. The third girl followed Bunty's example and, to the demented screams of the audience, stood with wide open legs to present the icicle to her snugly warm orifice. Bunty was already on her back with her legs high in the air. She gritted her teeth apprehensively easing the frozen thing into her tremulous twat.

'Ooh, aah, hell,' she gasped, 'it's bloody cold. It's freezing my poor little pussy!'

Her grimaces and squirming were aimed at amusing her audience, but the laughter really began when the ice started to melt and the condoms became floppy with a mixture of ice and water. To all the world they looked like three sexy young women on heat striving to satisfy their needs with three very limp dicks. While the pantomime continued the MC brought two stools into the centre of the room. A saddle had been thrown over each stool and into the seat was stitched a leather wedge like a huge phallus for the rider to sit upon. Whoever was to ride would be mighty uncomfortable!

'Come on girls. I want two experienced horsewomen to ride our two bucking broncos.'

Two society girls who rode point-to-point and to hounds stood up unsteadily. Jilly'd noticed they'd dipped into the snuffbox more than most.

'You don't expect us to sit on that?'

'Why not? You won't fall off so often with that stuck up your fanny!'

'We never fall off,' they replied with dignity.

The audience watched the two uninhibited females strip off their clothes and rise naked into the saddle. Being competent horsewomen they stood with their feet in the irons high above the saddle, and teased the watchers for some minutes before lowering their naked rumps onto the perpendicular leather wedges. With simulated squeaks of girlish excitement they sank slowly down until the cheeks of their bums were flush in the saddle and the leather phalluses were tucked away snugly inside their nice, warm quims.

'Ride 'em, cowgirls,' came a cry.

'Yoiks.'

'They went thataway!'

The two society girls had attended more wild parties than the rest had had hot dinners. It was a part of their lives. They entered into the game with a zest that none of the other women displayed. They sat tall in the saddle with the enthusiasm of young girls on their first rocking horse. Their long hair flew around their flushed faces as they urged their mounts on, bouncing up and down on the thick wedges as if they were in pursuit of a fox. The audience cheered. The women, aroused by their own wild abandon, rode lewdly, their tits bouncing as their glistening bodies pumped thirteen to the dozen on the big phalluses. They came together in a photo-finish.

When the audience had recovered its breath the MC spoke again.

'We have four lovely girls left to entertain us and nothing arranged for them, so I leave it to their own ingenuity to finish the show.'

Two women, who Jilly had placed as professional girls, strolled indolently forward as if on cue. Even as they walked towards the cushions they were unfastening their dresses and allowing them to fall where they stood. Neither had bothered with underwear, and as one nonchalantly took her place on the cushion by lying on her back so the other produced a box of coloured balls. They appeared to be smaller than billiard balls, and although solid, not nearly so heavy. The first woman stopped to take her partner's ankles and swung them above her head. Thus she was doubled up on her back showing her all, when her partner casually inserted one of the balls between the gaping lips of her wide open twat. No sooner had the ball disappeared into that glorious tunnel than she contracted her vaginal muscles to shoot it out as if launching a missile. The ball bounced across the room accompanied by loud guffaws of rude laughter. The show continued in the same vein with one woman feeding the balls into the other's quim for despatch into space as if from a rocket launcher. It was obvious to Jilly that the women had performed the trick many times – she'd heard of so-called cabarets which provided such entertainment. She wondered what the other woman would do for an encore. Maybe someone would produce a donkey out of a hat.

She didn't have long to wait to discover the second woman's party piece. She saw them change places, and watched the first woman produce a long king-sized cigarette. She dragged on it until the end glowed brightly, and then with a flourish took the cigarette from her mouth to present it to the lips of the second woman's cunt. She inserted it just far enough into the consenting vagina for the woman to grip the end. Thus the lighted end glowed a few inches from the soft mat of pubic hair and the audience watched in amazement as the tip burnt redder and redder. Such was the control she had over her vaginal muscles that she was now sucking smoke into her vagina.

'Blow us a smoke ring, darling,' drawled a male voice.

'Better than that. Send us a smoke signal!'

Sure enough, when her partner removed the cigarette, puffs of smoke drifted from between her legs. One was a perfect smoke ring. Jilly looked around the audience. The women were watching with a mixture of curiosity and disgust. She wondered if the vulgar spectacle did anything to arouse the men. She glanced around, but couldn't really answer her own question by the expressions on their faces.

'We have two lovely ladies left to give us a turn, so who's going first?'

Poor Jilly really had no idea what she could do. She wasn't frightened to perform. She was a born extrovert and exhibitionist, but what was she to do? A big-breasted woman walked forward confidently. She was probably the oldest woman present and the bored ease with which she took the stage made it clear she'd done it all a million times before. She stripped off her blouse and eased her enormous tits from her bra with the minimum of fuss. Jilly guessed her bust must have been every inch of forty-four. She had perfectly shaped knockers which were as fat as butter. She produced two coloured tassles which she proceeded to fasten to her huge gourds with nipple clips. Having prepared herself she swung into action. The tassles spun around like frenzied windmill sails as her great fleshy globes shook and swung like ripe fruit in a high wind. She was good, damned good. She twirled the tassles independently and in unison, first one way, and then the other. Jilly guessed she'd done it on the stage at sometime during her life. The audience clapped and whistled. At least they were in a good mood for Jilly, but the woman would be a hard act to follow.

'What shall I do?' she whispered to Bunty.

Bunty shrugged her shoulders, but the woman who could blow smoke-rings heard her and bent across.

'Twirl, like she's doing.'

'I can't do that. With my luck my tits would fly off'

The woman grinned and pushed something in her hand. 'You can wiggle your backside, can't you?'

She realised the crowd was beginning to slow handclap her. She found herself urged to her feet and was pushed forward onto the floor. She glanced down at what she was holding. The woman had given her two of the coloured balls she'd used in her act, but they were joined together by some nine inches of cord. She began to slowly undress to give herself time to think. By the way all the men had looked at her she'd known that she would be saved until last. Some seemed to be slavering at 'the

57

mouth. She knew she was by far the most beautiful woman in the room and she had youth on her side. She was easing her bikini briefs down her long shapely legs when she realised what the woman had meant. Standing naked, as she was, didn't embarrass her, but what she was going to do with those coloured balls made her hot and flustered.

The men who had been silent while drinking in her naked beauty began to slow handclap. Swallowing her nervousness she steeled herself for action and, taking one of the balls between her forefinger and thumb, she bent her knees and stuck her rump out towards the impatient audience. The idea of inserting the ball into her rectum before an audience appalled her, but that was what she meant to do. She curved out her posterior until her nether-cheeks were spread wide before presenting the ball to her tight little brown hole. Wishing she was a thousand miles away she fought to relax her body, her arse in particular. And then, taking a deep breath, she pushed the ball firmly against her anal muscle. She was surprised how easily it surrendered. The ball had slipped into her back passage before she realised it. For an instant she remained lewdly bending towards the circle of interested spectators with a coloured ball suspended from her anus by a piece of cord. Every eye was quite mesmerised by the coloured ball swinging gently between her open thighs and, taking advantage of their curiosity, she began to move her derriere in wide deliberate circles. The ball started to swing on the end of the cord until she had it turning behind her like an aircraft propeller.

'Hey, that's good!'

'Flap your arms, lady, you'll take off!'

'Move your arse, girl.'

She relaxed and smiled to herself. She was enjoying the applause, proud of the rude exhibition she was making of herself. Well, they say you're as good as the company you keep. She suddenly had a mental picture of Sonia, her stepmother. Would she have acted like this? she wondered. She knew she wouldn't, even though she possessed more eroticism than Jilly would ever have. She suddenly felt dirty, sullied. She realised the only part of the day she'd enjoyed was her meeting with Sonia.

On the way back to The Dame Edna Wallis Academy for Young Ladies she cried on Bunty's shoulder. Bunty thought it must be the alcohol, unless Jilly had dipped into that silver snuff box.

It was striking three when Paul left them outside the gates. He said nothing about meeting them again. Paul was a bit of a sadist and they'd disappointed him. He'd thought they'd be terribly embarrassed and shocked in the face of all that unadulterated sex. He'd looked forward to laughing at their discomfort but both girls had joined in the rudery as if they'd been raised in bordellos.

The two girls climbed the wall and ran across the

vast lawns which fronted the rambling old building. In a thrice they were through the boiler-house window and tiptoeing across the big kitchen towards the dining room. They were halfway across when light flooded the room. The caretaker stood by the door with one hand on the light switch. The care-taker wasn't a popular man. Their hearts sank into their shoes.

'My, my, what have we here?'

The two girls stood motionless. Neither attempted to reply.

'Been out on the town, have we?'

They looked at him silently. He loved to get one up on the girls, and there were a hundred tales about what he'd demanded of his victims and what they'd done to bribe him. Nobody believed half of them.

'Lost our tongues, have we?'

'No, Mr McNab, we've been out with our families.'

'Dressed like two tarts?'

'It was a disco to celebrate my young sister's six-teenth birthday.'

'So you'll have permission to be out late?'

'Oh, yes.'

'So the headmistress will know all about it?'

'Why, yes.'

'And she told you to come in through the boiler-house window, I suppose?'

'That's right,' they lied innocently, 'so we wouldn't wake anybody up.'

He laughed harshly. 'You're a pair of little toads.

Tomorrow I shall report you. Now goodnight, ladies.'

He switched off the lights and walked towards his own office, which was nearby. They scampered after him to catch him up as he pushed open the door.

'Please can we talk?'

He shut the door behind them. It was a big room combining a workshop with the office.

'What is there to talk about?'

Both girls knew the strict rules of the Academy. The punishment for breaking a major rule was expulsion. Staying out half the night certainly qualified for that. There was no excuse for not asking for the permission which was invariably granted in valid cases.

'Couldn't you forget you'd seen us?'

'Why should I do that?'

'Because we'll get expelled.'

'I know.'

Bunty was on the verge of tears. 'I can't be expelled. I mustn't be. I couldn't face my parents. It would break Daddy's heart,' she sobbed.

'It's no good crying. You should have thought of that before.'

'Isn't there anything we could do to change your mind, Mr McNab?'

McNab paused deliberately. 'Well to be honest I've always thought you girls should be punished properly instead of being allowed to leave.'

'Punished properly? What sort of punishment did you have in mind, Mr McNab?'

'Corporal punishment, young lady.'

That wasn't a viable alternative to Jilly. She wasn't prepared to have her backside tanned. Apparently Bunty felt differently. She sniffed away her tears.

'You mean we should have our bottoms smacked?'

'Speak for yourself,' snapped Jilly quickly.

'The offence is very serious. If it was up to me you'd both be given the cane.'

Bunty wiped her eyes. 'All right, Mr McNab, say you gave us the cane. You wouldn't have to report us then, would you?'

Jilly was about to object, but Bunty stopped her. 'Please, Jilly,' she whispered, 'this means a lot to me.'

McNab appeared to consider the suggestion. 'I suppose not, Miss Bunty, but it would have to be done properly.'

'How?'

'Like it was official discipline.'

'I'm willing,' gasped Bunty, 'I know I've broken the rules and as punishment I agree to be caned, but it must go no further.'

'It won't Miss. A quick dose of the cane and no more said. That's how it should be, girls.'

Jilly said nothing, but nothing would persuade her to let that nasty old man cane her bum. He saw her reluctance.

'It will have to be both of you, mind.'

It was the ravishing Miss Jilly who really excited

him. It was her he wanted to teach a lesson. She'd flaunted her female charm since the day she'd arrived, and his eyes had followed her everywhere, dreaming up things he could do to that gorgeous body.

Jilly smiled calmly. 'You wouldn't want to cane two girls at once, would you? Why not save me until tomorrow?'

His eyes lit up. So she was willing. It would certainly be something to look forward to until tomorrow. 'All right, if you promise to come here immediately after lunch.'

Jilly crossed her fingers. 'I promise.'

He turned to Bunty. 'Right, young woman. Let's commence your discipline. Fetch the cane.'

He pointed to a cupboard which she found contained half a dozen school canes of varying sizes. She selected the thinnest and carried to to him. It made her feel like a naughty little girl, but she supposed that was the idea.

'Raise your skirt, young lady and pull down your knickers.'

Bunty did as she was told. She knew the rules. She'd seen pictures in dubious magazines of girls being caned by so-called schoolmasters. It would probably sting, but it couldn't be as bad as what she'd already submitted to that night. Anyway, if it saved her from being expelled why not humour the old boy? She stood passively with her skirt raised displaying her softly rounded buttocks.

'Spread your legs and bend over to grasp your ankles.'

She obeyed without question and found herself in a position which made her feel more vulnerable than she could remember. Her body was bent double, her head just clear of the ground. Her delectable bare bottom rose high in the air as she clasped her ankles and peered through her parted legs to see the salacious old bastard swinging the cane.

'How many are you going to give me?'

'I think you deserve a dozen, don't you?'

'My God, that's too many!'

'I think not. Just make certain you count every one.'

'Yes, sir,' she groaned holding tight to her ankles.

She'd kicked off her shoes and her toes dug into the carpet about two feet apart. The silky wobbly flesh of her plump derriere seemed to invite the cane, and when it struck an extraordinary sensation of tingling pain shot through her. She yelped, straightened her back and clasped the blazing cheeks of her rump with both hands. Sizzling waves of fire scorched her abused tail. He waited a moment before placing the tip of the cane in the middle of her back to urge her forward again. She reluctantly resumed her position.

'You won't get up like that again, Miss. If you do I shall have to add another stroke.'

Again she grasped her ankles, and again the swishy cane descended upon the arrogant globes of

her seat. Bunty squealed like a little pig as Jilly
looked on aghast. Rather her than me, she thought
as she gazed at her friend's ignominious posture. Yet
she found herself watching fascinated as the
remaining strokes stoked an intense heat in Bunty's
outraged arse, turning the milky white skin to an
angry red. The unfortunate girl winced and snivel-
led at every lusty whack before shouting out the
number, arching her back and rotating her blazing
bum before pushing it out to meet the next stinging
stroke.

After Bunty's ordeal was over they tiptoed quietly
upstairs to their rooms. Although the tears were still
glistening in Bunty's swollen eyes Jilly was surprised how well she'd taken it. However, there was
no way Mr McNab was going to cane her.

Once inside her room she began throwing a few
things into a case.

Bunty watched her. 'What are you doing?'

'He's not going to cane me.'

'But you agreed.'

'I did nothing of the sort. You agreed.'

'You said you'd report to his office after lunch.'

'To have him take the skin off my backside? Not
likely.'

'I took it, Jilly. It's not that bad.'

'It would be for me. He fancies me. Didn't you see
the way he looked at me?'

'So?'

'He'd lay it on twice as hard.'

'Why should he? Especially if he fancies you.'

Jilly paused. 'You don't know the half of it, Bunty.'

'I know I'd rather have a sore arse than be expelled.'

Jilly exploded. 'Well, I wouldn't. Okay?'

Bunty was silent for a moment. 'What will you do?'

'I'll go home.'

'What will your father say?'

'I don't know, but he won't cane my backside.'

Jilly arrived home at a bad time. Her stepmother was busy arranging one of her parties. Her father listened to her, told her she looked like death warmed up, and suggested she go to bed. He'd speak to her the next day when he returned from his meeting in Brussels.

'I can't say I'm pleased with your behaviour, and your mother's furious.'

'She's not my mother.'

'And we'll have no more of that. She's your mother as long as you remain under this roof.'

'I'm sorry, Dad.'

'And I'm wondering what can be done with you.'

'I won't go back to that school.'

'I don't expect you to, Jilly, but what do you want to do with your life?'

'I want to work.'

'A career?'

'Not really.'

'Then what, for heaven's sake, girl?'

'I don't know, give me time to think.'

Her father stood up. 'Take your time, Jilly. I don't want to chase you away. I love you, you know that, but I'd like to see you settled down doing something. Not just gaddin' about.'

She grinned. 'Like mother, you mean?'

'I didn't say that.'

'Oh, by the way I saw Sonia.'

'Good heavens, where?'

'At Ayr races.'

He looked thoughtful. 'Do you know I've never heard from her since the divorce.'

She said nothing. She knew her father had often been sorry he got rid of Sonia. In retrospect it certainly wasn't something he could be proud of, especially since she'd just walked out of his life without demanding anything. That had surprised and hurt him.

'You thought a lot of her, didn't you?'

'I still do, Daddy.'

'What was she doing at the races?'

'She's the assistant trainer to a big stable. Apparently she's been abroad working as a stablegirl, and now she wants a yard of her own.'

'She'll probably be very successful. She was always good with horses.'

'She hasn't changed a bit. She's even more beautiful if anything.'

Her father ignored the remark. 'You like horses,

Jilly, why don't you look her up. Maybe she'll give you a job working for her.'

She brightened. 'Hey, that's a good idea. I might just do that.'

Chapter 3

Barney swung indolently into the saddle, which took a bit of doing considering he had over two stone of lead in his waistcoat. Sonia had waited to give him a leg-up knowing he'd never get up under his own steam. He gave her a half smile as he moved Man Samson forward to join the rest of the string.

'Ride away,' shouted Bart from the back of his old hack.

The horses moved out in single file towards the gallops and Sonia mounted to fall in behind them. Man Samson had been taken away from her as he was officially back in training. He would be too fit and highly strung to be used as a hack. A thin watery sunshine was beginning to penetrate the clouds on a typical early morning in late September. Barney had put an anorak over his waistcoat and realised he'd soon be sweating cobs.

'Yer blood runnin' thin, Barney?' joked one of the lads, 'feelin' yer age, are yer?'

'Thought it was going to rain,' he grunted.

Sonia was feeling nervous as she helped Bart to supervise work. It was make or break time for Man Samson. The gelding had to have a really good blow but he mustn't appear too fit. She'd arranged with Barney to gallop with a five-year-old mare who usually proved a good yardstick, but that was knocked on the head when Dilly Jacks drove onto the gallops. Dilly was a top jockey who often rode work for the guv'nor. Bart didn't retain a stable jockey. Instead he engaged one of several who were only to happy to ride for him when they were free. Dilly was the most regular of these, and as he lived nearby he often popped over to ride out. His opinion of a horse was invaluable to a trainer. He strolled over to Bart, who was sitting astride his hack some way from the gallops, swinging his hard hat by the strap.

'Morning, Bart. Anything special you want me to ride?'

'The big chestnut's going in the Wherry Stakes at Sandown next week. See what he feels like.'

Dilly began to strap on his hard hat, and Bart shouted to the horses circling nearby.

'Terry, bring the chestnut over here. Dilly's going to give him a spin.'

The stable lad moved the horse towards Dilly as Bart continued shouting instructions.

'Barney, I want you to give Dilly a lead over seven furlongs. It'll give me a chance to have a look at your gelding, too.'

Sonia's heart sank. That wasn't what she had in mind. A strong gallop under Bart's eagle eye would put Man Samson under the microscope, and with Dilly on the other horse nothing would go unnoticed. She prayed Barney was up to it.

'Okay, Barney. Let's be having you,' shouted Dilly.

Barney kicked Man Samson into a gallop. The gelding was into his stride in a flash and fighting for his head. Barney held him hard cursing his luck that the gelding was playing up. The big horse tossed his head as he ran with Barney standing in his irons, fighting to keep the gelding's head up. They'd covered a furlong when Man Samson deigned to grab his bit and race sensibly. Barney rested his hands on the horse's neck and the gallop became as smooth as silk. He felt the gelding stretch out under him, but all the time he was conscious of Dilly's presence behind. He could hear the chestnut snorting as it thundered on Man Samson's heels. At the four-furlong mark he still had a lot of horse under him, and let out a notch. The gelding lengthened his stride and the pace quickened. At five furlongs he heard Dilly shout he was coming through, and saw the chestnut's head creep up to his knees. He daren't let Man Samson down, the gelding was pulling double under him. He was convinced Dilly would see how much he had left in the tank.

'Press the button, Barney,' screamed Dilly, 'make a race of it.'

He knew he must do as he was told, and prayed

the weight the gelding was carrying would slow it down. He changed his hands and the gelding slipped into another gear. The two horses thundered side by side for nearly half a furlong before Barney felt his mount tire. He dropped his hands a trifle and, with a sigh of relief, saw the chestnut accelerate away. It had been a really good work out for Man Samson, who was beginning to want to race again after his injury. He hoped Dilly hadn't noticed just how well Man Samson was going. They made their way back to where Bart was waiting for Dilly's opinion of the chestnut.

'What do you think, Dilly?'

'He's a hundred percent, Bart. He'll win next Wednesday without a doubt.'

'And you'll take the ride?'

'Try and stop me!'

Barney held Man Samson on a long rein allowing him to crop the lush grass. He watched Sonia ride over, but didn't appear to look at her.

'What about your gelding?' she called. 'Do you reckon he's on the way back?'

'He looks good,' answered Bart. 'What do you think, Barney?'

'Yeah, guv. He went about his work well, but he tired quickly.'

'I noticed he faded. Still he's got another couple of bits of fast work before Sandown next Thursday.'

Sonia chanced a quick glance at Barney and smiled. All had gone well, better than they'd hoped.

It was hardly surprising that Bart thought the horse had faded considering it was carrying over eleven stone.

Back in the yard Barney prepared to interview a new girl who, if she passed muster, would take over Man Samson and two others. Barney had only just got rid of his weighted waistcoat when he was called to take the new girl to the office. She stood by the gate, a forlorn soul weighed down with a gigantic backpack and a guitar case.

'You're early, luv. The guv'nor's not expecting you just yet.'

The girl looked at him blandly.

'Your interview was arranged for 11 am, wasn't it?'

'I haven't got any interview. I'm here on the off-chance.'

He laughed. 'I'm sorry. There's been a mix-up.'

She looked disappointed. 'You mean you've got nothing for me?'

'No, we can always use someone else. A lad gave his notice this morning.'

She grinned. 'Can I try for that?'

'Why not? I'll see if the guv'nor's free.'

He took her to the office. Bart was drinking coffee and fuming over the price of feed. Barney stuck his head around the door.

'Guv, there's a girl here. Come on the chance of a job.'

'Wheel her in, Barney.'

Without her luggage weighing her down she looked altogether more spritely and presentable. She'd obviously pulled a comb through her short black hair and put on a touch of lipstick while she waited. She wore very tight blue jeans over cowboy boots, and an expensive-looking waistcoat over a polo-necked sweater. Barney noticed the pleading little-girl-lost image was gone, replaced by a confident young miss who knew the ways of the world. She was a good little actress if nothing else.

'What's your name?'

'Tess Shea. I was passing so I thought I'd see whether you had a vacancy for an experienced stablegirl.'

'Passing from where, Tess?'

'Mr McMallery's yard. I just left there.'

'Why?'

'I walked out.'

'Why?'

'One of the owners kept trying to get inside my knickers.'

Bart looked steadily at her while trying to keep a straight face.

'I wouldn't have minded, but he wasn't invited.'

'Why didn't you tell Mr McMallery?'

'I did. He seemed to think it was funny.'

'So you haven't got a reference?'

'I haven't even got my cards!'

Bart looked uncomfortable. 'I'm sorry, Tess. I don't think we can fit you in at present. Another time, perhaps.'

But the girl wasn't to be discouraged that easily. 'Your head lad said you had a vacancy coming up.'

'That's right, guv,' Barney explained, 'we might be able to use her.'

Bart looked dubious. 'Okay, Barney. If you think so. She'll be your responsibility.'

He turned to the girl. 'Barney will look after you. You'll be taken on temporarily. I'll speak to Mr McMallery and we'll see how you get on. I'm promising no more than a week's trial.'

The girl smiled happily. 'Thanks, guv.'

Barney swung her backpack over his shoulder and led her to Man Samson's box.

'You'll be doing this gelding today. I'll get Betty to show you the ropes and we'll meet again later.'

It was evening stables when he saw her again. Bart began his tour of inspection at 4 pm every afternoon. There was the evening feed and grooming to be done. It takes about forty-five minutes to groom a horse: twenty minutes each side, plus the feet to be picked out, eyes and muzzle to be washed and the dock cleaned – and each lad had three horses to do. This was an ideal time for the trainer to do his rounds, when he could have a good shufti at every horse and a word with its minder. Barney would follow him, watching him pat each horse, examine his legs, and ask about its general wellbeing. Man Samson's box was one of the last to be visited. Bart paused outside to listen to the chatter of the new girl. She was busy strapping the horse's coat with a soft body brush, while she whispered sweet nothings

75

to the great beast as if she was speaking to a child. Bart smiled – perhaps they'd found a good one in her. She looked up when they came in.

'Settling in, Tess?'

'I am, thanks.'

'Has Betty been looking after you?'

'Yes, guv'nor, she's been very helpful.'

He looked quickly at the horse. 'All right, I'll leave you to Barney's tender mercies. Anything you want to know, ask him.'

'I will. Thanks, guv'nor.'

Barney stayed in the box with Tess as Bart continued on his rounds. He watched her take the dandy brush and conscientiously begin working on the gelding's mane. He thought she must be about twenty, and her dark sultry looks gave warning of a quick temper and perhaps the promise of an erotic nature. She'd changed into a loose blouse which showed enough cleavage to stiffen his interest. He could see she had firm breasts like two luscious ripe peaches. Her face was elfin-like, with a cute pointed chin and mischievous brown eyes which appeared to turn black when she flirted. He studied her agile hands as she worked, and had a sudden mental image of her tiny feminine fist wrapped around his rampant cock. He was half ashamed to feel a stirring in his trousers and turned quickly away, but she seemed to sense the train of his thoughts and smiled impishly.

'This is a lovely horse,' she drawled, 'fit as a fiddle. Almost ready to race I'd say.'

He saw that she knew her job. 'You'd be right. He's entered at Sandown Park next week.'

'Will I have a chance to go with him?'

'Mebbe, if you keep your nose clean.'

'I will, I've had enough of moving around.'

'Where've you been then?'

'All over the country. Six yards in the last year.'

He said nothing. Either she had gypsy blood or there was something wrong with her work. Time would tell.

'I'll settle down here. I'm certain of that.'

'Good.'

'I like you, too, Mr Barney!'

'I'm pleased.'

'I owe you. If it hadn't been for you I'd never have got this job.'

'Oh, I don't know.'

She stopped work and looked at him. 'You know it's true.'

He fidgeted, patting the horse's neck to keep his hands occupied. She made him feel embarrassed. He caught sight of the guitar case in the corner of the stall.

'You play that?'

'Sure do.'

He felt foolish. 'Will you play it for me sometime?'

'Why not.'

There was nothing for it but to go. He wondered why this young woman made him feel strangely uncomfortable. He turned to leave.

'Don't go. Hold the horse's head for me.'

He took hold of the gelding and tweaked its ear. He was expecting her to lift the horse's leg and begin picking out the feet. Instead her agile fingers began busily unfastening his fly as she ducked nimbly down in front of him. Her hand was inside his breeches and winkling out his sleeping dick almost before he'd had time to draw breath.

'Hey, what are you up to?'

She peeped up knavishly. 'I was going to give you head, unless you don't go in for that sort of thing.'

He chuckled. 'Be my guest!'

'Anything for a quiet life, eh?'

His prick was now as stiff as a poker between her sexy fingers, and the thought of her soft red lips encircling it brought a tight band of excitement to his chest.

'You don't have to,' he murmured, and immediately felt silly.

'I know!' she grinned mischievously. 'But I'm an impulsive girl, and I like you. Anyway, I like to pay my debts.'

'You're not in my debt.'

She squeezed his agitated prong. 'Do you want me to suck you off, or not?'

'Yes . . . please.'

'Then be quiet and enjoy it.'

The instant her mouth closed over his chopper he knew she was good, really good. Her soft red lips teased and tantalised the smooth sensitive helmet of his cock with a host of butterfly kisses while her fingers slid under his testicles. Swiftly moving her mouth away from his impatient member, she began massaging the deep crease of his crotch with her lithe fingers and, ignoring his great pego, sticking up in the air like a mast, she nosed between his balls, licking them one by one. He could feel his pulsing knob quivering against her smooth forehead, and when she took it between her fingers to guide it into her warm wet mouth she thrust him into the realms of pure ecstasy. He could feel his charger swell to bursting as she rolled it languidly between her moist young lips. She drew her teeth back along its length and lightly kissed its tip.

'My goodness, you've got a mighty thick dick!' she cooed.

He was silent. Surely she didn't expect a reply.

'I'll try and get it all into my mouth without choking.'

He said nothing. He didn't think he was capable of speech.

'Shall I try?'

He nodded his head and held his breath. His short thick wedge stood up like a gorilla's thumb and he could feel the blood pounding through it like a thousand African tom-toms. She carefully held the root of the shaft with one hand while cupping his sac with the other. He watched her ease the tip of his stubby pole downwards until it was horizontal. There she held it for a second in such a way that he could view her lips moving towards the thick pulsing helmet and, as her mouth opened and her red lips closed over his anxiously waiting cock he was close to swooning. The sight of his penis slipping into her sweet mouth, of her lips closing over the thick shaft, combined with the feeling of her warm welcoming tongue was almost too much. He was certain he must either ejaculate or die.

Gently, and with infinite patience, she drew his prick into her mouth, accepting it deeper and deeper into her throat until her nose buried itself in his groin and the swollen tip was nudging her tonsils. She held him like that for a very long moment. A moment which seemed like a lifetime. A moment when her hand, which was nestling in his crotch, started to move backwards. A moment when the index finger of that dainty hand suddenly jabbed into his arsehole. To him it came like a thunderbolt out of the blue. It was so unexpected that the instant her finger penetrated his anus he shouted and ejaculated into her throat. Waves of sheer unadulterated ecstasy swept over him as his hot spunk shot down her open gullet and, beyond reason, he let go of the horse's head to clasp her face between his palms. Startled by the shouts, the gelding shied. Seeing the danger, Tess pulled away and the remainder of his cream splattered over her face. Simultaneously he grabbed the animal to quieten it. A female face appeared over the top of the stable door. It was full of concern.

'Are you all right, Tess?' said Betty, goggling at the scene that met her eyes – the head lad with his willy hanging out and great globs of semen all over the new girl's face.

'Yes, we're okay, Betty.'

The girl grinned. 'More than okay, I'd say!'

'Just remember what you didn't see, my girl!'

'None of my business, is it? Just don't frighten the horses!'

On Friday Man Samson had his last bit of fast work before the race. When he pulled up he wasn't blowing enough to snuff out a candle. Bart pronounced himself satisfied and Sonia was happy.

On Saturday Bart went to Newcastle to watch the stable's entry in a Group three race, while Sonia was left to saddle two no-hopers at Salisbury. She wasn't a great lover of Salisbury racecourse. Some miles outside the town, near the village of Wilton, it had a dogleg near the start of some races which was the cause of hard-luck stories, bad temper and even accidents. The saving grace was that the course was less than an hour from the yard and she could do a bit of shopping before the races. She'd just watched one of her charges trail in tailed-off, and was busy saddling the second when a welcome voice interrupted her.

'Hello, Sonia.'

'Jilly,' she smiled, 'twice in a month. This is becoming a habit!'

'I must speak to you.'

'How did you find me here?'

'I rang your stable.'

'Then you'll know I'm working. I'll meet you this evening at the White Hart, we'll make a night of it.'

'Great.'

'Let's do it properly. Book a twin room.'

Sonia had spoken impulsively when she'd suggested staying the night, and afterwards she wondered whether she was doing right by cultivating Jilly. After all, they came from different worlds. She changed her mind over a splendid dinner, a bottle of wine, and a good old gossip.

'I told Daddy I'd met you.'

'Really.'

'I think he still fancies you!'

'It's a bit late for that.'

'He'd be a fool not to, you're beautiful, Sonia.'

'He's better off with Lady Elizabeth. She can do more for his social life than I could manage in bed.'

Jilly giggled. 'Isn't he very highly sexed then?'

'Let's say he never put himself out.'

'He suggested I came to see you.'

'Why?'

'Now I've left school he feels I should have a career or something.'

'And how can I help?'

'I love horses. They're about the only things I know anything about – other than sex!'

'You want me to help you get a job in a racing stable?'

'I thought I could work with you?'

'Bart's got no vacancies, except for stablegirls, you wouldn't like that.'

'You said you were getting your own yard?'

Sonia hesitated. 'That's pie in the sky I'm afraid.'

'You mean it won't happen?'

She didn't know how much to tell Jilly of her plans, if anything at all. She liked the girl and guessed she'd be an asset, but it would be taking a chance. Then suddenly, quite out of the blue, she found herself babbling out the whole plan.

'I've no money. The whole thing depends on a betting coup.'

Jilly's face lit up. 'You're going to pull off a betting coup? Crikey, I'd no idea you knew anything about betting.'

'You have to in the racing game. It's what it's all about.'

'I suppose it is. I hadn't thought.'

'If it comes off I shall be able to afford a mortgage on a yard and set myself up in business.'

'Why don't you ask Daddy for some money?'

'I couldn't do that. I swore I'd never take a penny from him.'

'If you agree to employ me I'm sure he'll help you.'

'No.'

'At least let me ask him to buy a couple of horses for you to train.'

Sonia hesitated. She knew attracting good horses

would be a problem. 'I suppose that would be all right.'

'Fine, you let me help you in your yard and I'll get him to buy two racehorses for you to train.'

'It's a deal. Looks as if you're going to make a good businesswoman.'

Jilly grinned happily. 'When's this coup you're planning?'

'Next Thursday at Sandown.'

'Cripes, there's not long to sit and suffer, is there?'

'You'll know, one way or the other, next Thursday after the fifth race.'

Sunday morning Sonia got back in time to take out second lot for Bart, who'd wanted to spend an hour in the office going over the declarations and riding arrangements for the week. It was when she got back to stables that the balloon went up. Bart's voice boomed out as she approached the office.

'Sonia, is that you?'

She stuck her head 'round the door.

'Do you know what my bloody secretary's done? She's declared my gelding for the wrong soddin' race on Thursday. How she managed that, I don't know,' he fumed, 'it's not even a race I considered. I can't imagine how it was entered in the first place.'

'Which race it that, Bart?'

'Some bloody C grade at Sandown on Thursday when I put him down to be entered in the B grade earlier in the afternoon.'

Sonia smiled inwardly. All was well so far. Man Samson had been declared for the race she favoured. Now she had to make certain he ran.

'It's the race I wanted for him, remember?'

'Did you? Well, how did my secretary get mixed up? I'll kick her backside tomorrow, good and hard.'

'It's not her fault, Bart.'

'Whose it is then?'

'Mine.'

'Yours? How, for Christ's sake?'

'I made certain she entered and declared the gelding for the race.'

He went off the deep end. 'That's not bloody good enough, Sonia. I decide the entries, you know that. You're not the bloody trainer, not yet you aren't.'

'I'm sorry.'

'Sorry! That's easy to say now you've got your own way. Well, I shan't run him at all this week.'

'That's just spite. The horse's jumping out of his skin. He needs a race.'

'He'll have a bloody hard gallop this week, and I'll find a race for him next week,' he said triumphantly.

She paused. 'Look,' she said softly, 'it's all my fault. Why not just slap my backside and forget about it?'

He looked incredulous. 'What?'

'Take me upstairs and spank me,' she grinned mischievously. 'You'll feel much better after that!'

'I've a good mind to do just that, my girl.'

She turned towards the stairs and held out her

85

hand to him. 'Come on, Uncle Bart,' she lisped coquettishly, 'it's time you gave a naughty girl a good slap-bottom!'

During the three years Sonia had been with Bart she'd treated him to nearly every whim in and out of bed, but never had she allowed him to spank her delectable derriere. It wasn't a major fetish with him so he'd never insisted, but he'd noticed she fought shy if he slapped her playfully during their love-making. Often he'd gazed at the exquisite twin globes of her arse and imagined their plumpness wobbling like jelly beneath a good spanking, but he'd never once dared to go to work on those inviting mounds of feminine flesh. Now his chance had arrived. The thought of tanning her arrogant seat relegated any care about racehorses to the background. Who cared which race the damned gelding ran in?

Upstairs he pulled off his sweater and menacingly rolled up his right shirt sleeve. She stood before him smiling wanly, dressed in a white turtle neck jersey and tight cream jodhpurs which outlined her gorgeous rump to perfection.

'Well, young lady, you know what's going to happen to you now?'

'I'm going to be spanked, sir.'

'You certainly are, so prepare yourself.'

She undid the waistband of her jodhpurs with a slow sensuality before easing them down over her thighs until they fell in a rumpled heap around her ankles. The long white jersey dropped down to hide her brief blue knickers.

'Pull that jersey up. I'm going to give you a tanning you'll remember all your life.'

She looked uneasy. 'Not too hard,' she said anxiously.

'Oh yes, Sonia, my love. You asked for it. Now you're going to get it.'

She gulped. 'Please, Bart, it's only fun.'

He grabbed the offending jersey and jerked it up to her shoulders. 'Fun, is it? I'll show you fun, my girl.'

He plonked a hard-backed chair beside her and sat down on it. Snatching her wrist he pulled her to his side.

'Over my knee, you conniving bitch.'

Her mature posterior, covered by the briefest knickers, seemed to jut out ludicrously between the rumpled jodhpurs around her ankles and the jersey which encircled her shoulders. She obediently draped herself over his knees so that the palms of her hands were flat on the carpet and her long shapely legs were stretched out behind her.

'Legs straight, both hands on the floor, please.'

She was completely helpless over his lap, her cute bottom raised prettily for spanking. And spank her he did. Each time his hand whacked down across her plump nates the hearty slap echoed like a gunshot. Sonia found herself squawking like a schoolgirl now the walloping had begun. Then, as her derriere began to warm, he jerked down her knickers. She shrieked, endeavouring to cover her bare bottom with her hand, but he roughly twisted her arm behind her back.

'Stop it. My God, it hurts. That's enough, Bart.'

He paid little attention to her squeaking and continued to smack her blazing bum with stinging thwacks.

'No more, please. I'm sorry. Really I'm sorry.'

The ordeal went on until the reddened globes of her scorching behind were ablaze.

'Please, Bart, no more. I can't take any more.'

When the torment concluded she lay sobbing over his knees, her body limp, her butt glowing. It was as if her chosen punishment had lit a fire in her tail. She stood up. She'd paid her debt and she supposed it hadn't been too much of a price to pay. She'd ensured Man Samson's place in the race, even though her behind stung like billy-o. She moved to the wall mirror and surveyed her abused fundament over her shoulder. The cheeks were rosy red.

'Look what you've done to my bum, you bastard.'

He knelt behind her and began to soothe the damaged skin with gentle caresses of his fingertips.

'Your fingers are too rough. Kiss it better.'

She was surprised how horny she felt. The sweet kisses of his lips and the long licks of his tongue on the hot flesh of her buttocks heightened her randiness. She'd never been spanked by a man before, she'd never allowed it. She knew of a woman who loved it, who said it made her feel like a bitch on heat, but Sonia had never thought it was for her. Now she realised she'd been wrong. The hot sting that had begun in her derriere had spread to her loins, ignited an inner fire and brought a sensual warmth to her whole body. When she closed her thighs she became conscious that she was wet between her legs. Such was the excitement at the feel of his palm upon her haunches that her vagina was leaking love juice. For a brief second she was ashamed, but swiftly brushed the feeling aside. She'd learned early in life that shame had no place in lovemaking.

His long wet tongue had found its way into the deep valley between the cheeks of her bum, and his hands were gripping those twin moons to pull them apart so that his tongue would have full access to her two hidden orifices. She bent forward to aid his invasion of her privacy. She wanted to be licked, sucked, screwed. Her body yearned to be filled. His tongue stroked the length of her vulva, travelling smoothly between the engorged folds from her risen clitoris to her puckered bumhole. And when she was dripping with his saliva and her own love juice, she could wait no longer to be entered.

'I want you inside me, Bart,' she panted. 'Now. While I'm hot for you.'

He grabbed an upright chair and swung it round so that the seat faced her, and immediately it was in place she flopped forward so her hands were flat on the seat.

'Come on, man. Shaft me. What do you want, written permission?'

She heard him laugh sharply as he pulled her jersey to her shoulders and dragged her breasts free of her bra without bothering to undo it. His trousers were already around his feet and she could feel his rock-hard pego nudging between her twin moons. He moved back slightly, positioning his lusty tool at the entrance of her secret grotto: and then he simultaneously thrust into her and grabbed at her swinging tits. She gasped as he squeezed her big breasts in his fists, and groaned as his stiff penis filled her.

Content just be be impaled on his prick she moved her arse in a circular movement until he began shafting her in earnest. The long slow thrusting inside her gradually increased until it became a frenzied pumping which made her grab the sides of the seat to hold on for dear life. Miraculously they approached climax together and, as she shrieked with the release of her orgasm, so he came deep within her.

On Monday morning Sonia woke up smugly happy. Four days to the race and everything now looked like plain sailing. But she'd reckoned without Bart's racing arrangements for the week. He collared her over breakfast.

'I've decided to go to the three-day meeting at Sandown. You can go to Redcar on Thursday.'

Sonia's heart sank. 'I thought you were keen to go

to Redcar to see Lord Alfred's two-year-old run?'

'I was, but I've changed my mind. We know he can't win, and you can tell me how he runs.'

'Okay, if that's what you want.'

She wondered why he'd suddenly changed his mind. Perhaps it was the long drive to North Yorkshire. He'd been quite sweet on the two-year-old's chances in the race. He'd confided to her that he thought the colt was in with a squeak. She wondered what had changed. Maybe he fancied the stable's senior runner in Man Samson's race. She knew she wouldn't be able to change his mind so she kept her mouth shut but knew she had to find a way to keep him away from Sandown on Thursday. If he attended the race not only would Man Samson's odds tumble, but he might instruct his rider to take it easy and blow the race. She puzzled over the solution as she munched her way through bacon and eggs, and he read the daily racing paper.

'Bart, how about lunch today? Remember that new place we went to on the Devizes road?'

He looked over the newspaper. 'Yes, that was nice. What was it called?'

'The Knight Templar.'

'I remember. I'll meet you there just after one o'clock.'

Sonia had the outline of a plan which might just work. She rang Jilly and found her at home.

'You recall I said I needed time to finally decide whether to take you on when I get my yard?'

'Of course. Have you decided?'

'Are you still keen?'

'Yes, I'd love it.'

'Okay, that's settled then. Only thing is I might not have a yard now.'

'Why not?'

'I thought I had everything under control, but over breakfast Bart suddenly sprang it on me that's he's going to Sandown on Thursday. I have to go to Redcar.'

'Can't you get him to change his mind?'

'That's what I'm ringing about.'

'What do you mean?'

'I can't but you might.'

'Me? What can I do?'

'You can win your spurs, my girl. Save the day and get yourself a job for life!'

'I'll do what I can.'

'How're your seduction techniques?'

'I'm no Mata Hari but I've been known to turn a few heads!'

'Do you think you could manage Bart?'

'I don't know. Am I his type?'

'Blonde, young and female!'

'Do I have to wear my gymslip?'

'No, he likes 'em grown up and knowledgeable!'

'Seriously, what do you want me to do?'

'Keep him away from Sandown on Thursday.'

'How do I do that?'

'Use your imagination. We're having lunch today at The Knight Templar on the road between

Marlborough and Devizes. Do you know it?'

'I'll find it. What time?'

'We'll be there after 1 pm. I'll introduce you.'

'Who am I supposed to be?'

'Just a friend. He won't make a pass if he thinks we're close.'

'Gallant is he?'

'No, just afraid of being found out!'

'Anything I should know? Any tips?'

'He likes long hair worn loose, plenty of cleavage and thigh. Go easy on the make-up, but use plenty of expensive perfume.'

'And if I pull this off you're in the clear?'

'All that's left is for Man Samson to win.'

'I'll be keeping my fingers crossed.'

'So shall I, Jilly, for you!'

Jilly arrived at The Knight Templar at half past one and steadied herself with a large vodka. Sonia and Bart were already sitting at their table in the restaurant. She took a small mirror from her handbag and carefully arranged her long blonde hair until she was satisfied she appeared suitably windswept. Ordering a second vodka, she carried it into the restaurant.

'Why, Sonia. It is you, isn't it darling? It's been simply ages.'

'Hello, Jilly. How are you?'

'Fabulous, darling. Still waiting for the big part to take me to Hollywood.'

Sonia turned to Bart. 'Jilly's an actress,' she

explained, 'Jilly meet Bart. He trains racehorses.'

'Super. I adore horses.'

'Do you ride?' he asked politely.

'Not horses, darling,' she simmered suggestively.

'Care to join us?'

'Sorry, darling, I'm off to make a phone call. I'll be in the bar later. Stop by for a word before you go.'

They finished their meal and decided to take coffee in the bar with Jilly. It took her only seconds to catch Bart's interest and soon he couldn't keep his eyes off her. She chattered inanely, giving the impression of the original dumb-blonde with much more sex appeal than brains. She rarely spoke directly to Bart, but everything she said and did was angled towards him. She made it very clear she fancied him and that she wouldn't be averse to a tumble. She used her short skirt and low neckline to full advantage and, by the time he'd finished his coffee, Bart had been given vistas down to her navel and up to her crotch. He was as familiar with her stocking tops as he was with his own socks, but in spite of all this over-the-top behaviour she was a prize any red-blooded man would still try to capture.

'We must leave now, Jilly,' said Sonia, 'it's been lovely seeing you.'

Jilly tried to rise, but fell back into her seat laughing. 'Whoops, I do believe I'm tipsy.'

'Have you got your car, Jilly?'

'Yes, darling.'

'You can't drive in that condition.'

'How am I going to get home?'

'Bart could you take her?' pleaded Sonia.

'Where do you live, Jilly?' he asked.

'Just the other side of Melksham. About a twenty minute run.'

'You better get into my car. You certainly can't drive like that.'

She reached up and pecked him on the cheek. 'Isn't he sweet, Sonia?'

She tottered out to Bart's BMW and draped herself over the front passenger seat. Sitting close to her in the enclosed space of the car Bart was overcome by her nearness and her perfume. He let out the clutch and was a bit surprised to become aware of a rising between his legs. It was Sonia all over again. He wanted this dizzy young blonde almost as much as he'd first desired Sonia. She talked aimlessly and continuously for the first few miles, casually touching his sleeve or thigh as she spoke and each time her fingers sent a little jolt of sensual electricity through him. As she approached her destination she stopped chattering.

'Can I see you again, Jilly?' he ventured.

She touched him again. 'I'd love that, darling,' she cooed, 'but it will be a little difficult.'

'Why?'

'I'm going away tomorrow. I shall be in York for a couple of days, and then I'm off on tour.'

He looked crestfallen and she quickly continued. 'But you must travel as a racehorse trainer, watching your horses and things. Are you ever in the north of England?'

'I have a runner at Redcar on Thursday.'

'That's near York, isn't it? Why not travel up on Wednesday. We could spend the evening together.'

'And the night, maybe?'

'That sounds nice, darling. I shall be at the Post House.'

'I'll drive straight up from Sandown after racing. I can easily get back for Thursday afternoon.'

Her heart sank. 'Oh, I was hoping you'd take me racing at Redcar. I'd enjoy that.'

'All right, if that's what you'd like. We'll go racing.'

The car stopped. She touched his lips with her fingers. 'See you on Wednesday, darling. Don't forget the champagne.'

After the racing on Wednesday, Bart did the distance between London and York in record time, certainly beating anything Dick Turpin had managed. He asked the receptionist at the Post House to ring the room while he collected a couple of bottles of champagne from the bar. Jilly was waiting, dressed in a short white towelling robe with her long honey-coloured hair falling loose, and while he stripped for a bath she opened the champagne.

He was relaxing in the bath when she walked in carrying a bottle and two glasses. She handed him one, and knelt by the side of the bath sipping from the other. With a teasing smile on her lips she took the soap and slowly lathered her hands. He watched her silently. Very deliberately she dipped her fingers under the water and fished for his dick. With a giggle she pulled it above the surface and held it between her index finger and thumb in a vertical position. Very slowly it began to swell, and she took a nonchalant sip from her glass as she watched it grow to a size and stiffness where it could stand perpendicular without her support. That objective achieved she started fondling the shaft above the water with her soapy fingers, paying particular attention to the smooth bulbous helmet which she squeezed playfully between her fingers and thumb.

She chuckled merrily. 'Hey, it's more fun than a rubber duck!'

'Just mind he doesn't spit at you.'

'He wouldn't, would he?' she giggled.

'He might the way you're pulling him about.'

She slapped the surface of the water with her palm. 'Naughty Mr Duck,' she scolded.

He sipped from his glass and, as he did so, found himself dragged to his feet by his penis. Jilly had her fist tightly around the shaft and was pulling him upwards. Gripping his rampant tool she urged him to step out out of the tub and led him across the bathroom to the shower cubicle like a prize bull. She stood him under the shower and switched it on. As the warm water tumbled down she slipped out of her robe and joined him under the spray. It was the first time he'd seen her naked, but the water driving into his face got into his eyes so he couldn't properly appreciate her beauty.

She stood facing him for a second, playfully kissing each of his nipples before she knelt at his feet. He drew in a sharp breath as he felt her soft lips encircle his throbbing prick and when she began to suck he knew he wasn't far from ejaculation. His pego had been the willing victim of her busy fingers for so long that it was throbbing with lustful need. At first her wet mouth had soothed it, but as her tongue began to explore his foreskin and her lips caressed the shaft he knew he must come. He would have loved to have enjoyed a long bout of fellation, but his swollen cock was fit to burst. He felt his moment approach: it built up inside his balls, unstoppable, delicious, now! After he'd exploded into her throat he looked down to see her serenely swallowing a gushing mixture of semen and shower water.

He dried himself as she stood under the shower, and when she stepped out he wrapped her in a big white towel and patted her dry. She looked like a little girl wrapped in that big towel and he carried her bodily into the bedroom. There he swung her on top of a chest of drawers. She sat with her back jammed against the wall, and he parted her legs wide by grabbing her ankles and swinging them high above her head. Eagerly, he dipped his mouth between her open thighs to drink at her lusciously juicy fount. She lay back passively, content to let his tongue caress the deep folds of her shell-like vulva. He gorged like a glutton upon her sweet honeypot, licking up her nectar like a cat at the cream and forcing her legs wider and wider apart to flatten her mound of Venus, and to part the lips of her labia. She moaned a little as his probing tongue excited her tiny clit and gasped as it entered her vagina.

'Mmm, that's delightful. Eat me all up. More. More. Swallow me, darling.'

And when she began to tremble uncontrollably and the nectar from her body was flowing like wine he grabbed her in his arms and threw her onto the bed like a rag doll. The indignity of being dumped on her backside seemed to bring her to life. She hung around his neck and pulled him down onto the mattress. He fell on his back laughing helplessly as she sprang at him, her sharp teeth biting his belly and shoulders and thighs with little nips which soon had him begging for mercy. The savage passion she showed thrilled him, and by now he was frantic to enter her. She straddled his thighs, her rapacious cunt hovering above his eager tool and lowered herself inch by exciting inch, sucking him into her juicy hole until she was corked. There she paused, her buttocks flat against his groin, his knob held prisoner within her velvet tunnel. Outwardly she was as still as a statue, inwardly her vagina was milking his pego with the skill of a practised courtesan.

Without warning she fell forward onto his chest, her hands winding around his neck, her lips covering his. Their lovemaking became more frenzied. It was almost violent, their passion threatening to rip them apart as they became hotter, quicker. He spunked fiercely and she screamed as the warm seed creamed into her at the very moment of her orgasm.

'How good am I?' she whispered huskily. 'Did I live up to your expectation, master?'

'You were great, Jilly.'

'Did the earth move?'

'Move? It exploded!'

'So it was worth the drive?'

He pulled her down and kissed her. 'You bet,' he murmured.

After several heavenly minutes, as they lay with their bodies entwined, she urged him to roll over on top of her.

'Now fuck me gently,' she whispered in his ear, 'make me come, and come and come again!'

Jilly was up early next morning, but she left him to sleep. She soaked in a hot bath to soothe away the soreness in the more intimate parts of her body before waking him with a champagne breakfast. It was past 11 am before she allowed him to get up. By then it was too late for him to change his mind and go flying off to Sandown Park.

True to his word Bart took her to Redcar. His two-year-old ran a good third in a high-class race, but she didn't really notice it. It was a chilly afternoon with a cold wind blowing off the North Sea, and quite honestly she'd rather have been in bed with him than standing out in the open. She had the first two winners which cheered her up a bit, but her thoughts were far away. She spent the afternoon anxiously awaiting the result of the fifth race at Sandown Park.

Chapter 4

On the morning of the race Tess was singing happily
as she tended to Man Samson. She'd settled in at
Collyer's End. She liked Barney and had struck up a
thing with him even if he was old enough to be her
father. She'd been badly hit by a relationship which
went wrong soon after she left school, and ever since
she'd taken her sex straight without the sugar. The
rest of her stable workmates seemed a decent lot,
and although she found Bart a bit snooty she liked
Sonia.

In another hour she'd be off to Sandown Park with
Man Samson. She loved going racing. She felt
strangely excited as she gathered together all the
bits and pieces the horse would be wearing to stop
him knocking himself in the horsebox. Although
Barney hadn't said anything she instinctively knew
that Man Samson was expected to run a big race
that afternoon.

'Best foot forward,' she cooed in the gelding's ear,
'you've got to be at your best, fella. You'll win for me
this afternoon, won't you?'

She began sorting out the tack she'd collected from the Tack room, and all the odds and ends she'd need at the course; all the time she chatted to the big animal.

'You've never been to Sandown, have you, fella? You'll like it there. I'm sure you'll win,' she murmured planting a kiss on the gelding's nose. 'You'll show 'em all, won't you?'

At about the same time Barney was on the phone to a bookie friend he'd known for many years. They'd been buddies from way back and trusted each other implicitly. Nowadays Barney would feed him bits of genuine racing information to earn himself a bob or two. Sonia had been very worried about the betting side of the coup, without which the whole thing would be pointless. The race wasn't important enough for an ante-post book, yet if she asked for the morning price she knew the big bookies wouldn't accept much before the price tumbled drastically. She decided to take the starting price and spread her bets around as many bookies as possible. However, to achieve that she would need both time and help, and she had neither. She couldn't ask outsiders to stake her money without letting them into the secret. Barney solved the problem. He would enlist the aid of his bookie friend.

'Sam, this is Barney. How's tricks?'

'Fine. Have you got something for me?'

'Not the usual, but a favourite that will get stuffed.'

The usual was a tip from the stable that a horse was at the races to win. This type of information was especially useful to a punter, but a favourite that couldn't win was a bookie's delight. He could lay the horse at slightly longer odds than his rivals and attract money for an animal which was very unlikely to win.

Sam seemed dubious. 'That's not like you, Barney.'

'There's nothing dodgy, Sam,' he replied quickly, 'no question of stopping the horse. No drugs involved.'

'I've got your word on that?'

'On my life, Sam. The deal I'm offering is snow white.'

'Oh, it's a deal, is it?'

'I'll give you the losing favourite if you'll spread a bit about for me on an outsider?'

'Both in the same race?'

'Yes.'

'Both from your stable?'

'Yes.'

There was a pause. 'It's the fifth at Sandown, isn't it?'

Barney laughed. 'You're a smart old sod, Sam.'

'I have to be.'

'Are you on?'

'What makes you think your horse will be favourite?'

'Come on, the chestnut's the obvious choice with Dilly Jacks up.'

'Golden Times, you mean?'

'What else?'

'And he can't win?'

'He can't beat Man Samson.'

The reply was hesitant. 'Are you certain? I haven't heard any whisper about Man Samson, and he's been off injured a long time.'

'He's as fit as he ever was. You can take my word for it.'

'Okay, Barney. I'll do it as a favour but only because we go back a long way.'

'Thanks, Sam. You won't be sorry.'

'How much have you to spread about on the gelding. I take it you're angling for a long price?'

Barney told him the figure Sonia had to spend. He knew Sam employed faces to bet with other bookies on his behalf. These people were completely trustworthy, and nobody ever knew where the money was coming from or going to.

While Barney went about his day's work in his usual phlegmatic way, Sonia was preparing to hit the betting shops in all the big towns between Wiltshire and London. As she crossed the yard towards her old Cavalier Estate she saw Eddy, the Travelling Head Lad, supervising the loading of Golden Times and Man Samson into their horse box.

'See you at Sandown,' she called, 'have a good journey.'

Eddy didn't look up. 'Thanks, mam,' he grunted.

Eddy was a slow careful driver and Tess enjoyed the plod up the motorway. Once on the course she led Man Samson to the stables and began to prepare for the big event. She liked to turn her horses out looking neat and tidy but she never went in for the grooming niceties that won the best-turned-out prizes. She loved being at the races and, after a quick snack in the canteen, walked the course with the stable apprentice, Billy Barkes. Bart had given Billy the ride on Man Samson as he thought the seven pounds the boy's allowance would take off the animal's back would be valuable. He didn't worry about the boy's inexperience as he gave the horse no chance of winning. Billy was nineteen and had ridden six winners, but he was beginning to get too heavy to have much future as a Flat jockey. Only that week he'd sought Bart's advice as to whether to transfer to a National Hunt stable to continue his career in the jumping game. Tess turned to him as they trudged along the back straight.

'Have you ridden here before?'

'Once in an Apprentice race. I was nearer last than first.'

'Perhaps my fella will give you a winning ride today?'

'I'd like to think so.'

'He's fitter than they let on. I'm sure of that.'

'You think so?'

'I'm certain. He'll give a good account of himself, you see.'

'Yeah, maybe: but the chestnut's here to win.'

'Then I'll bet you'll be in the frame.'

He sighed. 'It's not the same as a winner.'

'But it would be nice, wouldn't it? To be placed in a Class C race.'

'Oh sure.'

Sonia was late arriving and Eddy instructed Tess to take her charge into the pre-parade ring. Tess was quite happy to walk the horse round as she knew it would loosen him up for the race – anyway she liked to be on the move herself.

Sonia arrived in time to supervise the saddling of both horses and she watched them being led into the parade ring. Golden Times was owned by a syndicate of twelve, and nine were on the course to watch the horse race. Sonia, therefore, had to spend most of her time entertaining, which left Eddy to calm the nerves of Man Samson's young pilot. Standing in the middle of the ring, watching Dilly Jacks arrive, she was surrounded by the syndicate. However, most of them drifted away from her to crowd around their famous jockey, so she was able to cross over to have a word with Billy. The bell rang as she arrived at his side and, after giving him a leg up, she walked at the horse's side towards the course.

'Billy,' she whispered hoarsely.

'Yes, Mrs Beechly?'

'Can you hear me?'

'Yes.'

'Well, listen very carefully.'

He bent his head down obediently.

'The gelding can win this afternoon.'

The lad said nothing.

'Did you hear me? The horse is here to win.'

'Yes, I heard you.'

'I want you to win.'

He looked puzzled. 'Yes, mam.'

'You don't sound very enthusiastic?'

'It's a surprise, that's all, mam.'

'You want to win, don't you?'

'Of course I do.'

'Okay, keep him up with the pace and out of trouble, and kick on from three out.'

'Yes, mam.'

'Just keep at him, Billy, and he'll run to the line. Is that clear?'

'I know he's got past form, but is he ready, Mrs Beechly?'

'He's ready to run for his life. Take my word for it.'

'You really believe he can win?'

'I'm certain of it, if you ride to win.'

The lad grinned. 'Don't worry, mam. I'll be bustin' a gut.'

'This is between us, Billy,' she said urgently, 'you must say nothing to Dilly Jacks, understand?'

There was no love lost there. 'It'll be a pleasure to beat him,' he muttered.

'I'll see you get a good present out of it, Billy.'

'Thanks, Mrs Beechly. Don't worry, I'll win for you.'

Billy liked Sonia. She was pleasant and kind, and

by far the most beautiful woman he'd ever seen. He wondered who'd set up the coup he was being entrusted to land. Had she organised it herself, or was the guv'nor in on it? He hadn't heard so much as a whisper around the yard so it was a secret well kept. So well kept it was almost unbelievable. He realised they were on the course and Tess was preparing to let go of the horse's head so he could take it to post.

'Good luck, Billy boy,' called the stablegirl.

Sonia fell in beside her as they walked back from the course. 'Did you hear our conversation, Tess?'

'Most of it.'

'It mustn't go any further.'

'I understand that.'

'Good.'

Tess's excitement suddenly gushed out. 'Do you really think Man Samson can win?'

'He'll win if Billy plays his part.'

'Billy won't miss an opportunity like this.'

'No, I don't think he will.'

'Can I put a bet on, Mrs Beechly? Will that be okay?'

Sonia produced a tenner. It was about what a hopeful young stablegirl might chance on her charge. 'Here put this on for yourself.'

She watched the girl sprint towards the line of bookies before she sauntered casually back to the stands to watch the race. For all her nonchalance she found she was trembling and sweating freely as she climbed the steps. She saw the horses hadn't yet reached the post, and she wondered what sort of state she'd be in when they came under starter's orders.

Barney walked into the betting shop a few minutes before the fifth race and immediately glanced up at the TV screens. Golden Times was firmly installed as favourite. It had opened at 7–4 and hardened to 5–4. Even as he watched, 11–10 was flashed up. On the other hand Man Samson had opened at 14–1 and drifted to 16–1. He heaved a sigh of relief. Nobody at the course had got wind of their attempted coup. The fact that Dilly was on the favourite, and the boy was on the gelding, was enough to allay any suspicion. He wrote out a slip staking £25 to win on Man Sansom, and waited as late as he dared before handing it to the cashier. She accepted it without question and as he took the receipt he heard the tannoy blare.

'Under orders Sandown. Off Sandown four twelve.'

On the course Sonia stood by herself with binoculars glued to the start of the ten furlong race. She was much too nervous to stand near anyone she knew. She had to experience the joy, or the sorrow, alone. The next few minutes would decide her future, and that was a very personal thing. Although there were twelve horses circling in front of the stalls she only had eyes for one. She followed Man Samson as he circled quietly with his head down like an old cart-horse. In her tense state she couldn't decide whether that was good or bad as she scanned horse and rider for any visible sign that might hint at their coming performance. The gelding looked fine. There was no sign of sweat on his coat or between his legs. Billy appeared as cool as a cucumber. It was almost as if she hadn't spoken to him, as if he had no idea of the responsibility on his young shoulders. She watched them file behind the stalls and begin to load up. Man Samson was one of the first to enter the stalls and because she could no longer see him she became even tenser. She swung her binoculars around to focus on the bookies' boards and glanced at the prices offered. The chalked prices were mostly hidden by the madding crowd, but she clearly saw 20s offered by one firm. She smiled. That was a good sign, perhaps things were going her way. They certainly should after the work she'd put into preparing for this race.

'They're under starter's orders, they're off and running . . .'

As the course commentator began his work her binoculars swivelled back to the runners. Billy had got a good break and was urging his horse up towards the leaders. After fifty yards the field settled down and some kind of pattern formed. Two horses shared the lead, and two were tucked in behind them. Following the first two pairs the remainder of the field was bunched with Golden

Times tucked in at the rear. Man Samson was the outside horse of the second pair. Billy had him perfectly placed and Sonia's pounding blood pressure eased a little. Maybe the lad had it all in hand. She knew she could do nothing to help him, but in spite of that she was with him mentally on the horse's back following his every move.

Five furlongs from home and the field began to bunch. She realised the leading pair had slowed the pace and fear stabbed at her again. Something would creep up on Billy's outside and box him. He'd never get a clear run. 'Oh, God,' she groaned. Even as she anticipated the problem she saw a horse being urged up on Billy's outside. It was all happening exactly as she feared, but Billy had seen the danger of a slow pace and kicked on. The two horses accelerated into the lead and because the horse on his outside began to lean, Billy was forced onto the rail.

'Keep him out of trouble,' she muttered desperately, 'keep him clear.'

Billy rode the rail around the bend with a head as cool as a jockey twice his age. He kept Man Samson so close that he seemed to be tied to the rail, his right boot almost scraping the paintwork. Once into the straight Billy balanced his horse and kicked for home. The gelding instantly lengthened his stride and started to race as if the only thing he wanted to do was win. Sonia watched through her binoculars with baited breath. They shook violently in her trembling hands, as the gelding gradually increased its lead with every ground-consuming stride.

'Come on. Come on, my son,' she breathed through flared nostrils.

The rest of the field watched Billy's arse disappearing out of sight as their mounts were hopelessly outpaced. Only Dilly Jacks had the horse under him to give chase and he'd been taken unawares. He pulled the big chestnut out and went in pursuit but Billy had flown. He was crouched, in the drive position, over Man Samson and pushing and pushing at the horse with his hands and heels. Fifty yards from the post and Golden Times was cutting back the gelding's lead under Dilly's flying whip, but there was no way he was going to pass him before the post. Sonia watched the final furlong with her heart in her mouth, her chest pounding like a drum as she gasped for breath. The exhilaration was so great that it was painful. It was like an orgasm. She heard herself scream like a dervish as the gelding flashed passed the post. *She'd won*! She'd pulled off the coup of a lifetime. She punched the air, kissed the woman standing next to her and didn't care that she had wet herself.

In the betting shop Barney watched the final furlong in complete silence. Not a flicker of emotion showed on his weatherbeaten face. Barney was an experienced gambler. He continued watching until he saw Man Samson returned at 20–1 before he turned silently on his heels and left the shop. Outside he allowed himself a smile. A 20–1 winner. It meant Sonia Beechly would be able to afford the mortgage on her own yard and he would be starting a new life under her. He grinned to himself, he'd rather be on top of her. Well, maybe one of these days.

Tess watched the final furlong with tears in her eyes as her charge flashed past the post the winner. Suddenly she was crying openly. Her pleasure at watching her pet win was in no way motivated by cash, and for that reason was much more heartfelt than either Sonia's or Barney's. In the short time she'd looked after the horse she'd struck up an affection that most girls reserve for their very own pony. She dashed wildly onto the course to meet her conquering hero, wiping her eyes with the back of her hand as she ran.

'Well done, Billy,' he enthused, 'smashing ride.'

'Thanks, Tess. It all went right.'

She fondled the gelding's nose. 'And you, fella. We can't forget you, can we?'

She proudly led the victors into the winner's circle, but although it was a very special moment for them nobody clapped. The hot favourite had been stuffed by a 20–1 shot. It had hit the punters in the pocket and they weren't pleased. Only the bookies would be grinning. Sonia waited for Man Samson and saw very few of the syndicate had bothered to come forward to welcome their horse into second spot. She watched Billy dismount and unsaddle the horse.

115

'Well done, Billy. It went like a dream.'

'Certainly did, Mrs Beechly. He did everything you said he would.'

She could see he was over the moon, having ridden a winner at a big meeting like Sandown. 'I'll see you right, Billy.'

'Thanks. I can't imagine I'll get anything off the guv'nor.'

She grinned. 'I doubt it, lad.'

'He didn't know about it, did he?'

'No, but I'll assure him that you had nothing to do with it.'

'Thanks, mam, but you'll get the sack, you know that, don't you?'

'That's my worry, Billy.'

Billy left to weigh-in, and Tess led the horse towards the stables to walk him and wash him down in preparation for the journey home. She wondered how far the coup went. She was ninety-nine percent sure Barney was in it, but who else? She was smart enough to realise that neither Sonia nor Barney would be at Collyer's End much longer, and wondered what they had planned for the future. Perhaps Sonia was after a yard of her own and Barney was going with her. If that was the case she wanted to go with them.

Tess searched out Barney after she'd bedded Man Samson down for the night.

'Have you got it on video, Barney?'

He knew what she meant without asking. 'Sure have.'

'I thought you would. Can I see it?'

'Come home with me now. We'll have a film show.'

'Just give me time to change.'

'Into something sexy, eh?'

She chuckled. 'What! Just to watch a horse race?'

In his small one-up and one-down cottage Barney poured a couple of large scotches and they settled down in armchairs.

'Cracking race, wasn't it?' she said.

'Sure was.'

'Where'd you watch it?'

'In the betting shop.'

'I bet you ejaculated when he won!'

He laughed. 'Young ladies aren't supposed to say things like that.'

'All right, but I bet I make you come this time round!'

'Just watch the race, girl.'

Even as he spoke she moved towards him, perching herself on the arm of his chair just as the video showed the horses circling behind the stalls. Without further ado her nimble fingers began to unfasten his fly, and by the time the horses were installed she'd delved into his trousers and pulled free his slumbering prong. Leaning over him, she wrapped her right arm around his shoulders and buried her face in his neck. As the horses came under orders her left hand began to massage his dick which now

117

lay exposed like a sleeping serpent.

It awoke to her magic touch. 'Oh, it's alive!' she giggled.

'Shut up, and watch the race.'

'Don't you like me playing with him?' she asked like a small girl who'd been told off.

'Let's see the race first.'

'No,' she pouted, 'I want to toss him off so he shoots when our horse wins.

He grinned up at her. 'Bet you can't!'

'How much?'

'I get to screw you if you don't.'

'And if I do?'

'You get to screw me.'

She walloped him. 'Big deal!'

'Well, are you on?'

'Wind it back. Then we'll start.'

No sooner had her fingers encircled the short thick shaft of his cock than she had it standing as upright as a soldier on parade. The magic of her fingers made it respond like a cobra to a snake-charmer. They watched until the point where the field swung around that final bend where Man Samson galloped into the lead. Now Tess dug her nails into the throbbing helmet of his pulsating pole.

'Hey,' Barney bawled, 'gently does it!'

The horses thundered into the straight and Billy slipped the gelding into the lead as Tess's hot fingers wrapped around Barney's foreskin and commenced to massage with all the expertise of a masseuse handing out a special. She timed it perfectly. As Billy brought his mount to the winning post so she brought her stallion to orgasm. At the very instant Man Samson crossed the line she jerked a volley of spunk from her victim's zealous charger.

Barney watched his juice pool in the palm of her hand.

'Wow,' he sighed, 'what a finish!'

'I bet you've never had a winner like that before?'

He chuckled. 'Never, but I intend to take you to bed and ride another very soon.'

She smiled wickedly and, holding her hand up in front of her mouth, she stuck her little pink tongue out provocatively to lick the blobs of semen from her palm.

'What did you get out of it?' she asked softly.

'Out of what?'

'Sonia's coup.'

'What makes you think she pulled off a coup?'

'Oh, come on!'

He poured them each another drink. 'She's starting her own yard. I'm to be head lad.'

'I guessed it was something like that.'

'Did you now.'

'Take me with you?'

'Take your clothes off and we'll talk about it.'

She chuckled. 'I was applying for a job as stable-girl, not your own personal tart.'

'They're one and the same. Take it or leave it.'

Sonia left Sandown Park on a cloud and stopped for a couple of drinks in the village, but she was more intoxicated with the excitement of the afternoon than the alcohol when she arrived back at Collyer's End. In her room she went straight to the video and rewound the tape. Like Barney, her first priority was to watch the race again and, like Tess, she was sexually aroused by it. The feeling of winning any race increased her blood pressure and made her pulse beat faster, but to win such an important race not only filled her with adrenalin but seemed to unbalance her hormones. She was desperate for a sexual experience while she watched.

She threw her clothes off swiftly leaving each item where it fell, until she was naked. She took her favourite dildo from its hiding place and, switching on the television, positioned herself in a chair with her legs spread wide. As the TV warmed up she hastily fingered herself, exciting her sweet clit by rubbing it vigorously with two fingers. The stimulation of that tiny organ aroused her erotically until she was at one with the sweating straining horses as they strode around the bend into the final straight. Her fingers were working at her throbbing button in time with the horses' galloping strides and, as Man Samson approached the winning post, she grabbed the dildo and thrust it up into her hot hungry cunt. She gasped in pleasure as it penetrated deep into her willing vagina, threw back her head in ecstasy and groaned lustily. A deep voracious cry that echoed from her very soul through the cavity of her chest up into her hot dry throat. At the crucial point of her self-induced sexual Nirvana came a loud knocking at the door. It was an angry knock. She climbed into a pair of jeans and pulled a sweater over her head.

Bart had been watching the fifth race at Sandown on the TV at Redcar racecourse. It had been an experience he didn't want to repeat. He'd promised his syndicate that their horse would win and there was Dilly Jacks trying desperately to catch the stable's second string. He exploded as Man Samson flashed past the post as the winner, grabbing Jilly's arm and dragging her to the car park. He had the good grace to return her to York before driving like a maniac towards Collyer's End. He was in no doubt what had happened. That bastard female had double-crossed him – she'd set up a coup using his own horse. When it got out he'd be a laughing stock. As he drove the miles separating them he imagined what he'd do to her. He'd kick her arse all around the yard, take a bull whip to her, beat her brains out . . . He hadn't cooled down much when he banged at her door.

'You cow. You fucking bitch.'

'I'm sorry, Bart.'

'Sorry! I could throttle you.'

'I know how you must feel.'

'You have no idea, you tramp. I could swing for you.'

'I'm sorry, what else can I say?'

'Say nothing. Pack your kit and clear off.'

She had been expecting that. 'Yes, Bart.'

'I suppose you did it to get your own yard?'

'Yes.'

'Well, you won't have any horses to train. By the time I've finished, your reputation will be such that no owner will trust you with a bloody donkey.'

She bridled. 'That's sheer spite, Bart.'

'It's what you deserve. Now sod off, before I strangle you here and now.'

She threw a few things in a case. She couldn't really blame him, but he had made good use of her over the past three years. She'd shared his life and given him freely of her body although he'd never once shown her any love or affection. She decided to stay the night at a hotel. She'd ring and book a room from the office, but first she must watch the video once more. Just to make certain it really had happened and it wasn't just some wonderful dream.

Chapter 5

Mandy was on top of the world. Yesterday she'd celebrated her sixteenth birthday and today she was going to ride a hunter-chaser. Sam was there waiting for her by the stables at the rear of his small isolated farm when she pedalled up on her bike. Sam was forty, an ex-National Hunt jockey who'd come down in the world after a fight against alcohol and was now scratching a living farming and training a few chasers. Mandy had met him at Fontwell Park races when she'd been there with a party from school. Like her elder sister, Jilly, she was dead keen on horses and had been a member of the Pony Club and gymkhanas since she was old enough to sit on her first pony. Now she attended boarding school in Sussex, she had little opportunity to ride during term time, so when Sam suggested she came over to ride out for him she jumped at it.

'Hi, Sam.'

'All ready, are we?'

'Sure am.'

'Got over yesterday's celebrations?'

'What celebrations?' she laughed.

'Didn't they give you a party?'

She giggled. 'Not what you'd call a party.'

He knew exactly what she meant. For all her tender years her idea of a party was a bottle of rum and a snog in his parlour after riding out.

'So you're all ready for Lumberboy?'

She threw her bike in the hedge. 'Lead me to him.'

'You remember our bargain?'

'Yes.'

'Is it still on?'

'Yes.'

Lumberboy was a big bay hunter-chaser whom she'd wanted to ride the first moment she set eyes on him, but Sam had said no. She'd badgered him until he promised she could ride him after her sixteenth birthday. She'd waited impatiently for the day to come, and while she waited she inveigled him into promising her the ride on Lumberboy in his next race under National Hunt rules. She hadn't got it for nothing though. Since the beginning she'd liked to pay her debts to Sam with a kiss. Later when he'd suggested she toss him off, she'd cried. She soon fell into line, however, and discovered a bit of slap-and-tickle worked wonders. To get her leg over Lumberboy she'd agreed to get her leg over Sam after her sixteenth birthday, and to get him to enter the horse for her to ride at Plumpton she'd already gone down on him.

'Okay, Mandy. Into the barn and get your clothes off.'

She looked surprised. 'Don't be in such a hurry. We can do that afterwards.'

'That's what I had in mind, but I want you naked when you ride Lumberboy.'

'Oh, come off it. Someone will see us.'

'Nobody comes up here. You know that.'

Reluctantly she went to the barn and began to undress. She sat on a straw bale to pull off her boots before easing down her skintight jodhpurs. It was a warm spring day and she was wearing only a silk blouse over her white bra. She stripped them off, running her fingers over her nipples as she did so. She was proud of her boobs, she always had been. She'd matured early and she recalled with a smile how jealous Jilly had been when at thirteen she took the same-sized bra. Mind you, she never pretended to be as beautiful as her older sister – Jilly was something special. But Mandy had the same blonde hair and soft feminine features. Unfortunately she was a couple of inches shorter and a bit tubbier. 'More comfortably built' she liked to say, when her sister teased her about her puppy fat. She decided to keep on her briefs as she knew her naked quim on the smooth leather saddle would overheat her. Sam, however, had other ideas.

'Get those knickers off'

She pouted. 'That's rude!'

'So it may be, but I want to see your bare arse.'

She slid them quickly down her legs. 'You're disgusting!' she pouted.

He'd tacked up the horses while she was in the barn, and gave her a leg up into the plate. She noticed he was bare-chested and bare-footed, but wore jeans. She felt very vulnerable and a bit ridiculous sitting the horse wearing nothing but her hard hat. He swung into the saddle of his own horse.

'Okay, let's go.'

He took her up the short gallop he'd laid out for himself, and over the practice fences. She jumped perfectly, if a trifle slowly. She'd been used to the gentler discipline of the show-jumping ring. He rode beside her and when she rose from the saddle, her backside high in the air as she stood up in her stirrups and bent forward over the horse's neck, he flicked his riding crop across her lovely bare rump. She squealed lustily. The sharp cut across her twin moons had left a thin pink stripe on the tender white skin.

'You pig, I might have fallen off.'

'Come on, get down to work. You're riding like an old woman.'

'Put that whip down then.'

But he didn't, and thrice more the flexible crop stang her naked posterior to the echo of her girlish squeals and curses. However, she increased her speed at the fences, taking them at near racing pace. His unorthodox urging had done the trick. As she dismounted she became very aware that she was feeling hot and horny and ready for the fucking she'd been promised. Her arse tingled from the four parallel pink stripes across it and her quim itched mightily from contact with the smooth warm leather. She'd ridden in just her knickers before, but her naked crotch against the saddle made her feel unbelievably randy.

He'd chosen a secluded shady dell and tethered their horses. Then he jerked his jeans down over his thighs. She saw his cock was standing out rock hard for her.

She chuckled. 'I see you're dead eager now I'm sixteen and ready for plucking.'

It was a reference to his insistence that she must reach her sixteenth birthday before he'd enter her. He probably thought she was a virgin. She certainly wasn't, but she'd say nothing about that. He squatted before her adoring her nakedness with lascivious eyes. Although she felt timid and rather shy she wanted to appear worldly and sophisticated. She raised her arms and rested her hands upon the top of her head to display the soft feminine curves of her young body to perfection. He reached forward to rest his hands upon her hips. The swell of her thighs was sufficiently voluptuous to show her maturity, yet the gentleness of the curves still hinted at adolescence. He allowed his fingertips to stray over her round belly as he rose on his haunches to kiss her delicious young tits which hung like two ripe pears. Gently he brushed her large pink nipples with his lips and watched them swell and harden.

He gorged on her young breasts awhile before running his tongue down her stomach. There, he reached out for the pure silken hair which partially hid her most precious jewel. His teeth teased the fine hairs until she obediently parted her thighs. She was eager to feel the lick of his tongue along the length of her burning crack. The fig of her slit, shrouded by a bouquet of curls, wetly offered itself. He could only comply. She whinnied like a foal as his tongue slithered over her spread vulva and the feel of his lips pulling at her petals made her gasp. No tongue had pleasured her with cunnilingus before and she found it quite wonderful. She wanted to be sucked forever but he had other ideas. He was hot to enter her. He squatted before her on bended knees, forcing his great ramrod between her legs in search of the opening into her sweet young body. A hunger to be filled welled up inside her. She grabbed at the bulbous tip of his monster and took it to the very edge of her hole. Sam impaled her in one long slow hot thrust.

She threw back her head, violently tossing her mass of short golden curls, and screamed to the heavens as he penetrated her. She burst into tears as he stretched her tight. She was well and truly corked – and she loved it.

'I'm full of you. You've filled me right up,' she sobbed.

'Don't you like it?'

'Yes. Yes, I do. Now fuck me.'

He began moving slowly inside her.

'No, quicker. Harder. Make me come.'

She felt him roughly clasp the cheeks of her bum and straighten his legs. She was swung bodily upwards until she sat straddling his thighs with his cock still deep within her. She wrapped her legs around his waist and her arms around his neck so he was forced to support her weight with his hands under her buttocks.

'What position do they call this?' she murmured happily.

'Lord knows!'

She giggled. 'I'm like a necklace around your neck.'

'Or a huge crab?'

She hit him between the shoulder blades. 'That's not nice.'

He was beginning to work his prick inside her and she responded by grinding her crotch against his body and pumping her sweet young twat up and down his pulsing organ until the sweat ran from them both.

'Come,' she gasped, 'come inside me.'

'In a minute . . .'

'No. No, now.'

'I can't yet.'

'Please. I can't wait to feel your hot spunk inside me.'

She increased her tempo, slapping her thighs

against him as she fought to drag an ejaculation for him.

'Oh, Christ,' she wailed, 'I'm coming.'

She dug her nails passionately into his back and squeezed at him with her legs.

'Too late,' she lamented, 'I've come. You're too late.'

But even as she spoke his semen shot into her and the palm of his hand slapped her spread buttocks with a blow that made her wince. Her answer was to sink her teeth into him.

'You bastard,' she shrieked.

He held her close. 'Who would have thought it?' he whispered.

'Thought what?'

'That such an innocent little girl's look could hide such a hot-arsed young doxy!'

She grinned from ear to ear and stuck her tongue in his mouth.

'More,' she whispered, 'more . . .'

During the next month Mandy sat on Lumberboy several times in preparation for her day at the races. It was no secret, for her parents had had to give their permission for her to ride. The school allowed a party to travel to Plumpton to support her. When the day finally arrived she was calmer and more confident than she'd thought she'd be. Sam had been wonderful, patiently grooming her for her big day.

There was a nip in the air and a slight drizzle falling as she walked nervously from the weighing room towards the paddock. It was a hunter-chaser steeplechase for amateur riders so she'd had the company of several other women in the changing room. They were a tightly knit group who rode against each other regularly and mostly ignored the new girl. However, an older woman showed her the ropes, and helped to guide her through the preliminaries of her first race under rules.

Sam was waiting for her in the paddock as the owner and trainer of Lumberboy, and his one and only stableboy was leading the horse round. She glanced at the busy scene. It was a mid-week meeting, and because the weather was dull and overcast there weren't too many spectators. The bell rang and she walked towards the big bay hunter.

'Just remember, he's got more experience than you. He'll take you round and keep you out of trouble, so don't go pulling him about.'

'Don't worry, Sam. I'll let him do the work.'

'If you are a position to get into the frame he'll run for you if you keep pushing him.'

'I'll do my best.'

He gave her a leg up. 'Sure you will, girl. Just enjoy yourself.'

She jogged slowly to post as Lumberboy appeared to be in no hurry, and she certainly wasn't going to upset him this early in the proceedings. She joined the rest of the field for a look-see at the first fence and was the last to turn back to the start.

There were ten in the field and she urged Lumber-

boy forward when the tape flew up. Unfortunately
the big bay horse didn't seem too keen about the
whole business. Mandy pushed at his neck, kicked
with her feet, and screamed diabolical unladylike
oaths in his ear. Panic engulfed her as the rest of the
field galloped away leaving her flatfooted. Oh, God,
what a disgrace. All her schoolfriends were watching
and her horse was refusing to race. She was nearly
in tears.

'Come on, boy. Gee-up,' she shrieked. 'Move your
arse, you lazy bastard. Quick, quick.'

Suddenly the big horse decided to gallop and shot
forward, nearly chucking her out of the saddle. She
was all of ten lengths adrift as she approached the
first fence, filled with a terrible dread of her horse
refusing. Fortunately he sailed over like an old cam-
paigner and settled down to run a sensible race.

Passing the post on the first circuit, Mandy was
still very much at the rear, but Lumberboy gradually
pulled himself up to the remainder of the field and
tucked himself in behind the trailing bunch. Mandy
hadn't planned to be on the rail but she had no
intention of fighting the horse. He appeared to have
a mind of his own when racing. At the sixth a horse
fell in front of her, but Lumberboy avoided it cleverly
and, when at the seventh another refused, he took it
into his head to run. The big bay hunter put himself
into the race and when Mandy felt him lengthen his
stride she pulled him off the rail to gallop past two
opponents. At the ninth he took off like a stag to

outjump the horse in front and land in fifth place.
She could see the leading four horses approaching
the tenth some way in front of her. Although she
couldn't possibly win from that position she realised
that if she could keep Lumberboy up to his task they
would finish in a respectable position. She wouldn't
be disgraced after all.

And then, without warning, it happened. The
whole race changed in seconds. The leader fell at the
tenth. It was a nasty crashing fall and it brought
down two other horses. The rider of the fourth horse
panicked, attempted to change direction, unbal-
anced her mount and was unseated. Mandy remembered what she'd been told. She held the horse
together, sat tight and prayed. Lumberboy sailed
over the fence, instinctively avoiding the mayhem on
the other side, and galloped away happily as if he
was in the hunting field.

It took a few moments for Mandy to realise she'd
been left clear. The only horse in front of her was
riderless. She was in the lead with two fences to go.
She felt a tingle of excitement run up her spine. She
was in a position to win the race. In fact if she didn't,
Sam would have every right to slap her backside. A
dozen ways to ride flashed through her mind and she
dismissed them all. She sat tight and let the horse
do the work. After all he hadn't done so badly up to
now. Lumberboy galloped relentlessly at the last two
fences and took them as surefooted as a goat. Mandy
chanced a quick glance over her shoulder. She was

clear by a mile. A feeling of disbelief swamped over her to be replaced by a glow of satisfaction. It was only when she crossed the line that she was fully aware she'd won.

Never had she experienced such exhilaration, such rapture. It surpassed passing her school exams, or opening her Christmas presents, or even an orgasm. She was led into the winner's circle in a haze of purple enchantment. It was like floating on air.

'Well done, Mandy,' screamed her schoolmates.

'Nice race, girl,' murmured Sam.

'Congratulations, my dear,' smiled the rider of the second.

'Lucky young tart,' muttered the rest of the crowd, 'if it hadn't been for that pile-up at the tenth she'd be nowhere.'

But Mandy didn't care what they said. Her name was in the record books. She'd jumped all the fences and jumping is the name of the game. She looked so young and flushed with joy that she positively oozed sex. When she dismounted Sam could have dragged off her jodhpurs and shagged her on the spot. Instead he had to be satisfied with an arm around her shoulders and a quick peck on the cheek.

'You gave him a lovely ride,' he murmured in her ear.

'I never dreamt I'd win, did you?'

'Everyone deserves a little good fortune.'

'It was all those fallers that did it. They were all well ahead of me.'

'Jumping is what it's all about, Mandy. You've got to jump 'em all to win.'

Her best friend, Helen, came running towards her as she walked towards the weighing room. 'Miss Ales says I can go back with you after the races. Is that okay?'

'That's marvellous. See you when I've changed.'

Sam began his celebrations immediately after the weigh-in, and stayed in the bar until after the last race. The two girls helped the stable lad wash down the horse and walk it, prior to loading up to go home. Sam was already staggering when he climbed into the box, and he produced a bottle of cherry brandy for the two girls. Although he drank a lot of it himself, the girls drank enough to be merry by the time they arrived back at the stables. Sam was so plastered he was unable to walk and the two girls had to help him into the house. He lived alone and insisted on being taken into his bedroom where he collapsed and was asleep in seconds. Helen looked at Mandy as if she was concerned.

'We can't leave him like this.'

'Why not? He's as drunk as a fiddler's bitch.'

Helen giggled. 'Shouldn't we loosen his clothing, or something?'

'You want to undress him, don't you?'

She blushed. 'Of course not.'

'We could.'

'Could what?'

'Could undress him and put him to bed. I bet he wouldn't remember anything about it tomorrow.'

Helen looked uncomfortable. 'That wouldn't be right.'

Mandy grinned at her. 'I bet you've never seen a man naked.'

Helen contradicted her quickly. 'I have.'

'Who?'

'My brother.'

'He's not a man.'

'He's sixteen.'

There was a long pause. 'Go on then, I dare you,' challenged Helen.

'Only if you help.'

'All right.'

The cherry brandy had loosened their inhibitions and taken away their modesty. They began to undress the soundly sleeping Sam with quick nimble fingers which would have been the envy of many nurses. Soon his shoes and shirt and tie were draped over a chair, and being a well-brought-up young lady, Helen had even taken off his socks. It was then they paused and looked at each other. Should they continue? Next would be his trousers. He was still fast asleep. He hadn't moved a muscle since the two girls had gone about their task.

'Now for his pants,' grinned Mandy.

'Should we?'

'Why not?'

'There'll be no going back.'

'What do you mean by that?'

Helen blushed. 'What if he wakes up?'

Mandy laughed. 'You're afraid he might go berserk and rape us?'

'Something like that,' Helen giggled wildly.

Mandy grabbed at his belt and began to unbuckle it. Helen stood back nervously and watched as she unzipped him. She took a good hold of the trousers and underpants around his waist and jerked them down over his hips.

'Come on,' she urged Helen, 'grab the legs and pull. Let's have 'em right off.'

Helen looked dubious but began to pull the trousers over his feet. She couldn't help but notice that Mandy had stripped off his underpants as well.

'Don't look so shocked,' chuckled Mandy.

'I can't help it. He's naked!'

'I said you'd never seen a naked man, didn't I?'

Helen gazed down at him. 'He's lovely, isn't he?'

Mandy shrieked with laughter. 'What!'

Helen was flustered. 'I mean he has a good body. All lean and muscled with a nice flat tummy.'

'And a nice big prick!'

'Mandy! I didn't say that.'

They sat on the bed, one on either side of Sam's nude body, and peeped at each other saucily. Mandy's slim fingers strayed towards his sleeping dick.

'Shall I wake it up?'

'Won't that wake him?'

'I don't know. Perhaps if I'm very gentle we can get it to stand up without waking him.'

'What do you mean, we? I'm not touching it, Mandy.'

Mandy grinned. 'You've never touched one, have you?'

'I have.'

'Whose?'

'My step-brother's.'

'That doesn't count.'

'Why not? He had an erection.'

Mandy gasped. 'You jerked your brother off. You dirty little cow.'

'I didn't say that.'

'No, but I bet you have.'

Helen looked sheepish. 'Once or twice,' she admitted with a touch of pride.

'You little raver. What else did you do to him?'

'I gave him head once,' she confessed quickly.

Mandy was flabbergasted. 'Well, I'm damned.'

'What makes you say that?'

'I never thought it of you. Did he stick it up you?'

'No,' she answered sharply, 'he did not.'

While they talked Mandy's sexy little fingers had brought Sam's slumbering organ to full erection. They both looked at it pointing proudly towards the ceiling like some fleshy monolith.

'Go on,' urged Mandy, determined to embarrass her friend, 'it's your turn. Get your lips around that.'

'Mandy, you're disgusting.'

Even as she spoke Mandy's willing fingers were caressing the smooth helmet of that rock-hard weapon, and the alcohol, combined with the strange situation, made her blood pump faster with sexual desire. She dipped her head and lightly kissed the smooth blunt tip.

'Has he fucked you, Mandy?'

'Once.'

'Was it nice?'

'Nice enough.'

'You suck him first. Then I'll follow.'

Mandy was filled with an overwhelming desire to see her friend's mouth full of Sam's cock. She wanted to watch her suck at it. The mental image of Helen's mouth greedily fellating that rampant weapon aroused and stimulated her. She had no idea why — perhaps she was a voyeur at heart. She parted her lips and moved her head downwards to cover the bulbous red tip with her open mouth.

'Mmm, lovely,' she murmured as she swallowed the monster lollipop deep into her throat.

Helen giggled nervously, her eyes like saucers as Mandy gobbled the throbbing prong with all the expertise of a high-class call girl.

'Your turn.'

Helen gave a fleeting smile, shy and flirtatious, before her fresh young lips dived at the ramrod glistening with Mandy's saliva. Her lithe tongue slithered hungrily down the stiff shaft of his organ, wrapping it around his prick as if it were an ice cream cornet. Mandy watched, eagerly urging her to accept more and more into her mouth until the girl almost gagged upon the thick shaft wedged in her gullet. Almost choking, Helen withdrew her head, and her place was immediately taken by Mandy whose sweet lips covered the upright pole with repeated kisses. As Helen watched, fascinated, she became aware of the sexual tension within her. She was ready to fuck. She wanted to be penetrated, filled, abused. Mandy appeared to read her thoughts.

'Do you want it inside you?'

Helen nodded and, while Mandy gently massaged the root of the pulsing wand with her cool fingers, she stripped off her skirt and had her knickers down like lightning.

'Put one foot either side of his tummy, and crouch down over him,' Many instructed, 'I'll guide his cock into you.'

Helen crouched astride the stallion ready to ride, her hands between her open thighs, her fingers holding apart the swollen folds of her pretty pussy, while Mandy guided the blunt end towards the entrance. She wanted to see her friend shag herself with this living dildo, and almost purred with pleasure as the pego slipped into her like a well-oiled bolt. She heard Helen groan at the deepness of the penetration and urged her on until she was impaled to the hilt.

'Make him come, Helen. Slide up and down his slippery pole.'

As her friend began to move her arse Mandy suddenly felt an overwhelming desire to join in. She thrust her hand up her skirt, pulled her knickers down and off, and stood up on the bed so her snatch was hovering under Helen's nose. Grabbing the girl's head between her palms she thrust her hot groin into Helen's face.

'Suck me, Helen. Eat my pussy.'

This was a situation familiar to Helen. She'd eaten girls before. There was a time when she was convinced she was a lesbian. She grabbed the cheeks of Mandy's buttocks and pulling her closer, began to frantically tongue her slit. Revelling in sensation, Mandy opened her eyes and happened to glance down. Sam was wide awake. She saw him wink lecherously up at her. She wondered when he had woken from his drunken stupor.

'You bastard,' she squealed, 'how long have you been awake?'

'Oh, my God,' shrilled Helen in muffled tones from deep between Mandy's legs.

'Fancy pretending to be asleep, and letting us carry on like this.'

'Don't let me stop you, girls,' he laughed, 'just you enjoy yourselves!'

Mandy jerked herself free and, without warning, fell backwards to bury his face under her warm naked seat. The two girls were now facing one another. Grinning, they wound their arms around each other and kissed. The threesome quickly developed into an orgy of erotic movement as Mandy squirmed her hot tail into Sam's face, grinding herself against his mouth to feel the whole of his tongue inside her vagina and his lips searching out her clitoris. Then Helen screamed her climax.

'Golly, I'm coming. Oh Jesus, I'm going to orgasm,' she squealed.

Mandy sat back and watched her. Helen's face was a picture. Her eyes tightly shut, her cheeks sucked in, her lips drawn back over her teeth. It was the ultimate mix of pain and pleasure. Mandy envied her the moment and wished it was she who'd mounted that rampant penis.

During the summer months Mandy spent more and more time at the stables working with the horses and pleasuring herself with Sam. She rode several point-to-points and two more steeplechases, but her school work suffered and the teachers began to question her activities. As she had the blessing of her father they tolerated it until her torrid affair with Sam was sensationally disclosed. She was expelled and packed off home within the hour. Her father wasn't pleased.

'I've just had all this with your sister,' he growled. 'What's wrong with you girls?'

'I'm not going back to school, Daddy.'

'That's what your sister said.'

'You can't make me.'

'I suppose I could leather your backside. Your stepmother would.'

'You won't let her, will you, Daddy?'

'I would if I thought it would do any good. What is it you want to do?'

'To work with horses.'

'That's what your sister said. You didn't plan this together, did you?'

'No, we didn't, but you let her, didn't you?'

'I said she could join Sonia when she opened her new yard.'

'Did Jilly agree?'

'Yes, she did. But if you join her you're there to work, not arse about.'

'Sonia will train Flat horses. I want to work with jumpers.'

He father looked exasperated. 'You'll work with her, or you'll go back to school.'

Mandy pouted. 'All right, but buy me a jumper I can take with me.'

'We'll see.'

'Please, Daddy, pretty please,' she wheedled as she slung her arms around his neck.

He grinned. 'Be off, you minx!'

Chapter 6

Jilly was disconsolate. Nothing was going right. She and Mandy had moved into The Billings, Sonia's new yard at East Hipton, but things just weren't working out. The stables were nice enough, with a comfortable house and boxes sufficient to accommodate fifty horses, situated in the heart of the beautiful countryside of Wiltshire. The yard had its own gallops and all-weather strip, but most of the boxes stood empty. Jilly could have cried for her stepmother.

Sonia had got her dream, a yard of her own, but she was universally blamed for the way she got it. Bart had vented his anger in no uncertain way. He'd made sure that everybody vaguely connected with racing knew she'd pulled off a coup at his expense. She'd done it when she was under his wing, accepting his hospitality, and by using his own horse. The sauce of it amused many but overtly everybody sided with Bart. Most of the racing hacks, sensing a juicy story, printed every bit of vitriol Bart spat out, and

Sonia was ostracised. Many turned their backs on her at the races, few spoke more than a few words. Certainly no owners sent horses to her. The stable housed ten horses, and six of those belonged to her ex-husband. The remaining four had working-class owners, who'd made good the hard way and admired her for putting one over on the establishment.

After a month her ex walked unexpectedly into the yard.

'I hear you're being given the cold shoulder?'

'That's about it. Don't tell me you've come here to take your horses away?'

He chuckled. 'No, my word's my bond. You know that. Even if we disagreed about everything else we were always honest with each other.'

'Why have you come?'

'Not to gloat, my dear. I wish you well. You pulled a stroke, but really I can't understand the spite of the chap from Collyer's End. It should be forgotten by now.'

'Thanks for your vote of confidence, but I haven't exactly repaid you for giving me your horses.'

'What do you mean?'

'I'm still waiting for my first winner.'

'Don't worry about that. I've written off the capital outlay.'

She smiled. 'I know it was really for the girls, but thanks anyway.'

'You do realise you'd have owners lining up if they thought they could get you into bed?'

She chuckled. 'You haven't improved. You always were a dirty-minded old devil.'

'True!'

'I'd only have to do that once for it to be around the whole racing set. That would make things even more intolerable.'

'I'll do my best to put in a word for you, Sonia, but I don't move amongst the racing set.'

In spite of what he said he managed to persuade two of his business friends to transfer their horses to her, which brought her total up to twelve. It was already well into April and the Flat had been going for a month, and still The Billings hadn't saddled a winner. It wasn't for want of trying for Sonia had had runners on the all-weather at Lingfield and Southwell before the Flat began.

Even so, she was convinced she'd spent the £100,000 her ex had given her to buy six horses, wisely. She'd spent a large sum purchasing one well-bred yearling at the Newmarket Tattersalls sales, but the rest had been bought at the Breeze-up sales and the Horses in Training Sales. At the Breeze-up, young horses were allowed to canter before their potential buyers, while the Horses in Training Sales were a bit like an annual used-car auction. She still remembered with a great deal of pleasure the lush interior of the glass-domed mock-classical pavilion of Tattersall's Sales paddock with its high windows and electronic board flashing bids in four currencies. She'd felt she was a member of some high-class club and wished she could do all her shopping there. She dreamed of success so she could travel to Ireland and the USA, to the sales at Goff's and Keeneland. Maybe some day she would.

She came down to earth with a bump. That afternoon she was at Leicester where she hoped to have the winner in a D class handicap sprint.

It was drizzling at Leicester, nasty thin wet rain which soaked her to the skin before she realised she needed a raincoat. She walked back from the paddock and stood silently in the old-fashioned wooden stand, watching her horse go down. It was a miserable time when a stable failed to produce winners. She wondered what was going wrong and who was to blame. Maybe she'd never make a trainer. Maybe she was missing that bit of magic which was necessary when working with animals. She watched over her charges, both on the gallops and in the yard, like a mother hen; and she worried continuously about what she'd left out or hadn't done right. She'd got the vet to test the whole yard for everything she could think of. This afternoon she'd engaged Dilly Jacks to ride her entry. She watched the race with her heart in her mouth but the run Dilly conjured out of her colt fizzled out before the post.

'Mrs Beechly, isn't it?'

She looked around. A tiny vivacious young woman stood smiling up at her.

'Yes, that's me.'

'You don't know who I am, do you?'

'I'm sorry.'

'My name's Peggy-Sue Rhyma.'

Sonia's face lit up. 'Of course, the jockey. I thought I knew your face. I do apologise for not recognising you.'

Peggy-Sue laughed. 'Good heavens, why should you. I'm a has-been now.'

Sonia thought she looked like an effervescent young gypsy girl with her short brown curly hair, cute pixy face and dancing hazel eyes that sparkled like diamonds when she laughed. Standing facing her she felt like a giant for Peggy-Sue was a slightly built four-foot eleven. But however small her body, she was one-hundred percent female with all the right curves in the right places.

'You had that terrible accident at Epsom last June, didn't you?'

'Yes.'

'It was dreadful. I saw it on television.'

Peggy-Sue laughed lightly. She wasn't looking for sympathy. 'I'm over that now.'

'I'm so glad, but it put an end to your riding career, didn't it?'

'The doctors thought it had. My vision was affected and I suffered dizzy spells without warning. Race riding was out of the question, but I kept faith that time might heal me.'

'And has it?'

'Yes, I believe so. My doctors think I'm fighting fit.'

'I'm so glad for you. Will you be able to ride again?'

'I'm hoping so. I've an appointment with the Jockey Club doctors tomorrow for an examination.'

'Racing has missed you. You were the most outstanding woman jockey to come into racing. You rode for the notorious Mr Norster I seem to remember.'

'Mr Norster no longer trains.'

Sonia recalled the whispers that had gone around racing after Peggy-Sue's accident. It was rumoured that Norster had been doping his horses, and his stable's success rate was so high that many people believed it. Naturally Peggy-Sue, who rode for him, was tarred with the same brush. A lot of racing people, especially the men, thought she must be crooked. They refused to believe that a female jockey could be that brilliant. The whispers appeared to be confirmed when Norster closed his yard and went abroad. Nothing was ever proved, but mud sticks.*

'I read somewhere that he married his secretary, and they emigrated?'

Peggy-Sue didn't answer, but looked her straight in the face. Sonia was well aware that the young woman had approached her for some purpose and she was now about to come to the point. 'If I pass my medical I'd like to ride for you, Mrs Beechly.'

Sonia was flabbergasted. 'Why me? You can do better for yourself. My stables are new, and you must know I'm not exactly flavour of the year.'

'I know, but then neither am I. However, you've got

*See *Under Orders* (Headline Delta 1994) for an account of this scandalous affair the guts to stand up to them, and the brains to pull off that coup, so I'll take it on trust you're a first-class trainer.'

'Thank you, but . . .'

'You need horses to fill your boxes, don't you? A couple of rich influential owners to send you good horses to win top-class races?'

'I certainly need a rich and influential owner, but I don't know one.'

'I do. I could help you.'

'I don't think so, not in the present anti-Beechly climate.'

'I rode for Prince Sojo last season. I could ask him.'

'Why should he help? He doesn't know me.'

'Give me the nod and I'll try for you.'

'Okay, Peggy-Sue, if you really want to.'

'And you'll retain me if I get my licence back?'

'I'd be a fool not to, you've proved yourself a top jockey. But you must realise money's tight – your retainer would be peanuts.'

'We'll talk about that when you're a success!'

Peggy-Sue spat on her palm like a gypsy horse dealer and offered it to Sonia. Sonia grinned and took the offered hand.

'Tell me, Sonia – how far are you prepared to go to fill your boxes with good horses?'

Sonia recognised a wicked gleam in her eyes, like a naughty girl suggesting a bit of mutual mastur-bation to her best friend.

'How far did you go to get the best rides?'

'All the way!'

'And so will I, but only if complete discretion is assured.'

'You make me sound like a pimp.'

Sonia chuckled. 'Well . . .'

Peggy-Sue had mentioned Prince Sojo's name without any real idea of how she could contact him. She knew he had a racing manager to supervise his horses in Europe. She recalled his name was Guy and that he'd fancied her something rotten when she was riding. It wouldn't be difficult to discover his haunts. She wanted to meet him privately, away from the racecourse.

It rook her two days to discover he had a flat in Pimlico, not too distant from her own, and that he worked out every morning at a nearby health club. The next morning she donned her track suit and made her way there. She met him on the step. He was on the point of coming out. He recognised her immediately.

'Peggy-Sue Rhyma, what a pleasant surprise! What are you doing here?'

'I live nearby. I thought I'd give it a try.'

'I can recommend it. I come here regularly.'

'You're leaving very early. Is the club open all night?'

He laughed. 'I know the owners, and because I like to work out so early they give me a key.'

'Can I work out with you tomorrow?'

'Certainly. Are you completely over your accident now?'

'More or less.'

'Will you be able to ride again?'

'I've put in for my licence.'

'That's marvellous news. I never thought you'd sit on a horse again after that terrible fall.'

'I've got a retainer lined up.'

'Really, who?'

'Mrs Beechly.'

'Oh.' The tone of his voice was flat.

She ignored it. 'I'd like to speak to Prince Sojo. Could you arrange it?'

He answered quickly, furtively. 'He's not looking for a jockey, I'm afraid.'

'It's not about that.'

'I see. Is it very important to you?'

'Yes.'

He paused. 'What do I get in return?'

She smiled inwardly. 'We could make tomorrow's work out a bit special . . .'

He leered. 'How special?'

'I leave that to you.'

He was already at the club when she arrived very early the next morning. She wore a new sky-blue track suit with a large white towel wrapped around her neck. Her short brown curls had been brushed out to frame her pixy face, and it gave her the look of a fluffy photogenic model rather than a hard professional jockey. She saw he'd set up a badminton net.

'Do you play badminton?' he asked.

'Not very well, I'm afraid.'

'You'll make out.'

She picked up a racquet and wandered unenthusiastically onto the court.

'Not like that, my lovely. I want you out of that track suit.'

She hesitated. 'But I'm not wearing sports kit underneath. Only my knickers.'

'We'll have them off, too.'

'I'd be naked,' she exploded, 'I can't play like that.'

'Why not?'

'All my bits will wobble.'

'I'll enjoy that!'

Even as she spoke her fingers hooked into the elastic waistband of her trousers and jerked them down with one swift movement. She'd been prepared for this. In fact, she'd have been surprised if he'd allowed her to keep her track suit on. On court she quickly discovered that he was a first-class player, and she was kept running around like a mad thing to give him any sort of game at all. Soon the sweat was flowing freely from her overheated body as she stretched in pursuit of the ever-elusive shuttlecock. Endeavouring to concentrate on the game, she didn't properly realise the extent to which her sexy body was being revealed. Her gorgeous white boobs bounced like rubber balls for his delectation, her pumping thighs displayed her curly fleece, which only partially hid the luscious folds of the long pink slit between her legs, while the plump cheeks of her voluptuous bottom quivered as she rushed about the court. Her exertions were such that soon her muscles ached.

'Enough,' she cried, 'you win.'

He stripped off his clothes and fell on his knees before her. She stood with hands on hips trying to recapture her breath, her pretty breasts moving seductively as if they had a life of their own. She felt him clasp her thighs as he bent forward to kiss her flat belly. She was so petite that he could reach up to suck her lush tits and she revelled in his hot kisses covering those tender silken orbs. As she panted, so her breasts and stomach rose and fell rhythmically, and the perspiration trickled between those swollen hills to flow down to her navel. Suddenly his wet tongue began to lick the sweat from her body like a cat lapping milk. She vaguely wondered what strange sexual gratification her perspiration was satisfying, for he was sucking her damp flesh as if he was feeding on the nectar of the gods.

'Run,' she heard him command. 'Go on. Run on the spot.'

Obediently she began to pound her feet up and down on the wooden floor with military precision until her breath was coming in quick gulps and the sweat was pouring from her open pores. She wanted to get down to her racing weight again, but there were easier ways. When she stopped, his lips fastened onto her sweating heaving globes once more, but this time she, too, was feeling sexy. His fingers were invading the intimacy between her thighs, and no sooner had she spread her legs for him than he was exploring her short curly hair and touching the sensitive folds of her succulent fig.

She was saturated between her legs, and when his middle finger slid inside her it was like a diver questing for a pearl, her pearl. He stood up urgently, the tip of his knob hovering between her legs. Suddenly he sliced into her like a knife into butter and when he had impaled her she wound her legs around his waist and clasped her arms around his neck. Holding his ramrod deep within her she clung to him hungrily only to be disappointed when he suddenly flooded her with his come. She slid to the floor. It was her turn to feel randy. Her turn to want to screw. She knew that having ejaculated he would want to dress and leave. If she wanted another poke it was up to her to take the initiative. She led him from the court.

'We can't go in this state. Let's have a sauna.'

'Wouldn't a shower do?'

'No, I want to lose weight.'

He led her to the sauna cubicle and lay on his stomach on the wooden bench. The dry heat immediately opened their pores, and she sat watching the beads of perspiration form on his buttocks and back. Suddenly she was taken by an urge to taste his body as he'd tasted hers. She began to suck the sweat from his back, licking the hot flesh with long strokes of her tongue. Warming to her task, she moved slowly downwards to his firm buttocks, pulling the cheeks apart to insert her long tongue into the cleft. Reaching far beneath his legs she forced his thighs apart so she could cup his hairy scrotum in her palm and fondle it. Then, surrendering to a dark impulse that inexplicably surged through her, she jammed her mouth into the cleft of his bum and ferociously sucked at him.

She heard him groan in ecstasy as her tongue scoured his ballbag and licked at his anus. She was like a bitch on heat, as horny as hell to have his prick inside her again. With the strength of a trained athlete she grabbed his shoulders and, urging him onto his knees, slipped under him so she could be taken in the missionary position. She took his tool and guided it to the entrance of her tunnel of lust. It was as hard as a rod of iron and throbbing with the need to be inside her. One long fierce thrust impaled her and she shrieked as she flung her legs upwards for him to grab her ankles and shaft her until she orgasmed and orgasmed again. It was sheer lascivious pleasure.

Guy kept his word and phoned her to say the Prince would be at Ascot on Wednesday as he had a fancied runner in the Victoria Cup. Peggy-Sue put on her best bib and tucker and painted her face with a hint of make-up and, with her most ingratiating smile at the ready, set off to Ascot. Guy welcomed her and they were deep in conversation when the Prince joined them.

'Peggy-Sue, how nice to see you. Have you fully recovered?'

'Yes, sir. I hope to be riding again soon.'

'Excellent. The sport cannot afford to lose such a colourful character as Peggy-Sue Rhyma.'

'Thank you, sir.'

'Will you be riding freelance, or have you a retainer up your sleeve?'

'Mrs Beechly has promised to retain me.'

'Really? I don't think I know the lady.'

'An elegant redhead, sir. She looks more like a film star than a racehorse trainer.'

'I believe I've noticed her. She's always in the company of a very attractive blonde girl?'

Peggy-Sue laughed. 'They do tend to turn heads when they're together.'

'Are they sisters?'

'No, sir. The blonde is her stepdaughter and assistant trainer.'

He went to walk away. 'You must introduce me, Peggy-Sue,' he said casually.

'I will, sir. I understand she's a very good trainer, but her yard is in need of horses.'

'I'm afraid I couldn't help there. I'm not increasing my number of horses in training at present.'

'No, sir. I didn't expect that, sir,' she smiled humbly, 'but should you hear of any other owner . . . Mrs Beechly would be very very grateful.'

'Would she indeed? I'll see what I can do.'

It was all very non-committal, and Peggy-Sue had

no idea whether she would hear from him again. However, two days later, when she'd received news that her licence was renewed and she'd put her London flat on the market to search for a cottage in Wiltshire, her phone rang. It was Prince Sojo.

'Are you alone?'

'Yes, sir.'

'I have a proposition I wish you to put to Mrs Beechly.'

'Yes, sir.'

'Have you heard of Prince Khaneme El Bessis?'

'No, sir.'

'He has a string of thoroughbreds in France.'

'Who trains for him?'

'M de Lalec.'

'Yes, I remember. Pink and yellow colours, but he never goes to see his horses run, does he?'

'He's a recluse. He rarely leaves his chateau.'

'Does he live in France?'

'For four months during the racing season he resides at his chateau in the south of France.'

'How does this affect Mrs Beechly?'

'The Prince has decided to take part in the British racing scene. To initiate this operation he means to transfer his twelve horses from M de Lalec's stable to a yard in England.'

'Mrs Beechly's?'

'That is the proposition.'

'What is, sir?'

'If Mrs Beechly and her stepdaughter care to

travel to France and put themselves at the disposal of Prince Khaneme for forty-eight hours he is prepared to send them the twelve horses.'

She paused. 'Exactly how much will they be at his disposal?'

'Completely, Peggy-Sue. Completely and utterly.'

'And during that time?'

'They will have no more status than his concubines.'

She breathed out slowly. 'I see.'

'You don't like it, Miss Rhyma?'

'It's not up to me. I'll see his proposition is conveyed to Mrs Beechly.'

'I'll give you a number to ring before midnight tomorrow if she is interested.'

'She mightn't like the idea of taking horses from another trainer's yard.'

'Khaneme intends to take them from M de Lalec, whether they go to Mrs Beechly or not.'

'One question, if I may, sir? Why does Prince Khaneme live for several months in France and own racehorses there if he never goes to watch them?'

The Prince's voice flattened. 'He uses his thoroughbreds to cover his real interest in western Europe which could not be made public.'

'European women, I suppose.' she muttered half to herself.

The Prince appeared not to hear, and was gone.

Sonia spoke to Jilly, and after much deliberation

they decided to go ahead with the plan. Sonia rang the number and the Prince's contact informed them he would meet them at Nice airport. Three days later they flew from Gatwick. Sonia had grave misgivings at the last moment, worrying whether she'd done the right thing to allow Jilly to accompany her. She'd offered to go without her stepdaughter, but had been told bluntly it was both of them or the deal was off. On the other hand Jilly was young enough to be excited at the prospect of meeting an eastern prince. Deep down she still harboured the western picture of Rudolph Valentino look-alike sheiks, sultry romantic desert nights and majestic white horses.

Their contact met them at the airport and took them to a large black Mercedes. He was a tall Frenchman who introduced himself as Claude. They travelled for well over an hour in the enclosed saloon, and although they both tried to question Claude he would indulge in no more than small talk. Finally they turned off the main road into a narrow lane which was signposted Château de Tours. The building was a renovated mansion standing in its own spacious grounds. The surrounding lawns and flowerbeds which bordered the long gravel driveway were truly magnificent. As they approached the house they could see that the outside had been modernised. A vast residence had been built around the remains of the old castle.

They were escorted to the central building which

was laid out like the great hall of a medieval castle.
It was completely enclosed and had been turned into
the Prince's personal quarters and harem. The windows were so high they couldn't be overlooked and
the only entrance was guarded by a burly servant.
Awaiting Sonia and Jilly was a throng of silent
inquisitive women but, instead of being welcomed,
they were bustled into two separate side rooms.
Mother and daughter were upset at being separated
but no heed was paid to their loud protests.

Jilly attempted to push her way out, but was
restrained. She sat down on a wooden bench wondering just what she'd let herself in for. She was soon
to find out for she was led through the main hall to a
smaller, dimly lit room, and handed over to two
women. These women had the air of authority and
she assumed they were wives rather than concubines. One was a brown-skinned Arab, but the other
was a black Ethiopian. To Jilly's surprise the black
woman spoke almost perfect English.

'Where did you learn to speak English like that?'

'My parents were servants to a very rich British
merchant. When Prince Khaneme saw me as a
young girl he wanted to buy me. My father would
only agree if he took me as a wife.'

'And do you like your life?'

'It's more comfortable than being married to a
poor man, and a thousand times better than being
a concubine. But you? You have no intention of staying long, have you?'

Jilly grinned. 'No. It's a very temporary arrangement.'

The woman smiled pragmatically. 'Whatever, you have been summoned into your master's presence.'

'Crikey, I've only just arrived!'

'You are blonde. He lusts after you.'

'What must I do?'

'Satisfy him and, above all, be obedient.'

Jilly was ushered into an inner room by the eldest of the two wives, and left to stand some fifteen feet from the foot of the couch on which her temporary master reclined. She stood motionless, uncertain what to do. Never in her life had she felt at such a loss. She decided to stand demurely until he spoke.

'Your hair is as golden as the sunrise.'

His voice was nasal and his accent thick, but she was able to understand his French. He was a big man. He must have weighed eighteen stone. She was unprepared for that. She'd imagined all princes to be young, slim and handsome. He popped a sweetmeat into his mouth, fastidiously licking his fingers, but his eyes never left her face.

'Take off your clothes, Englishwoman. I will have you now.'

Far from being frightened or upset Jilly was on familiar ground. After all, this was what she had come for. Besides, she enjoyed sex. She disrobed slowly and tantalisingly before the big man, occasionally glancing towards his crotch to see whether he was rising to her performance. She slipped her simple pale blue cotton dress over her head with all the splendid eroticism of Salome shedding her sixth veil, and stood shyly before him like a young virgin on her wedding night. She looked the picture of demure femininity, her long shapely legs encased in black nylons and the narrowest of suspender belts circling her pretty waist. Her exquisite breasts were bare, hanging like the most succulent fruit in the orchard, ripe enough to tempt the fingers of a saint. The Prince sat watching like a statue, propped up on his soft pillows, as she unhurriedly removed her final garment with provocative grace. His face showed nothing. Even when she stood stark naked before him his expression never changed. Surely he hadn't possessed so many fair-haired European women that he could be that blasé? She willed him to speak.

'You may approach me, woman. On your stomach.'

There was no going back. She lay on her tummy on the soft-piled rug and wriggled her way inch by inch towards the foot of the couch. As she moved towards him she went over in her head why she was in this ignominious position. She was doing it for Sonia. She smiled inwardly when she tried to picture her proud stepmother going through this part of the agreement. She reached the man's bare feet, and in turn kissed the sole and heel while caressing the instep, before popping his toes into her mouth to suck each one as if she was playing little piggies with a child. Progressing with care, she wriggled up onto the couch beside him so that she was able to kiss and caress his body from his thick ankles to his large thighs. He hadn't spoken since she'd got down on her stomach for him, so she presumed her Lord and Master was satisfied with his new plaything. She glanced up from licking his fat thighs to be confronted with a monolith rising under her nose. She grinned wryly. It seemed that he was well satisfied.

Beyond the enormous phallus she could see his face above the vast expanse of his belly. He was expressionless, and it amused her to imagine herself bouncing on his huge belly like a trampoline. She reached up to finger the shaft of his upstanding penis. It was covered with the thickest foreskin she'd ever seen. She guessed he'd want her to take it into her mouth. As her soft hand closed around the shaft she found it greasy to her touch. She quickly guessed one of his wives must have prepared his weapon with oil. She really didn't fancy it down her throat. She was scared she might be sick. Her heart sank.

Fortunately this wasn't to be. She hadn't noticed the two women lurking in the shadows. They were the Prince's other two wives. They moved forward to grasp her under the armpits and behind the knees. She found herself lifted bodily and positioned so that her wide open thighs were immediately above her master's magic wand. With her arms around their shoulders she was held immobile above his large cock. The women spread her legs further apart so that her unprotected gash was poised above his monstrous prong. Then she felt her body being lowered and knew that soon she would be impaled on that threatening lance.

Although her legs were parted so wide that her quim lips hung open invitingly, the women failed to manoeuvre his impatient ramrod into her gaping hole. She wondered why they were in such a hurry. She wasn't sexually aroused and her welcome would be as dry as sandpaper. It was fortunate that his prick was soaked in oil or she would have been hurt, but when they finally lowered her body he slipped into her like a well-oiled bolt. Satisfied their job was done, the two women moved away to leave her sitting on the man's large expanse of stomach with her cunt filled to overflowing with oily prick.

The Prince didn't deign to move so she began slowly sliding back up his totem pole until she held only the tip between her gorgeous pussy lips – then she plunged down again onto his belly like a little girl bouncing on a trampoline. His great cock felt strange to the sensitive walls of her vagina. It was like being filled with soft putty, not that it was unpleasant. Exhilarated, she pumped faster and faster, all the while squeezing her vaginal muscles to achieve the sensations that would drive her towards orgasm.

Suddenly, without warning, he ejaculated. She felt herself flooded with his cream and moaned at the loss of her own climax. His manhood quickly shrank within her and she raised her buttocks to be rid of it.

He hadn't moved a muscle while she'd rogered him. Not a muscle, not an eyelid. Maybe it was some strange custom.

After her introductory poke it appeared Jilly was free to go where she pleased for nobody attempted to stop her. She went in search of Sonia, but she was nowhere to be found. As she had access to all the rooms she decided to look around. At the end of the great hall was a small man-made oasis with two palm trees growing around a pool of water. She peered into it, half expecting to see crystal-clear water alive with colourful fish but the water was dank. In the trees and surrounding shrubs, and playing on the ceiling beams above, were a number of small monkeys. Later she discovered they were kept as pets for the concubines, who delighted in feeding them while as they scampered around their feet.

Wherever she went there was no sign of life. She wondered where all the women hid themselves, not realising that most of them were in the many false alcoves surrounding the great hall. She saw that part of the floor around the oasis formed a mosaic and guessed the original castle had been built on a Roman site. She imagined it had once been a fabulous building, but now it was architecturally compromised. The outer rooms were blatantly twentieth century and had been added without thought to the remains of the castle. The Prince's entourage lived in the outer building. The women occupied the inner rooms, hidden from prying eyes.

At the main door her way was barred by a very large eunuch who beckoned a young concubine to look after her. The girl was a chubby youngster wearing loose robes. She led Jilly to the small room which was to be hers. The girl sat with her and gradually others joined them. They were nearly all brown-skinned Arabs, although she noticed several black Africans and a slim Egyptian. She stood looking out of a window at a small garden that had been built in the courtyard and when she turned she found she was alone. They'd gone as silently as they came.

Sonia's fate was very different. She was grabbed bodily by the four wives, and dragged struggling to a shallow water butt where her head was forced underwater. She screamed, fearful of drowning. The women reassured her.

'Don't be frightened.'

'How can I help it? What are you trying to do — drown me?'

'We are to wash your hair.'

'Why?'

'To see if it is dyed.'

'Of course it's not dyed,' she snapped.

'We must be certain.'

'Why?'

'Our husband won't touch you unless you're a natural redhead.'

'Hell, that's a pity. You'll find I'm red to the roots.' They began to soap her long red hair. 'I thought he was wild about blondes?'

They smiled. 'Red hair has a special significance.'

She left it at that, and when they were satisfied that she was telling the truth one of the women coyly lifted her skirt. Giggling wildly they took down her flimsy briefs to inspect the colour of her pubic hair. Finding it a golden red, they stroked her there until she felt quite aroused in spite of herself.

Later she was led into her temporary master's presence to find him reclining on his couch just as Jilly had before her. However, she wasn't expected to wriggle on her tummy towards him. He gazed at her steadily for some moments, a cold piercing stare which made Sonia pull the robe, which the women had given her, close around her body.

'Disrobe yourself, woman.'

The nasal tone of his voice took her by surprise, but she let the wrap slip from her shoulders. She did it with a certain teasing eroticism which seemed to arouse his interest for his eyes lit up as she revealed her nakedness bit by gorgeous bit.

'You may kiss my feet.'

She bit her tongue to stop herself replying, but knelt to obediently press her soft lips to his instep and toes. He appeared to be satisfied, for he waved her to a low stool and, as she sat, a concubine served refreshments. She noticed her silver goblet was filled from a different vessel, but she daren't question it. She found the taste sweet and pleasant, but that was the last thing she remembered.

When she woke, she found herself alone and naked. Instantly she knew that she'd been well and truly humped. Her body ached and there was bruising on her skin. She became aware of an unpleasantness between her thighs, and saw a mixture of dried love juices and semen caking her pussy. She moved her fingers to explore, and the soreness inside her vagina told her that she'd been put through her paces good and proper. As she lay motionless her befuddled memory began to recall flashbacks of the night. She remembered his big knob covered in folds of foreskin. She remembered being smothered by his sweating body as he shafted her time and time again. She remembered his wives inserting leather dildoes into her while they pinched her thighs and buttocks. She remembered she'd been the plaything of these women who had amused themselves by abusing one of the European women so admired by their husband. Then she shut off her memory – she didn't want to know anymore.

Sonia had to get away, away from this cloying atmosphere. She dressed and walked towards the outer door. There was no guard, no eunuch. She wandered in the outer building through what appeared to be a library and on to the terrace of the large garden. The sun was warm and the fresh air relaxed her. A gardener was busy with a bed of roses.

He told her it was unusual to see a European

woman in the castle. In fact, he said, it was unusual to see any woman unescorted. Sonia found it difficult to understand his broad accent.

'How long has the Prince lived her?' she asked.

'For ten years. But he only comes in the summertime.'

'Did he have the whole house rebuilt?'

'It is really a castle, madame,' he explained glumly, 'he has done all this to it.'

'I take it you don't like it?'

'No, madame, but I've never been inside.'

'Do you get many visitors?'

'Mostly Eastern gentlemen and some French horseracing folk, but I'd rather not talk any more.'

'Why not?'

'My employers don't like me to talk to the visitors, especially the women.'

Sonia walked away. She'd been upset by the gardener's obvious reluctance to talk to her and when she was hustled inside by a guard she was even more annoyed. It turned out that by talking to the gardener she had broken the rules of the harem. The Prince was informed and she was sentenced to be whipped. It was despotic, but Sonia knew she would have to suffer it or go home empty-handed. She only prayed that their idea of punishment wasn't a whipping which would lacerate the flesh. Surely they wouldn't dare do that to her.

She was locked away until noon when the flogging was to take place, and although Jilly tried to comfort her, she was on the verge of hysterics when they came for her. The Ethiopian wife led her naked to the centre of the great hall where she stood shivering in spite of the oppressive midday heat. The Prince, wrapped in a magnificent robe, sat on a raised dais at one end of the room, his wives by his side. The female servants and concubines sat in a semi-circle on the carpeted floor. Other than the prince and his eunuchs, no male eyes were allowed to witness her shame. She thanked heaven for that and glanced nervously around her. She'd heard the sound of sandals flapping on bare feet behind her. Somebody was approaching her from the rear. Blind curiosity combined with fear forced her to look round and she saw an old crone swinging what appeared to be a long flexible paddle; not the whip she'd feared. She breathed a sigh of relief. It was an elongated flat instrument rather like a bat used in a children's ball game – but it wasn't a child's game they were going to play on her behind.

At a clap of the Prince's hands, a eunuch took his place in front of her and she was mounted on his back like a little girl on piggyback. She wrapped her arms around his thickly muscled neck and felt his forearms tighten under her thighs, thus holding her legs close to his sides. In that position, she realised, the bare cheeks of her posterior were well-spread and thrust out towards her audience. So far everything had been done in silence. Not a word had been spoken, nevertheless she failed to hear the paddle swing towards her fundament.

The silence was broken by her scream and the crack of leather upon her bare female flesh. The flat surface of the paddle not only stung like a thousand bees, but on contact seemed to wrap itself around the whole contour of her derriere. It dawned on Sonia that this was no strange experience for the assembled audience. Hapless concubines and unsuspecting visitors probably got beaten quite regularly.

The stinging pain of the next blow drove all thoughts from her mind other than the searing throb the instrument brought to her rear end. The crone swinging it might have been old and weak, but she possessed the knack of raising a sharp tingle in an errant girl's bottom. Sonia squealed again. There was no point in being brave. It might even earn her a few added strokes. She tightened her grip on the eunuch's neck and pushed her shoulders and breasts into the warm comfort of his broad back. The paddle set her nates on fire once again, and tears sprang to her eyes. She sobbed unashamedly. Perhaps the old woman would take pity on an innocent English girl? She did no such thing. Sonia received twelve strokes, each more scorching than the last, until her poor butt was on fire and she was convinced it was shining like a beacon.

When it was over, Jilly gently massaged her stepmother's mistreated nether-cheeks with oils while she lay on her tummy bemoaning her fate.

'Is it very red?'

Jilly chuckled. 'Like a ripe tomato!'

'It's not, is it?'

'No, it's not too bad. Does it hurt much?'

'I've had worse,' said Sonia nonchalantly.

'Don't tell fibs, Sonia. When?'

She didn't have time to reply as Jilly glanced up to see a face she knew. It was the Frenchman, Claude. Jilly quickly covered her stepmother's nude derriere with a towel, but not before the man had caught sight of the exquisite pink globes glistening with salve. He smiled.

'I see you've managed to upset your host, Mrs Beechly?'

Sonia turned on her back to look up at him. 'It would seem so.'

'Perhaps I should have warned you of his short fuse with females who break the rules?'

'Maybe you should, but now I've learned the hard way.'

'Does it hurt much?'

'What do you think?'

'I think that you may wish to be released from your agreement. You realise you have another twenty-four hours at the disposal of the Prince. However, I have spoke to him and he agrees to terminate your contract so you can leave immediately.'

'What makes you think we'd want to leave?'

'Western women aren't used to being beaten, are they?'

'No, they are not, and if we'd realised it was part of our deal I doubt if we'd have agreed.'

Jilly interrupted. 'What would happen if we did call it a day now?'

'Your deal would be void. The Prince would send his horses elsewhere.'

'We'll stay,' said Sonia emphatically.

'Yes,' agreed Jilly. 'We've been here a day, we can live through another.'

The Frenchman bowed. 'As you wish, ladies. I will convey your decision to the Prince.'

They watched the Frenchman stride towards the outer buildings. Now their decision was taken they felt more relaxed. Then they noticed the old crone standing in the shadows watching them.

'Watch yourself, Jilly,' said Sonia with a grin, 'she's got her eyes on your backside!'

'Vicious old cow,' Jilly whispered, 'I'd like to push her into a heap of manure.'

'Now you've done it. She can speak English!'

'Oh, Christ,' wailed Jilly, 'she'll flay the skin off my bum!'

Sonia burst out laughing.

'You bastard!' groaned Jilly.

But even if the old crone couldn't speak English, she was swinging the paddle both menacingly and suggestively. Sonia fingered her sore rump and drew in a short breath. Jilly realised that she, too, would be on the receiving end next time. Never mind, the prize would be worth it.

The Prince kept his bargain to the letter. Three days after Sonia and Jilly had returned home, the first of the twelve horses arrived at The Billings, and the following morning the racing press was full of it. They reported that the fabulously rich Prince Khaneme El Bessis had arrived on the British racing scene and a part of his French racing empire was being transferred to England. Twelve horses were being transferred from the stables of M de Lalec to Mrs Sonia Beechly. Given the prevailing ill-wind blowing against Sonia, most of the papers questioned whether the Prince had made the correct decision. They were pleased that the Prince was entering the British racing scene, but had he done right to choose a new trainer with so little experience? Sonia smiled. She wondered what they'd have made of the real story.

The following week her stable totalled the respectable number of twenty-four horses and she hoped it marked the turning of the tide. Later that day she spoke to Jilly.

'You've done an awful lot for me, Jilly.'

'What, for instance? I'm only a learner at the job. It's nice of you to teach me.'

'There was no need for you to come to France with me.'

'I was part of the deal.'

Sonia grinned. 'An essential part. He fancied you more than me.'

Jilly laughed outright. 'No man in his right mind would do that.'

'Thank you, stepdaughter, for those few kind

words. Seriously though, there was no need for you to put your body on the line.'

Jilly cut her short. 'I love sex, you know that. I wouldn't have missed it for the world!'

'What I'm trying to say is that I want to reward you.'

'No, really. There's no need.'

'Let me finish. I believe you're committed to racing and I believe you'll make a success of it. I'd like you to be my partner.'

'Are you sure, Sonia?'

'Of course I am.'

Jilly hugged her stepmother. 'Then I accept.'

Chapter 7

Mandy was surprised to hear from Sam. It was over two months since she'd been expelled from school and, although she'd written to him once, he hadn't replied. Sonia handed her the phone.

'Hi, Mandy. I expect you're surprised to hear from me.'

'What's on your mind, Sam?'

'You said you were in the market for a chaser.'

'That's right. Daddy promised to buy me one.'

'Have you found one you like?'

'Not yet, but there's no hurry. I shan't be riding until early in the autumn.'

'Lumberboy's for sale. I thought you might like first refusal.'

Her heart skipped a beat. 'Thanks, Sam. I'd love him.'

'Pop down tomorrow and look at him. If we agree a price you can take him back with you.'

'You'll have to speak to Daddy about money, but he'll pay up as long as it's not too pricey.'

'You want him then?'

'Of course I do,' she replied hurriedly, 'but why are you selling?'

'I'm broke, Mandy. I'm selling everything and getting out.'

'I'm sorry.'

'No need to be. When shall I see you?'

'I'll be down tomorrow.'

Jilly was persuaded to go with Mandy, and afterwards they were to drive to Windsor for the evening meeting, where Peggy-Sue was riding a handicapper for Sonia. When they pulled up at Sam's place Jilly jumped into the driver's seat and headed towards Brighton where she'd arranged to meet a school pal for a couple of hours. Sam looked at Mandy. She seemed to have matured, probably as the result of leaving school and working in an adult environment. He noticed she wore a smartly cut skirt and pure silk blouse.

'You aren't dressed for riding. Don't you want to sit on him before buying?'

'I know him inside out, Sam,' she smiled.

'Maybe, but he may have gone lame or something.'

'I trust you, Sam. You wouldn't sell me a pig in a poke.'

'All the same, I'd rather you sat on him.'

She was reluctant. 'No, really. I'd rather not, I'm not dressed for riding.'

'You could slip your skirt off.'

She laughed. 'Oh, I see. That's it, is it?'

He smiled at her brazenly. 'Yes, that's it. I'd love to see my young pupil riding bare-bottomed again. What about it, Mandy?'

She looked dubious. 'I don't know.'

'Give a poor broken-down trainer one last wish.'

She chuckled. 'Okay, how could I refuse. Go and tack him up for me.'

'He's ready. I'll go and lead him out.'

'You lecherous old devil,' she said, smiling as she slipped out of her skirt. 'You were pretty sure of yourself, weren't you?'

She wore no stockings and her lovely bare legs made her appear alluring and sexy. Her loose silk blouse grazed the full swell of her hips. A light wind caressed the bare flesh of her thighs. She shivered. It was too chilly to remove the blouse, but she could guess what he'd say. He led out the horse and stopped beside her. He looked disappointed.

'Aren't you going to take off your knickers?'

She smiled to herself as she slipped the bikini briefs down and off. She'd guessed correctly, although she didn't expect any prizes.

'Satisfied?' she smiled.

He gave her a leg up and watched her exaggerate the swing of her leg over the saddle so that he could feast his eyes on her long gash, surrounded by its nest of silken fur. She trotted the big chaser around the yard, exaggerating each bounce in the saddle so every time her buttocks rose she revealed the whole curve of her exquisite derriere. The eroticism she felt by displaying her seat made her forget why she was on the horse. She was supposed to be judging whether he was sound, but she knew he was. She dismounted and watched Sam lead him back to his stall. He hadn't spoken once since she'd flashed herself for his delight and she wondered whether the sight of her nakedness had aroused him. She decided to find out. She slipped off the long blouse and moved up behind him.

As he closed the stable door he was standing with his back to her. She pressed her warm body against him and slid her arms around his waist so that her inquisitive fingers could discover the answer. She found an ominous bulge in his jeans and smiled.

'I see you still like me!' she whispered.

'If you mean do I still dream about screwing you night and morning, the answer's yes.'

'Stay still. I'll see what I can do.'

She jerked his shirt free from the waistband of his jeans and, still standing close behind him, reached around his body to unfasten the buttons one by one. Slowly she pulled the open shirt from his back and covered his back and shoulders with a delightful flurry of butterfly kisses, before sticking out her dainty tongue to lick the curve of his spine from neck to waist. She could feel his flesh shiver beneath the erotic movement of her wet tongue and she cuddled him, her slim arms circling his well-muscled torso. They stood entwined for a long silent moment like living sculpture, motionless but for her fingertips straying over his chest and belly with erotic intent.

'Now I'm going to have those trousers down,' she whispered in his ear, 'to see if Mr Dick's standing to attention for me!'

He said nothing as her agile fingers unzipped his jeans and dragged them down over his hips.

'Is he?' she insisted.

When he didn't reply she pinched his butt with a fearful nip that made him cry out.

'Ouch, yes,' he squealed, 'ready and waiting, mam.'

'And does he want to fuck my pussy?'

'Yes . . . please.'

'Say it.'

'He wants to fuck your sweet cunt, mam.'

'Nice and hard and long?'

'What do you think?'

'And make me come and come and come?'

'He'll try.'

'Don't you like me talking dirty?'

'I'm easy, Mandy, but I'd rather you took me inside you.'

She swiftly moved her fingers down to his weapon and, wrapping her fist around the shaft, began to wank him whilst her other hand cupped his ballbag. She gently squeezed his testicles and fondled his swollen joystick until he turned, picked her up bodily and carried her to a bale of straw. She realised she'd aroused him to the point of animal lust and, frantic to be violated, threw her legs high as he slung her down onto her back. The straw was rough and prickly but she was oblivious to it. She spread her legs above her head with wild abandon as she felt two, maybe three, of his fingers stab into her vagina.

She swooned as his lance speared into her, plundering the depths of her hot inviting tunnel. He strove to part her legs even wider as he forced her knees back behind her ears and, as she shrieked, he grew harder and harder, thrusting deeper and deeper, inside her. Suddenly her tension disappeared as he commenced driving in and out of her like a piston until her orgasm washed over her in thrilling ripples.

'Now you come,' she whispered urgently as she reached up to pull him down onto her heaving breasts, 'quickly. Now. Flood my pussy with hot cream.'

Her full breasts rose and fell rapidly, her breath coming in fitful gulps, as she dug her nails into his shoulders and back. As he climaxed his cock was deep inside her. She sighed contentedly and, after milking him of every last drop, tightened her quim muscles to keep him trapped within her throbbing pussy.

For several minutes they remained locked together until she reluctantly released him. It was the first time she'd experienced such wild carnality – her whole body had been on fire. She wondered what had made her want to talk dirty – she'd never done that before – not that she was ashamed. She found she was saturated between the legs. She took his hand as they walked back to the house. Jilly would be another two hours yet. Time for them to do it again. And again.

At Windsor, Peggy-Sue was about to have the first ride of her come-back. Surprisingly, she didn't feel at all nervous as Jilly gave her a leg-up into the plate. The horse was expected to do well, and it would be a real tonic to have a winner on her return to the saddle. Sonia had gone to Bristol for a seminar about equestrian blood-testing, but she'd assured them that the horse should win.

Windsor wasn't Peggy-Sue's favourite course. She disliked riding the loops since nearly going the wrong way on her first ride as an apprentice. Once out onto the track she cantered her horse slowly to the start.

Windsor is a pretty little course beside the river Thames and the evening meetings are invariably crowded, in spite of the buildings being dingy and unwelcoming and in need of renovation. It was handy for Londoners, and that's where most of the crowd had come from.

The race was over a mile, and Peggy-Sue kept her horse handily placed, just off the pace, until the final furlong when she pushed the button. The horse accelerated smoothly into the lead but she couldn't get rid of the top weight, who hung onto her coat tails stubbornly, niggling away at her slender lead.

She rode a hard finish but even with all the stops pulled out she couldn't hold the top weight who won by a head. She returned to the unsaddling enclosure disappointed. The horse had been fit enough but not quite good enough.

That was her one ride of the evening and she was preparing to go home when she received a message that she was wanted outside the weighing room. An Epsom trainer, whom she knew by sight, was waiting for her.

'My jock hasn't arrived. Will you ride mine in the third?'

'You're sure you want me? It's my first meeting back after injury.'

'I know. There's no one else.'

'Thanks a bunch!'

He blushed. 'I didn't mean it like that.'

'That's okay. I know not everyone likes female jocks.'

'I don't question your ability. I've seen you. You're good.'

'Thanks. What is it you want me to ride?'

He held out his hand. 'My name's Tony Bills, the horse is Sally Ewe.'

'Has she any chance?'

'Not a lot. The owner likes to see her run. I keep entering her in low-class sprints. She wins in her turn which isn't often.'

She met him again in the paddock with the owner. The owner's eyes were all over her and, if it hadn't been so public, she guessed his hands would have been too. The bell rang for the jockeys to mount.

'Have you any instructions?' she asked.

'Not really. You can ride her how you like. She'll be happy wherever you put her.'

'I think she's better when she comes late,' interrupted the owner.

'Okay,' smiled Peggy-Sue sweetly, 'you're the guv'nor. I'll hold her up.'

There were twenty runners in the race and it was a typical six-furlong cavalry charge. There was no obvious advantage to being on either side so the field stretched right across the track. Peggy-Sue, drawn at 10, tucked Sally Ewe in behind and ploughed a furrow up the middle. The trainer was correct in saying the filly didn't care where she raced, and was totally relaxed as Peggy-Sue allowed her to gallop freely behind the others.

Approaching the final furlong a group of six had forged ahead and Sally Ewe was lying in last place. Peggy-Sue had formed some sort of vague plan to come fast and late to finish with a flurry that would impress the owner. Opposite the Silver ring she set the filly alight. Two sharp cracks behind the saddle galvanised the horse into action and a high-pitched scream in the ears seemed to frighten the life out of her. Sally Ewe flew for her life to the line with Peggy-Sue pushing and kicking and shouting blue murder in the filly's ear. The owner and trainer watched open-mouthed as, one minute, their filly cruised

187

lazily in the rear and, the next, was sprinting through the field as if she was being chased by a thousand devils.

A photo was called, and nobody on the course had the slightest idea of the winner. Three horses had crossed the line together, with Sally Ewe finishing the fastest of all. The judge had to ask for a print to separate them and it was more than five minutes before Peggy-Sue knew she'd ridden her first winner on her return back.

She'd changed before she saw Tony Bill and the owner again, and they were busy congratulating her when a large man in a flashy hand-painted tie interrupted them.

'Miss Peggy-Sue, isn't it?'

'That's correct,' she said. 'Your face is rather familiar. Do I know you?'

He had an American accent. She guessed he was from New England. 'My name's Joe Ladd. My brother and I bought that lovely little grey filly you used to ride.'

'Misk Garnett? Of course, I remember. You bought her and took her to the States. How is she?'

'That's what I'm over here about.'

'What?'

'You'll recall we bought her as a three-year-old after a successful season over here.'

'I remember her well. Best horse I've ever sat on. She won three top-class mile races over here, and the Breeder's in Kentucky.'

'I'm afraid she flopped as a four-year-old. She

hasn't been placed in four races.'

'What went wrong?'

'We don't know. We've tried her on turf and on dirt and over different distances, but the zing's gone.'

'I'm sorry. She was so good, too.'

'She's entered at Aqueduct, New York, on Wednesday.'

Peggy-Sue smiled politely. 'I hope she wins for you.'

'We want you to ride. That's why I'm here.'

She was flabbergasted. 'You've come all this way to ask me that?'

'Yup. When we read you were back in the saddle we knew we had to have you. We won't take no for an answer.'

'If it's that important to you, of course I'll take the ride.'

'Thanks. I'll be flying back tomorrow. Can I make a booking for you?'

'Please do.'

'Let me have your number and I'll phone you with the details.'

She handed him a card. 'Tell me, why do you want me to ride? I appreciate the compliment, but there are jocks a lot better than me in the States.'

'That's a matter of opinion,' he grinned, 'but we have to make plans for the filly's future and we want your opinion of her. After all, you rode her when she was successful. Maybe you could pinpoint what's gone wrong.'

'I'll certainly try.'

It was as they shook hands on parting that Mandy joined them. She smiled sweetly at Joe Ladd and the big Yank stopped in his tracks at the sight of her. Her fresh youthful face, honey-blonde curls and complexion of peaches and cream was the type of English beauty so admired by Americans. Close behind this vision glided a second woman so beautiful she took his breath away. Peggy-Sue introduced Mandy and Jilly, and Joe Ladd took their hands as carefully and tenderly as if they were made of the finest porcelain.

'Mr Ladd's offered me a ride in the States.'

'Really,' gasped Mandy, 'when?'

'Wednesday. We're flying out tomorrow.'

'Oh, you lucky thing. Where in the States?'

'New York.'

Mandy's face lit up. 'New York. I've always wanted to go there. It's my dream city.'

Joe Ladd laughed. 'It's not what it used to be, young lady.'

'Can't I go with you, Peggy?' she burbled. 'Take me with you. I could be stable representative, or something.'

'I'm riding for Mr Ladd, not our stable.'

Joe Ladd held up his hand. 'Hey, hold hard. Are you part of the stable that retains Peggy-Sue?'

'Yes, I'm Sonia Beechly's stepdaughter.'

'Sure you can come. My brother and I want to talk to a representative from your stable.'

Jilly spoke for the first time. 'I doubt whether

mother would allow her to go alone. She's rather young.'

Mandy started at her sister and if looks could kill she'd have dropped dead on the spot.

Joe Ladd glanced at Jilly. She was a little older, a little slimmer, and a lot more woman. The younger girl was pert and attractive, this woman was alluring and seductive. Her long golden hair haloed a face which was serene and beautiful. She was both elegant and sexy. The long trip to Britain had been worth it just to look at them.

'Are you sisters?'

'Yes, she's Mandy, my name's Jilly.'

'Then you must come, too, Jilly. You can chaperone your sister. I'm sure your stepmother would agree to that?'

'Well . . .'

'It's settled. You'll travel with Peggy-Sue. I'll buy three tickets.'

He was gone before they could answer. Jilly was surprised at the generous offer and wondered what was behind it. Mandy's head was in the clouds just thinking about New York.

When they returned to The Billings the news of her horse's defeat into second place was relegated to the background when Sonia was told of Joe Ladd's offer. She was dubious and turned to Peggy-Sue for guidance.

'As far as I know, Sonia, the Ladd brothers are genuine racing men. They have a lot of horses in training all over the States and are very rich.'

'You think it's safe for the girls to go?'

'I don't think they'll be sold into white slavery, if that's what's worrying you. And if Joe said he wanted to talk to someone from the stable it can only benefit you to listen.'

The next day the girls flew from Heathrow to JFK airport from where Joe Ladd took them by helicopter to the centre of Manhattan. He checked them into a hotel on the corner of 58th Street and 7th Avenue, before saying he and his brother would pick them up at 7.30 that evening.

At 7.30 sharp Joe walked into the hotel and introduced them to his brother, Hank. Hank was a large, broad-shouldered man with an open face and thinning blond hair – Joe's twin. The girls were amazed at the similarity. They were like two peas in a pod. They looked, spoke and acted alike. However, they could easily be told apart, for Joe had blond hair and Hank's was light brown. The brothers had a flourishing frozen-food business in Detroit and Buffalo, and lived in the town of Lancaster in the county largely famous for the Amish people who farmed there.

They escorted the three women to a Broadway show, followed by dinner at a night club, before returning to the hotel.

'We'll pick Peggy-Sue up at six thirty tomorrow morning and take her to the course,' drawled Hank. 'Will you two girls be able to find your way on your own?'

They agreed they would and were pleased to be able to lie in.

While the sisters spent the next morning window-shopping on 5th Avenue, Peggy-Sue was hard at work at the track. She met the brothers' trainer, rode one piece of fast work and cantered Misk Garnett.

'What do you think of her, Peggy-Sue?' asked Joe.

'She's filled out a bit. Otherwise she's the same little grey rocking horse we knew and loved.'

'Grey rocking horse?' queried the trainer.

Peggy-Sue laughed. 'That was her pet name. We called her that because her dappled grey body with the white mane and tail give her the look of the old-fashioned rocking horse found in every British nursery.'

'Yes, I see. American kids love 'em, too.'

'She doesn't seem so full of herself, but then she's older.'

'A staid old lady, huh?'

'Not exactly, but she used to be very skittish and a bit stubborn in the nicest possible female way!'

'I've never seen it. She must have grown out of it.'

Peggy-Sue looked thoughtful. 'I thought the racing over here would have suited her. She loved to come off a fast pace.'

'She's been a disappointment, Peggy-Sue. She doesn't find any toe at the end of a race either on dirt or on turf.'

'Seems strange. Perhaps I'll be able to tell you more after the race.'

'Let's hope so.'

The race was over a mile, the filly's best distance. A few showers after a deluge the day before hadn't done the track any good. The pony outriders accompanied the runners to the stalls, something that didn't happen in Europe where the horses went down alone. Once in the stalls, a bell rang like the clappers of hell when they flew open. Peggy-Sue kicked the grey and she came out running.

Up to that moment there didn't seem anything different about Misk Garnett. She appeared relaxed and happy with herself. Determined to ride her off the pace, as she had in the past, Peggy-Sue settled the grey in behind. The penalty for this was that the horses in front kicked the loose dirt up into their faces. Some horses hated it, but Misk Garnett didn't seem to mind.

At the quarter, the grey was motoring smoothly and at the half Peggy-Sue was quite content to sit quietly with her hands on the filly's neck. In the back straight she determined to move up a bit and on the final bend she urged the filly to take closer order. Misk Garnett didn't respond. Coming off the final bend Peggy-Sue let her down, asking for an effort, but the grey rocking horse found nothing. She galloped on one-paced to the wire to finish eighth out of ten.

Peggy-Sue pulled her goggles down, her face was black with dirt. She was tired and disappointed. She patted the filly's neck and murmured endearments into her ear, but her heart wasn't in it. The grey was a ghost of her former self.

'What happened?' asked the twins.

'She found nothing. The tank was empty,' replied Peggy-Sue sorrowfully as she dismounted and unsaddled.

'I was afraid of that,' grunted the trainer. 'You'll have to face it, guys. The filly's fallen out of love with the game.'

Joe looked solemn. 'It's not your fault. You did your best with her.'

The trainer walked away. 'I'm sorry I couldn't do more.'

Hank looked at his twin. 'So it's over to the old country?'

'That's what we agreed.'

They joined Jilly and Mandy, who'd they'd left to watch the race from their private box, and waited for Peggy-Sue to join them. When she arrived, saddle over arm, Joe spoke to her.

'You'll be catching the plane back tonight?'

'Yes, I've got a taxi waiting outside.'

'I think you better stay while we tell the girls why we invited them over here.'

Peggy-Sue nodded. 'Okay, guys, shoot.'

'This afternoon was a last chance for the filly. We'd decided to send her back to England for the rest of the season if she failed.'

'To whom?' asked Jilly quickly.

'Mrs Beechly, if that's agreeable.'

'She'll be thrilled,' gasped Mandy.

'Why Sonia?' asked Peggy-Sue, 'you don't know her.'

'We want you to ride her in all the races and you're retained by Mrs Beechly. You don't object?'

'Far from it. I'm honoured.'

'That's agreed then. When you get back you can tell Sonia that Misk Garnett's on her way. And tell her the filly's entered to run in the Queen Anne Stakes at Royal Ascot, and we want her to go.'

'Well I'm damned,' smiled Peggy-Sue. 'You've had this in mind for some time, haven't you?'

The twins just grinned.

Peggy-Sue said her goodbyes and scampered for the taxi waiting to take her to the airport. Hank ordered a bottle of champagne and they settled down to watch the remainder of the card. The twins knew a lot of colourful characters who came to their table and the afternoon turned out to be fun. The champagne bottle emptied to be replaced by another, and the two British girls began to open out like exotic blooms.

'Now, girls,' exclaimed Joe, putting a fat cigar between his teeth, 'let's get down to business.'

Mandy's eyebrows shot up. 'What's that?'

'It's why you're here, girlie.'

Mandy giggled. They were being a bit blunt even for Yanks. Jilly kicked her under the table. 'You wish to talk racing business?'

'That's the idea. You see we're considering extending our interests.'

'But you race all over the States and Canada now.'

'We're thinking about England.'

'You mean by sending Misk Garnett to us?'

'No, not just the filly.'

'What, then?'

'We're seriously thinking of buying a dozen good horses and racing them in Europe.'

'That sounds entertaining. I'm sure you'd enjoy it.'

'We're taking a year off next year, and we thought we'd spend it in England following our horses.'

'Splendid idea. You must look us up.'

'You still don't get it, do you? You British women aren't much for business, are you? Any young American female would be lobbying like hell.'

Jilly smiled sweetly. 'We take it for granted that you will want us to train them for you.'

The twins laughed. 'I'll be Goddamned,' grinned Hank.

'And what makes you think we'd choose you?' asked Joe.

'Maybe because we've got legs all the way up to our asses?' ventured Jilly.

'And big boobs,' grinned Mandy.

The two brothers laughed loud and long. 'Jeeze, you've hit it. What other reason is there?'

Jilly raised her glass. 'So now that's settled, here's to winners all over Europe.'

They clinked glasses and drank.

They ate dinner at the New York Hilton where the

twins were staying. They drank cocktails and champagne until both girls were on a high.

'You'll have to come to England and sort all this out with Sonia.'

'We plan to do that soon. We've heard she's none too popular with your establishment.'

'It'll blow over.'

Hank laughed. 'It means nothing to us.'

'Tomorrow we'll take you to see our stables in Pennsylvania,' said Joe.

'Tomorrow we're flying home.'

'There's no need. Stop another day. You must see Niagara before you go.'

'Our flight's been booked.'

'We can change that. Have you seen the Falls?'

'No.'

'You must. We'll take you to the stables in the morning and the Falls in the afternoon.'

'And the night?'

'We'll see!'

'It sounds nice, but it's not reason enough to stay over. Sonia will be furious.'

'We have a champion sprinter called Crazy Face. He won everything at two- and three-years old, but lost his form at four. We think he might benefit from a change of environment.'

'Why not send him to England with the grey filly?'

'We were considering it. We just need a little push to make up our minds!'

Mandy looked at Jilly. 'It would be an excuse.

Sonia couldn't say it wasn't business.'

'Okay,' said Jilly, 'I'm persuaded.'

Fifteen minutes and another glass of champagne later their waitress approached them.

'Are you ladies staying at the hotel?' she asked.

'No.'

'I'm sorry to tell you that a transport strike has been declared in New York City. There are no cabs on the streets. No way to get back to your own hotel.'

'We can walk.'

'In New York, after dark?'

'What do you suggest?' asked Jilly.

'You could stay here.'

'Could you book a room for us?'

'I'm sorry, because of the strike all our rooms are taken.'

'Maybe we could sleep in the lounge?'

'The lounge has been booked by the Brooklyn Dodgers.'

'In the bar, maybe?'

'The New York Yankees will be in there.'

'And I suppose the Notre Dame football team will be in the kitchen?'

'Correct, miss!'

'Okay, so what do we do?'

'Your gentlemen friends have rooms. Perhaps if you asked them real nice?'

Jilly laughed. 'Don't you realise you're leading two innocent young girls into a fate worse than death?'

The waitress's deadpan expression didn't change. 'I was well paid, miss!'

The woman picked up the glasses and walked away smiling.

'And you two Casanovas. Fancy bribing her to do your dirty work for you.'

'You mean there isn't a strike?' murmured Mandy wide-eyed.

In the bedroom Joe proved himself to be a thoughtful lover. He undressed Mandy as if she were a young bride and gazed upon her nubile body with reverence. He carried her in his arms to the bathroom and bathed her body with gentle hands that explored every nook and cranny of her naked form as he soaped and rinsed her. She stood silently, as he towelled her dry. On the bed he kissed her eyes, her ears, her nose, before burying his face in her hair and throat – all this before seeking out her succulent red lips. And when he'd fed on her twin breasts and tiny navel only then did he approach the heart of her sensuality.

His tongue flicked teasingly at her clitoris, his lips sucked at the secret inner lips of her fig and his fingers infiltrated the intimacy of her inner channel. She hadn't moved while he adored her with busy lips and fingers, but when his cock penetrated her she cried out and took him into her arms to love him in return.

For Jilly it was a very different tale. If Joe was a man of love, Hank was a creature of lust. Once she'd consented to sleep with him he treated her as if she were a whore. He crudely fondled her buttocks in the escalator, squeezing the pliable twin cheeks through the material of her skirt, pinching the full soft gourds of her plump seat. She pushed his hand away when others joined them in the escalator, but he surreptitiously forced his middle finger into the cleft of her arse. In his large luxurious bedroom he poured out two bourbons.

'Strip, babe, and we'll watch a movie show.'

'Surely I don't have to undress to see a film?'

'For this one, you do!'

He pulled off his tie and slung his coat over the back of a chair. 'What's the matter, honey. You shy?'

'No.'

'Come on then, get 'em off.'

He perched on the arm of a chair to watch her, sinking the Bourbon and refilling the glass. She kicked off her shoes wondering whether she'd done right offering herself for the night. Being grateful was one thing, but she didn't want to be abused again – not after her experience in France. She was glad Mandy had chosen to go with Joe, he seemed a kinder, gentler man. Approaching him she turned her back and lifted her long golden hair clear of her collar.

'Unzip me please.'

She felt him unzip her top and pat her bottom with lecherous intent. 'I'm dying to see that ass of yours, girlie,' he said.

She wriggled the skirt down over her thighs and allowed the top to fall away to leave her big boobs naked.

'That's what I call a pair of knockers,' he growled appreciatively.

He stretched out his hand to squeeze the plumpness, but she moved quickly away. As the skirt came down over her thighs she hooked her fingers into the waistband of her briefs, pulling them down, too. She stood naked before him, bathing in the admiration she saw in his eyes, before reaching up and freeing her hair. When it tumbled loosely around her shoulders she heard him draw in his breath in one quick gulp. Turning round, she showed him her bottom and preened for a moment on tiptoe like a showgirl in a burlesque revue. He watched goggle-eyed for a few seconds as she displayed her charms, but soon became impatient to get on with the scenario he had in mind. She watched him push a tape into the video and beckon her to watch.

The video was pornographic. What else? But why did he want to watch girls on film, Jilly wondered, when he had the real thing sitting next to him? Maybe he was a voyeur. Maybe he got his nuts off by making girls watch porn with him.

The tape was pretty hard, with pervy sex she knew about but had never practised. Surprisingly he didn't attempt to maul her during the show, but immediately it finished he grabbed her and threw her backwards onto the bed. He was certainly acting the caveman. She half expected to be clubbed over the head.

She lay on her back looking up at him as he climbed onto the bed and stood towering over her, stark naked. His great tool stood out like a barber's pole as he grabbed it in his fist and wanked a couple of times. A sort of self-start, she thought to herself. She was certain most men would have preferred a female touch to awaken them but obviously Hank Ladd was a crude customer once the bedroom door was closed. She was momentarily frightened when he sat on her for he was a big man. His thighs came down over her face almost smothering her and, when she opened her eyes, she saw he was on his knees astride her face with his iron-hard cock quivering an inch from her nose.

'I'm gonna fuck your mouth, honey,' she heard him mutter, and so saying he manoeuvred his throbbing penis until the tip was resting against her closed lips.

'Come on, open up. Make a meal of Hank's meat!'

She parted her lips to allow his phallus into her mouth but, instead of letting her gently suck and swallow in her own time, he thrust all seven inches into her throat. She gagged. Her mouth was full of prick and she was unable to move for his belly was pushed into her face. She grabbed at his thighs and vainly tried to lever him upwards, but he didn't budge. She was forced to work her tongue around the wet pole which was jammed into the back of her throat. Slowly she relaxed and began to gobble him but it was difficult. The man was a maniac. Left to her own devices she would have willingly fellated him like an angel.

For what seemed an eternity she sucked at the dick in her mouth but there was no sign of an ejaculation. She realised he was full of alcohol and that was probably holding him back. And then, as suddenly as he'd fallen on her, he withdrew from between her wet lips. She watched him stand up by the bed grinning down at her and wondered what else he'd got in store for her.

'And now, honey, for the main event!'

She barely had time to guess at his intent than she was tossed over like a pancake and made to kneel on her hands and knees. He had her placed with her butt facing him. By peeping into the mirror on the opposite wall she was able to see him bend forward over her, his bulging knob threatening her arse. She expected to be taken doggie-fashion, which she usually enjoyed, and it wasn't till when the swollen tip of his rampant member foraged mercilessly between the cheeks of her bum that she realised what he had in mind. She was to be sodomised. She felt him grab her hips and pull her back onto him. The swollen helmet of his pego burrowed between the cheeks of her rump to nudge against her small tight bumhole. She automatically tightened her anal ring against the invader but he unceremoniously gave her buttocks a hearty whack.

'Come on, loosen up. I'm coming in your back door!'

'No. You're not to.'

'What?' he exploded, 'why not?'

'I don't want you up there.'

He laughed. 'You came here to be humped. What does it matter which way it is?'

'It does to me,' she replied indignantly, but it was too late.

'Oh, Lord, take it out,' she squawked loudly.

'Too late, Jilly, honey. 'Cos now I'm gonna screw your sweet young ass.'

He penetrated her anus in one smooth thrust and suddenly her arse was full of prick. She gasped at the strangeness and the lewdness of it. His belly was flush against her nether-cheeks and his testicles bounced against her bum as he began rogering her as he had promised. She felt as if she was being plundered. And, although the initial penetration had been painful, she found she liked it. It was brutal, perverse, intimate. She was outraged, yet excited. She gritted her teeth and flicked her head from side to side. She moaned and gasped and whinnied. She became aware of a corrupt pleasure stir and build in her bowels. She tensed, yielded, struggled. Then his semen flooded her in great warm ripples. A cry of passion and anguish flowed from her throat as she collapsed onto her stomach. It was over, she was free of him. She lay panting into the pillow. She felt dizzy and used, yet deep down she knew that even if it was the dark path she wouldn't be frightened to go down it again.

She awoke hours later. Dawn was breaking. He'd parted the curtains and a gentle light was peeping into the room. She turned her head. There was no man beside her. She vaguely wondered where he was before she drifted off into sleep again, only to be woken almost instantly by a gentle hand stroking her breast. She lay still as he made love to her and this time it was a gentle love. A love so undemanding that she turned over unable to believe it was him. Hank's face smiled at her. It was difficult to believe it was the same man. He had changed from night to morning like a Jekyll and Hyde. There was no question of refusing him and she enjoyed an hour of joyful coupling before their 6 am call. It was as they stood in the shower together that the answer came to her.

'You're Joe, aren't you?'

He grinned. 'Yes.'

'How do you do it?'

'People tell us apart by the colour of our hair. We have one hairpiece between us. Hank usually wears it, but we swap!'

'I knew it was you.'

He smiled. 'We've been discovered before but only by women who've slept with both of us.'

'I'm not surprised.'

'Why?'

'Your approach to sex is chalk and cheese.'

Two hours later they left Manhattan by the Lincoln

Tunnel and motored from New York City through Pennsylvania to the brothers' racing stables in the heart of the green countryside. They were shown how a typical American yard functioned and then the champion sprinter was paraded for them. He was a striking animal. A real champion, standing seventeen hands with a lively eye and a proud stance. He was as black as coal, but like many others before him he was called dark brown. Racing folk were naturally wary of black horses.

'Isn't he a beauty?' Joe asked.

'He's magnificent.'

'What would they think of him in England?'

'He'd be magnificent anywhere.'

'How would you like to train him? For the rest of the season anyway.'

'Could you bear to part with him?'

'We'll be over to see him, remember?'

'So you will.'

'Well?'

'We'd love to have him. He'd be the stable beauty and we'd do our best to win with him.'

'I'm sure you would. Misk Garnett went over today. We'll fly Crazy Face over next week.'

Then they flew by private helicopter to Niagara and it wasn't until they landed that the sisters were able to talk.

'Even if they've given us Crazy Face I'm not sleeping with them tonight, Jilly.'

'Whatever you say, Mandy.'

'We've spent one night with them. That should be enough. That's fair, isn't it?'

'There's no rules to the game, little sister.'

'I know,' she murmured, 'and if you think we should, I'll do it, but remember I'd rather not.'

'You had a bad experience last night, didn't you?'

'It was this morning,' she grumbled.

Jilly smiled. 'And is your poor botty still sore then?'

'What?'

'You got screwed up the arse, didn't you?'

'How did you know?'

'Because I got it the same way.'

Mandy groaned. 'It was so totally unexpected. He was so nice the night before.'

'It wasn't the same twin.'

'What?'

'They swapped during the night. It was Hank who bummed you. He did it to me the night before.'

'The bastard!' exploded Mandy, but she was laughing.

'What are you laughing at?'

'The thought of you getting it that way.'

'What's so funny about that?'

'You're usually so cool. I bet that put you in a tizzy.'

'Quite the reverse. I enjoyed it.'

'Oh, you fibber!'

'Am I?'

Niagara Falls was every bit as impressive as the twins had promised. They crossed into Canada to see it from that side, and they took the short trip on the Maid of the Mist which sailed right up to the torrential downfall of water. The noise was deafening and the spray like a summer storm, but they both enjoyed it.

That evening they were booked into a fashionable hotel overlooking the Falls and again they were entertained lavishly. They both swore not to drink so much, but the twins were such relaxed hosts that they were soon merry, happily allowing their glasses to be refilled. The following day was to be their last and, having had a taste of America, they both wanted to return. They were due to fly out of New York's Kennedy airport at 9 pm and Joe went over the instructions for Sonia. Misk Garnett was entered at Royal Ascot and they wanted Crazy Face to run at the same meeting. They would be over for the whole of Royal Ascot week, and would arrange with Sonia to buy several horses for her to train for them.

That night the twins booked a double room for the girls, but invited them to their suite for a goodnight drink. Neither girl felt she could refuse – at least they had their own room to return to.

Once in the brothers' suite the conversation became bawdy and Hank ordered champagne. The champagne was delivered by an attractive brunette waitress dressed in the hotel uniform of green waist-coat and skirt. Her name tag told the world she was Leila. She opened the bottle and filled the glasses.

'You were unpardonably late, Leila,' drawled Hank.
'Pardon, sir?'

'We waited much too long for our champagne.'

'I'm sorry, sir.'

'You're a lazy inefficient waitress, Leila.'

She looked angry. 'I've never been called that before, sir.'

'Will you be punished if I complain?'

She looked uncomfortable. 'I shouldn't think so, sir.'

'Then I shall punish you.'

'What?' she cried incredulously.

'I shall smack your bottom, Leila. For being a lazy waitress.'

She moved to leave. 'I'm sorry, sir. I must go.'

'Wait. Answer a question first.'

'What question?'

'Don't you think a lazy waitress deserves a spanking?'

While he spoke Hank took out his wallet and deliberately counted out four fifty-dollar bills in front of her. He carefully laid them out fan-like on the table by her hand.

She hesitated. 'I really don't know, sir.'

He slowly added another fifty-dollar bill to the fan of notes. 'I think you should be spanked, and my friends think so, too.'

Mandy and Jilly watched in disbelief. The sheer nerve of Hank was diabolical. They could see the girl was hovering on the verge of acceptance. They saw him add a further fifty-dollar bill to the little pile and put his wallet in his pocket.

'Now, Leila. It's up to you. Tell us you're a lazy

waitress who should have her bottom smacked, or leave us to drink our champagne.'

They watched the girl take a deep breath, grab the notes from the table, and blush to the roots of her hair. 'I'm a lazy waitress and I deserve to be slapped,' she babbled.

'I agree,' said Hank coldly, 'come here and bend over.'

The attractive young waitress edged forward nervously to stand in front of Hank's chair. Slowly she bent forward from the waist and clasped her knees with her hands. Quick as lightning Hank reached out and, circling the girl's slim waist with his left arm to hold her in place, he whipped up her uniform skirt and jerked her flimsy knickers down to her knees. She squealed with surprise.

'No. No, you mustn't. Not on my bare butt.'

She attempted to straighten her body and retrieve her knickers, but Hank's arm restrained her while he commenced to rain a barrage of sharp slaps on her bare behind. She squealed. Short sharp squeals coincided with each resounding thwack across her naked seat. The slaps from his open palm onto her fleshy posterior echoed erotically throughout the room. The two girls watched the scene open-mouthed. The spanking taking place before their eyes was bizarre enough, but when they began to realise they were enjoying it they felt awful. The flesh of the waitress's pretty behind was soon wobbling like jelly, turning pink under Hank's sound spanking. The girl stood up tearfully when it was over rubbing her abused flesh and pulling up her knickers.

Hank grinned at her. 'Now what about a dose of the strap?'

'Go to hell,' she spat at him.

He produced his wallet again and held up another fifty. 'I just fancy strapping a plump female ass.'

'Not mine, you're not. Whip one of your girlfriends.'

'Oh, Leila, what a good idea.'

'Oh, no,' reacted Jilly quickly, 'not us. Not now.'

'Okay. We'll take a raincheck.'

'What's that mean?' asked Mandy.

'Another time, another place.'

'We're flying home tomorrow,' said Mandy triumphantly.

'We're in no hurry. It will be something to look forward to.'

'You really don't think we'd submit to that sort of thing in England?'

'I thought you were big on CP in the UK. A sort of national kink?'

'Amongst public schoolboys, perhaps.'

'Never mind. Maybe we can popularise it as a sport!'

'Not on our bottoms!' grinned Mandy.

Yet the more they protested the more it was certain that they would be touching their toes when Joe and Hank Ladd crossed the pond for the Royal Ascot meeting.

Chapter 8

The gloom that had settled over The Billings lifted a little when they received the news from the States. The yard fell in love with Misk Garnett the moment she arrived, and the grey rocking horse was given to Tess to look after. She became the darling of the stables; that is until Crazy Face was led out of his horsebox. The gigantic black horse, with the head of a prince and the backside of a navvy, strolled arrogantly into the yard as if he owned it.

'Look at him,' breathed Tess, 'isn't he a beauty?'

'He's a powerhouse of an animal,' agreed Barney.

Sonia's eyes lit up. 'He'll make a fine stallion at stud.'

Tess was full of excitement. 'Can I have him, Mrs Beechly?'

'You've got the grey filly,' interrupted Barney.

'I've still only got two. He'd make up my three.'

Sonia grinned. 'What do you think, Barney? Do you think she could handle him?'

'I'm not sure. Perhaps we ought to give him to one of the lads.'

213

She punched Barney's shoulder. 'I'll kill you, Barney.'

Sonia settled the argument. 'I think you'd better take him, Tess. Then we'll have the same girl looking after both the American horses.'

She stuck her tongue out at Barney. 'Thank you, Mrs Beechly,' she said.

Tess's third horse was Man Samson, who'd joined the yard at the beginning of May. After the infamous race which had seen Sonia leave his yard, Bart had decided to sell the horse. There was absolutely no reason for such an action but Bart had a dark side to his nature. He flatly refused to sell to Sonia, who had immediately made a generous offer, and after much shilly shally he sold the horse to a Welsh businessman. The Welshman turned out to be an agent for The Billings so Sonia finally got what she wanted, leaving Bart to stick more pins into her effigy. Unfortunately, Man Samson had had a slight recurrence of his injury, but was now ready to race again. He was to go for a Class C handicap at Epsom on Derby day. When they left his stall after evening rounds, Sonia turned to Barney.

'Wouldn't it be something if he was our first winner?'

'Sort of poetic justice, you mean?'

'I don't know what I mean, but I'd give anything for a winner and it would be nice if it was Man Samson.'

'He'll win. See if he doesn't.'

'What makes you so confident?'

'I can feel it in my water!'

Sonia chuckled. 'That doesn't guarantee much.'

'I'll bet you a week's wages.'

'That he wins?'

'Yes.'

'I'd be betting against my own horse. I can't do that.'

'Okay. I'll give you a week's wages if he doesn't win.'

'And if he does?'

Barney paused. 'Remember the day all this began? On the way back from the pub.'

He daren't look at her. His heart was in his mouth. She'd probably think he'd led her into it.

Sonia didn't stop walking. 'You're a crafty bastard, Barney. You led me into that, didn't you?'

'No, honestly. Forget I said it.'

She turned to him. 'It's a deal. You can lay me if Man Samson wins. My God, if he wins the whole damned village can lay me!'

Barney grinned. He'd made certain the animal won even if he had to dope the rest of the runners.

The four-day Epsom meeting began on the Wednesday, the day of the Derby. It was on that day, exactly a year ago, that Peggy-Sue had her horrific fall and lost the Derby as a result. Now she parked her car and walked towards the course in trepidation. Her mind was a confusion of thought. She was more nervous today riding Man Samson in a handicap than she'd been riding in the Derby last year. As she approached the weighing room, a Channel Four interviewer caught up with her. She agreed to a short interview and faced the cameras smiling.

'It's good to see you back, Peggy Sue Rhyma.'

'Thank you.'

'I expect many viewers will remember that the last time Peggy-Sue was at Epsom she had that terrible fall in the Derby. Remind us of what happened, Peggy-Sue.'

'I don't really remember too much about it. My horse collapsed under me about fifteen yards from the post.'

'And that was in the Derby?'

'That's right. One year ago today.'

'And tell us what's happened to you since? Did you think you'd ever ride again?'

'I kept hoping, but the doctors were sceptical. I suffered dizzy spells and my sight was affected.'

'But you're okay now?'

'Yes, I was given the go-ahead three weeks ago and I've had several rides.'

'Any winners?'

'Two, but not for my retained stable.'

'This afternoon you ride Man Samson in the ten-furlong handicap.'

'Yes, for Mrs Beechly.'

'Your only ride this afternoon?'

'Yes, my other mount was withdrawn. It was found cast in its stall this morning.'

'For the benefit of our viewers, what exactly does that mean?'

'The horse was found lying in the stall and couldn't get back to his feet. He'd injured himself trying.'

'And what about the Derby. No ride this year?'

'I'm afraid not, but I'll enjoy watching.'

'Are you nervous at returning to the scene of your accident?'

'A little. I wouldn't be human if I wasn't.'

'How true. Well, we wish you luck this afternoon, Peggy-Sue.'

'Thank you.'

As she walked away she was surprised to find the interview had relaxed her. She was looking forward to riding the switchbacks of the world-famous Epsom course again.

Sonia was late arriving at the course and when she did she was like a cat on hot bricks. The race was getting to her almost as much as when Man Samson had run at Sandown. She patted his nose. If he won this afternoon she'd buy him a hundredweight of his favourite mints.

During the past months she'd done everything to try and break her losing run. Her latest fad was the horses' feed. She'd made Barney personally respons-ible for the hay, instructing him that there mustn't be too much clover mixed with the rye grass. She'd insisted the oats be bought straight from Scotland, and that they have plenty of weight and not too much husk. She gave strict orders that they were mixed fresh every day, while twice a week she personally supervised the mash, fussily mixing the vitamins and honey and nuts into the boiled linseed and oats. Heaven help the stablehand who failed to renew the salt licks in the stalls, or tell her when their charges weren't eating up.

She'd had so many disappointments she daren't bring herself to believe that Man Samson could win for her. She realised she'd been silly to have that bet with Barney, but if it helped bring about a winner she'd have frigged the stable cat. The Derby was run, and the favourite won, so everything else was an anti-climax. The bubbling excitement around the course had died down and the tension in the paddock was back to normal. She watched Man Samson plod round led by Tess, who looked as smart as paint and a credit to the stable. Sonia was in deep thought when Peggy-Sue arrived and tapped her on the shoulder with her whip.

'Penny for 'em?'

'I was thinking he looked a picture.'

'It won't be your fault if he doesn't win. He looks a hundred and ten per cent.'

'Oh Lord, Peggy, do you think there's any chance?'

'Every chance. How do you want me to ride him?'

'As we agreed. Take him to the front and make the pace. Let's just pray he lasts home.'

'You're certain? It's doing it the hard way.'

'He's happy making the running and he's fit, so let him have a go.'

'Okay, guv. You're the boss.'

'Just do your best. If he loses he's only one of a long string. We won't die of it.'

'Maybe not, but it would be nice to break our duck.'

Once on the course Man Samson acted like a perfect gentleman. He shuffled into the stalls as quietly as an old goat, but came out like a greyhound. There was no natural front-runner and, as Sonia had guessed, nobody wanted to make the pace. All the jocks were prepared to dawdle at the start, playing cat and mouse with each other. They were caught flatfooted when Man Samson shot into the lead taking some ten lengths out of the field. Peggy-Sue allowed the gelding to stride out and, as he had a naturally high cruising-speed, there was no need to push him.

Sonia watched through her binoculars as they came down the hill into Tattenham Corner with her horse swinging along in front. She saw Peggy-Sue guide him around the bend some two horses' width from the rail and, keeping him perfectly balanced, aim him for home. Man Samson was still galloping within himself but the field were beginning to close. She watched Peggy-Sue begin to push, putting the gelding under pressure, urging him to stretch out. Her skin began to tingle, her hands trembled on the binoculars, and her gut knotted with nervous tension. God, the stress would kill her. She'd end up with a heart attack.

Man Samson was galloping relentlessly past the

two pole and was still two lengths in the lead. She saw two horses closing the gap. Her heart was in her mouth. *Oh Lord, please let the post come!* She saw Peggy-Sue change her hands, swing her whip, and ask for more. The horse changed legs, momentarily faltering. Peggy hit him once, twice. The one pole had come and gone. One of the two challengers had fallen away, but the other was closing with every stride. Peggy was pushing and kicking and swinging her whip in front of the horse's eyes. The gelding responded. He put his head down and fought like a lion. Inch by inch he succeeded in pulling away from his rival until, at the line, he had half a length to spare.

Sonia went mad. She'd done it! The spell was broken. She was on her way. Nothing could stop her now. She scampered down to meet her winner. *Her first winner.* Tears streamed down her face. She was on a magic carpet. Tess was leading the gelding in, her face wreathed in smiles, a hint of tears in her eyes. Sonia grabbed her by the shoulders and planted the whopper of a kiss on her lips. It was a real smackeroo. Tess looked surprised. Several bystanders clapped at such spontaneous jubilation. Others frowned, thinking they were a couple of dykes. Peggy-Sue laughed outright, her peals of merriment displaying her own joy. Only the horse plodded on unconcerned. When Peggy-Sue dismounted Sonia threw her arm around her and kissed her cheek.

'We've done it, Peggy,' she babbled, 'we're up and away. Nothing will stop us now.'

Peggy-Sue unfastened the girths and pulled off the saddle. 'That elusive first winner at last.'

'He did it well. So did you. A race to remember.'

'I enjoyed it,' replied her jockey.

'We'll celebrate. I'll ring the yard and tell them there's a party on me tonight at the Spread Eagle.'

That night at the Spread Eagle was a real ding-dong. Chucking-out time saw a procession of legless stablehands helping each other home. Sonia left her car in the park and helped Barney carry a paralytic Tess back to his cottage. She didn't feel too bad her-self, a plate of sandwiches had served to soak up some of the alcohol.

'Goodnight, Barney,' she called.

'Hang on. I'll walk with you.'

'I'll be all right. You look after Tess.'

He fell in by her side. 'She's sleeping like a babe.'

Although neither said as much they both knew why he was there. Barney wanted to collect his win-nings. The house was empty – Mandy and Jilly were staying in Surrey for the remainder of the Epsom meeting. Sonia closed the front door and moved towards the lounge. She wasn't having Barney in her bedroom. She didn't mind him fucking her on the rug, or over the sofa, but she drew the line at her bed. She felt him tug at her sleeve.

'Not in there. Let's go into the office.'

She followed him. 'If you like.'

He pushed open the door and switched on the light. 'That's better.'

'What's so special about the office?'

'I've always fancied screwing you in here.'

She laughed. 'Why?'

'You look so damned cool and unapproachable sitting in that big chair.'

'Really?'

'It makes me want to drag you from behind the desk and stuff your posh arse.'

'You've got some sort of phobia, Barney.'

'I've got a hard-on just thinking about it!'

She moved silently behind the big desk and deliberately sat in the chair. 'Okay, Barney. You've won your bet, and I'm pleased you did, so why not make your fantasy come true?'

He stood motionless looking at her as if frozen to the spot. She couldn't believe he was unsure of himself. Not Barney. Did he really think she was so unapproachable? It was a different Barney to the man who'd shafted her over the back of her own car. And then, quite suddenly, he sprang at her. She found herself lifted from the chair and swung bodily onto the desk. She was surprised by his strength. Although it was rather undignified she went with the flow, allowing him to dump her on the desk with her long legs dangling towards the floor. He swept the desk top clear with one movement and grabbed a chair to sit facing her.

'Let's have that skirt up to your waist,' he said flatly.

Sonia felt a stab of annoyance. She didn't like being ordered about, especially in that tone of voice, but there was no point in arguing. She'd put herself in this position so she only had herself to blame. She recalled the last time he'd taken advantage of her. She'd quite enjoyed it. But then, she usually enjoyed sex.

She began to wriggle the tight linen skirt up her thighs, baring her trim nylon-stockinged legs until her stocking tops showed. She paused briefly to watch his face. His eyes were fixed on the hem of her skirt. She raised it another couple of inches to expose a strip of bare white flesh between her stocking tops and her panties. His face was blue and she was certain she saw steam coming out of his ears. She lifted her behind from the desk and quickly wriggled her skirt upwards until it was around her waist. She kept her legs firmly together as if they were glued. She'd done what he asked, now it was up to him. She was damned if she was going to seduce the man.

Barney was not the shy type who needed seducing. He reached up beneath the folds of her rumpled skirt, feeling for the waistband of her knickers, and jerked them down and off. Sonia found herself sitting bare-bummed on the cold, polished surface of the desk top. She shivered. Her skirt was around her waist, her knickers on the floor at her feet. He sat on the chair studying her limbs, modestly closed to hide her femininity. She looked down at him trying to guess his next move. Would he require her to fellate him? Or pleasure her with cunnilingus? Or take her in intercourse? Or had he some other trick up his sleeve?

'What are you going to do with me, Barney?'

He grunted something she couldn't understand.

'Something nice, I hope?'

Without warning he burst into action, grabbing her ankles and swinging her long legs upwards until she toppled over backwards onto the desk. Thus she found herself flat on her back with her legs high in the air. He clasped her behind the knees and, roughly forcing her thighs apart, pushed her knees back towards her neck. She was doubled over like an envelope, her pussy vulnerable and unprotected, winking up at him. He licked his lips.

She smiled up at him and spoke in a little girl's voice. 'You look as if you're going to eat me for your dinner, Mr Wolf.'

He laughed. 'I just might, m'lady. You've got a cunt like a peach, or should I say a peach of a cunt!'

She grinned. 'You're drooling, Barney!'

She wriggled her arse a little. Her thighs were spread so far apart that her mound of Venus stood up like a furry hillock and the swollen lips of her vagina gaped in welcome. He longed to suck and suck at her until his mouth was filled with her sweet nectar.

His mouth enveloped her soft nest of fur, his teeth

nibbling at the short red curls. She felt his tongue straying around the edges of her labia, and his hot breath playing on her genitals thrilled her. She realised she was alive with anticipation. She actually wanted to be eaten out. It was no longer a duty – she was eager. And when his tongue slid between her quim lips to move upwards towards her hooded clitoris she was avid with desire.

Even before the tip of his tongue touched it, her clit was pulsing with excitement. He teased and tantalised the sensitive organ with his tongue until she could feel an orgasm building within her loins. A scream trembled in the back of her throat and she shrilled as she orgasmed, fiercely pushing her crotch into his face. She reached down with her hands to drive his face even further between her legs until his tongue seemed to be right inside her, gobbling at the walls of her vagina.

She closed her eyes, lying placidly after the storm, and he sucked and sucked at her until she came again and again. Each time he swallowed her juices as if they were the food of the Gods. Sonia felt a pang of loss when he finally withdrew his head.

'Where'd you learn that, Barney?'

'What?'

'To suck like a dream.'

He half smiled. 'From a woman I knew years ago.'

'She must have been a good teacher.'

She watched him stand up. 'She used to pay me. I was only a lad.'

'You're joking.'

He slipped out of his trousers. 'Am I?'

She began to lower her legs, but he took her knees and urged them back behind her ears. She watched him climb onto the desk, one leg either side of her, his body kneeling above her.

'Don't you think you've collected your bet?'

He grinned. 'You're probably right, but I still need to shaft you.'

'Need to, or want to?'

He lowered his body down onto hers. 'Does it matter?'

She could feel his hot cockhead against her crotch and she had no doubt he knew she wanted to continue as much as he did. It would be hypocritical to pretend otherwise. Her quim was still moist from her juices and his saliva, still hot from his cunnilingus, still itching for further erotic adventure.

The palms of his hands were flat on the polished surface by her head as he raised his body to manoeuvre his impatient ramrod between her thighs. She reached up and wound her arms around his neck while hooking her legs over his shoulders. The blunt end of his penis was nudging into her and she swallowed with excitement as she felt him impale her. She felt a surge of sweet, aching pleasure sweep through her loins as she was penetrated.

As she began to writhe beneath him her overt sexuality made the passion rise in his groin. He allowed that passion full reign, driving into her while she gripped his throbbing member inside her vagina, fearful that he would slip from her. And when they came, they came together.

Once Man Samson had broken the ice, the winners began to arrive. They came in a trickle rather than a flood, but every one was like a breath of spring to The Billings. A new optimism blossomed in the yard. The two horses from the USA settled down without fuss. Misk Garnett appeared to appreciate the return to her old environment for she began to show some of her old skittishness while Crazy Face took it all in his stride and soon established himself as the king of the castle. However, it was only a fortnight to the Ascot meeting so little could be done with either horse.

The kudos of having runners at the Royal meeting gave a fillip to the stables as it was the premier meeting of the racing calender. Misk Garnett was entered in the Queen Anne stakes over the old mile on the Tuesday; Crazy Face in the King's Stand stakes over five furlongs on the Friday; while, on Wednesday, Sonia had entered Iskmak, one of Prince Khaled's horses, in the Coronation stakes.

Iskmak was a beautifully bred filly who'd only run three times in her life. As a two-year old she'd had one outing at Chantilly to run a promising fourth out of ten. As a three-year old she'd run in a seven-furlong race at Longchamp to finish a respectable second to a potential classic filly, so M de Lalec had sent her to Newmarket for the 1,000 Guineas. She'd completely flopped, finishing tailed off, and hadn't run since.

On the Tuesday Sonia was the guest of Joe and Hank Ladd, who'd been invited to share a private box with a rich and influential American who resided in Britain. The twins had rented from Moss Bros and looked like two elegant penguins while Sonia drew admiring glances from all who saw her. She wore a chic and simple dress in a shade of green that set off her magnificent mane of red hair which she'd allowed to cascade over her shoulders and down her back. Sonia rarely wore her hair loose so it was a sight to seduce friends and enemies alike. The twins gazed at her in awe.

'Mrs Beechly, we had no idea you were so beautiful. Your stepdaughters should have prepared us.'

Sonia laughed. 'Thank you, gentlemen.'

'Say, isn't this something?' cried Hank, 'a real old-fashioned British pageant.'

'The racing's good, too,' smiled Sonia.

'That's what we came for. I suppose people forget the quality of it amongst all this colour.'

'Most of the guests in the Royal Enclosure have little or no interest in racing. They're here to see and be seen.'

'Never mind,' sighed Joe, 'let's go and look at our horse in the paddock.'

'She looks well,' said Hank.

'Don't expect too much. She's only just arrived.'

'We know, Sonia. We're not expecting to win, but we'd like to talk about the filly's future.'

'Tell me what you envisage,' said Sonia.

'It's really up to you, but we'd like her to run in two or three Group One races before the end of the season. Races which we can pop over to see.'

'Do you have any particular races in mind?'

'We leave that to you, Sonia, although we've heard a great deal about Glorious Goodwood. Is that a possibility?'

'Why not?'

'And the same with Crazy Face. If you can get him anywhere near straight we'd like to see him contest the big sprints over here.'

'What exactly is wrong with him? Did your trainer give you any inkling why he might have lost his form?'

'No. It's a mystery.'

'I'll try my best with him, but I can't promise miracles.'

'Of course you can't, but you can allow us to entertain you tonight so we can get to know one another.'

'That sounds nice.'

'Good. We'll book a room for you at our hotel so we can make a night of it.'

She could guess what sort of a night they had in mind. Jilly had told her about their sexual appetites so she knew what to expect.

'I'm sorry, but I have to get back to the stables.'

'Nonsense. Your stepdaughters are capable of taking charge.'

She smiled. 'All right, if you insist. It will make a change.'

Here I go again, she thought.

The grey filly showed no temperament when Peggy-Sue took her to post. There was none of the skittishness or reluctance to go down that she'd shown in the past. This shouldn't have worried her jockey, but it did. She just didn't have the feel of the filly she knew. She showed little interest in the crowds lining the course and barely pricked her ears at the noise. On the other hand, Peggy-Sue felt excited. It was grand to be back. The horses circled in front of the stalls at the start of the old mile which is in Swinley Bottom at the far corner of the course. The bustling, crowded Stands could be seen but not heard, and the only noise was the passing traffic on the nearby A322. Once out of the stalls the filly settled in behind as was her wont, and Peggy-Sue switched her off until the final bend.

When she asked her, the filly responded grudgingly and they were well into the short straight before the horse really quickened. The leaders had long flown, and although the filly couldn't possibly get into the frame Peggy-Sue threw everything at her without resorting to the whip. Only in the last half furlong did she respond. The race was lost, but Peggy-Sue was rewarded when Misk Garnett suddenly slipped into overdrive. So, she was still capable of it when she wanted. She dropped her hands. It was all much too late.

'Well,' asked Sonia, 'what happened?'

'All's not lost,' grinned Peggy-Sue, 'she's still got the ability. She can still do it, but for some reason she's not willing.'

'Good work, Peggy. I thought you'd lost your marbles riding like a maniac when the race was lost.'

'No fear. I wanted to see if there was any sign of her former brilliance.'

'And is there?'

'I think so.'

'Then we must persuade her to show it.'

Joe and Hank Ladd entertained Sonia lavishly that evening. They talked horses and racing and had a supply of amusing tales. Later they discussed the horses they wished to purchase, the money they were prepared to spend and the Sales they'd buy from. Never once was sex mentioned and Sonia began to wonder whether Jilly and Mandy had been exaggerating their erotic adventures. It was almost as an afterthought, as they stood in the lift whizzing up to their floor, that Joe started the ball rolling.

'How about a nightcap, Sonia?'

'To cap a pleasant evening,' added Hank.

'Why not?'

In their suite they poured her a scotch and, making their excuses, disappeared. She sat sipping the whisky surprised to be left alone, they'd shown themselves so attentive throughout the evening. It was when they returned that she got one of the surprises of her life. They walked back into the room stark naked. It was so damned unexpected. She glanced from one to the other in amazement.

'Your mouth is open, Mrs Beechly!'

She chuckled. 'Are you surprised?'

'Don't tell us you've never seen naked men before?'

'It's a bit unexpected. Why?'

'Surely you can guess?'

'You wanted to shock me?'

'Not particularly. We just thought we'd like to get down to the business in hand as soon as possible.'

'And what is the business in hand?'

'To make a sandwich of you, Mrs Beechly. We've been dreaming about it since we met you.'

'Why didn't you tell me? I'm an adult.'

'A consenting one, we hope?'

'On this occasion. However, I won't be making a habit of it.'

She remembered saying the same thing to Barney. Perhaps she was too easy a touch.

'Nor would we expect it.'

'I'm not so sure I like the sound of this sandwich you speak of.'

'We're twins. We like to do things together.'

She looked at them. Hank had removed the hairpiece and there was no way she could tell them apart. They were big men, well-muscled, but running to a middle-aged spread. They had the same carpet of hair on their chests and, as far as she could judge, the same length of prick.

She stood up languidly. 'I'll undress in the bathroom.'

'No, please. Here, in front of us.'

'You're making it difficult for me. A lady likes her privacy.'

'And gentlemen like a show, especially when a lady of your beauty is the star.'

She laughed. 'Touché.'

She decided that if she had to strip before them that she would indeed put on a show. She turned to be unzipped, and once the simple green dress was unfastened it peeled off easily. She held it to her breasts with both hands spread like a stripper in a Parisian revue and, pouting sensually, shimmied before them with simulated dance steps to imaginary music. They clapped. She allowed the green dress to fall, revealing her shapely white breasts, so invitingly kissable. She held the dress at her hips for a moment before allowing it to tumble to the ground, leaving her naked. She posed in black nylons and a thin suspender belt, while between her thighs was looped the briefest of G-strings. It did little more than cover the folds of her quim and certainly didn't do anything to hide her beguiling nest of silken pubic hair. As she slipped out of the G-string they drank in her beauty. She was truly magnificent, a classical beauty with a mane of auburn hair. She bent to unfasten her stockings.

'Leave them on, please.'

She did as she was bid. She didn't feel so naked while she wore stockings, and she knew from experience that many men liked her to wear them when they made love. The sight of her exquisite nude body had made both men hard. She approached Hank until she was close enough to reach forward and take his pego. Simultaneously, Joe had moved behind her and was so close she could feel his warm breath on her back and imagine his stiff shaft hovering near her derriere.

It was Joe who spoke. 'You're quite willing to do this, Sonia?'

'What is it you want me to do?'

'Take both of us at once.'

She paused. 'Yes.'

At her answer she felt Hank's hands grab her shoulders and Joe clasp her hips.

'We shan't speak again, Sonia. Neither of us enjoys conversation during sex.'

'My sentiments exactly,' she replied.

'However, if pleasing both of us becomes too much you must tell us.'

'Thank you.'

She could have burst out laughing. They were so formal. It was like entering into a contract, although with all the weird litigation that took place in the USA, perhaps they were just covering themselves. She felt Hank urge her to bend forward at the same time as Joe's hands gently pulled her hips backwards. She ended up on her hands and knees with Hank kneeling in front of her, his stiff pole quivering about an inch from her nose. At the same time Joe had parted her knees and slid, on his back, beneath her. His face was directly beneath her crotch, his mouth just inches below her pouting crack.

The cock and cunt sucking that followed went on for a soul-searching age and every so often the twins would change places. They did it so smoothly that she hardly noticed, and anyway she couldn't tell one from the other. Their tools looked the same and tasted the same. However, she soon discovered that when he was beneath her Hank's sucking was more frenzied; and that he would try to fuck her mouth while Joe was satisfied to have her suck him.

In spite of the frantic oral sex neither twin ejaculated and when they carried her to the bedroom she realised the time had come for her to take them both inside her. They worked with military precision and Sonia wondered how many women had submitted to them in this way. Joe lay on his back on the bed and she found her place was to be astride him on her hands and knees. Whilst Hank watched from behind, Joe manoeuvred his rampant cock to the entrance of her wet pussy and thrust between her petal lips into the tunnel beyond.

She gave a low moan of satisfaction as she sank onto his cock, which turned to a high-pitched squeak when a foreign object stabbed at her back passage. It was Hank's index finger introducing itself into her rear. The initial surprise over, she fought to relax. She had known she was going to be taken that way. She was quite aware that being the meat in a sandwich meant taking two men from front and rear. She'd committed herself so there was no point fighting it.

She felt Hank smearing the sweetness from her honeypot around her puckered anus and it was quickly followed by the end of his dick nudging against her sphincter. She was already full of one prick that was working like a piston within her vagina, and when the second impaled her she felt as if she must surely cry out. She closed her eyes and bit her lip. Oh Lord, she was filled to overflowing. Two pricks were sheathed to the hilt within her. She had to speak, she couldn't be silent.

'God, I'm full up.'

Her words must have aroused a greater passion in them both for they pushed into her as if they were trying to cram their balls into her as well.

'Fuck me,' she pleaded, 'but gently, please.'

Obediently they began to shaft her: moving simultaneously, and then alternatively. A whirlwind of erotic sensation gathered inside her. She felt she must burst, but instead she found her body relaxing. She'd swallowed up two rampant cocks. The elasticity of her genitals had allowed her to take their male protrusions until gradually the initial hurt had become a deep sensual pleasure. She loved it. And after they'd ejaculated simultaneously and flooded her with their semen she slept between them, exhausted and strangely content.

Wednesday belonged to Prince Khaneme's filly, Iskmak. However, Claude, the Prince's racing supervisor, was in no way similar to the Ladd brothers. Since Sonia had acquired the Prince's horses, Claude had been nothing but a nuisance. He liked to arrive without warning at The Billings and demanded everybody's undivided attention. Sonia disliked the man and wondered how he held down his job. She spoke to Peggy-Sue, who promised to speak to Prince Sojo's racing manager, Guy. The two men were in the same line of business. A couple of days later Peggy-Sue walked into the office and closed the door behind her.

'Guy can't abide the Frenchman, Claude.'

'Why not?'

'I didn't ask, but he said Claude only got his job because of his attitude to women.'

'What does that mean?'

'As you know, the Prince has a harem in addition to chasing European women. Apparently he can't handle competition and won't have any men with an eye for the girls on his staff.'

'Are you telling me Claude's queer?'

'You mean gay?'

'Whatever.'

'Guy doesn't think so, but he can't abide feminine women. The fluffy submissive type get up his nose.'

'And all the Prince's females answer to that description.'

'That's correct, so Claude's tolerated.'

'That doesn't help us, does it?'

'Hang on,' chuckled Peggy-Sue, 'Guy reckons he's one of those men who get turned on by dominant women. You know the sort of thing?'

'The leather-clad mistress with a scowl and a whip?'

'Quite so.'

'So he's a submissive. I can't see that gives us any hold over him.'

'I don't know, think about it. What if you played the stern mistress for him?'

'Me? I'm not sure I could.'

However, Sonia did think about it, and decided if it got the prat off his high horse it would be worth it. She spoke to Jilly and Mandy, and between them they dreamt up a scheme. Claude was invited back to The Billings after Iskmak's race at Royal Ascot. He accepted.

Iskmak was entered in the Coronation stakes on the Wednesday, a Group One race over a mile for three-year old fillies. She looked way out of her depth, but Sonia wanted to assess her worth in the highest class. The filly had come to the yard with a bad reputation and initially had lived up to it. For the first few days she'd been stubborn and bad-tempered and thoroughly temperamental. She'd nipped her stable-lad, chased Sonia out of her stall and tried to bite Barney. Sonia had laughed when Barney had been forced to jump for his life.

'What are we going to do with her, Barney?'

'Get her a goat.'

'You reckon?'

'It might quieten her.'

'I'll look around for a billy as bad-tempered as she is!'

'Bloody good idea, but you'd better not. He might injure her.'

They settled for a nanny with a docile nature which did little else but eat everything within chewing distance. Iskamak accepted her without reservation and they became inseparable. The filly began to settle down, but she still wouldn't allow Barney into her stall.

At Royal Ascot she showed signs of temperament, fly-kicking as she paraded, and spooking at any quick movement in the crowd. Claude attempted to force his own idea of riding onto Peggy-Sue, but Sonia had already told her how she wanted the filly ridden. At the start she bucked and kicked, and dumped Peggy-Sue on her arse. However, Peggy-Sue was unhurt and quickly remounted, but the handlers had trouble getting the filly into the stalls. Finally, a blindfold did the trick, and she got away with the others. Peggy-Sue took her straight into the lead as the idea was to see exactly what the filly was. Sonia wanted to give her a hard race so she knew where to aim in the future.

After a furlong Peggy-Sue found she couldn't hold
the lead when two horses crept up on her outside
and took over. She pushed at Iskmak, trying to make
her lay up with the leaders, but the filly couldn't or
wouldn't go. At the five pole Iskmak was plumb last
and floundering. The pace had been fast and furious
and coming off the bend most of the field were under
pressure. Only one filly was on the bridle and when
her jockey let her down she went away to win by four
lengths. In spite of her position at the back of the
field Peggy-Sue kept on at Iskmak, swinging her
whip and hitting her several times behind the
saddle. It was only in the last half furlong that she
began to run through tired horses, to finish a
respectable sixth of ten. Sonia was there to meet her
as she dismounted.

'She needs further.'

Sonia frowned. 'Are you sure?'

'I'd stake my arse on it.'

'Her sire barely got a mile.'

'I realise that, but the filly definitely needs
further.'

'What makes you think so?'

'Her cruising speed isn't quick enough for a fast-
run mile and she resents being pushed.'

'That's not enough, Peggy.'

'She finished like a train as if she needed further.'

'You were running through beaten horses.'

Peggy-Sue looked angry. 'She gave me the feel she
needed further,' she shouted.

'Ah, now that's better. A gut reaction from a good horsewoman. I'll accept that.'

'Okay, Sonia. So now it's over to you.'

Claude was disappointed and said so. He criticised Peggy-Sue's riding but Sonia shut him up. It was the first time she'd snapped at him. He looked at her with respect and when she told him to be at The Billings at 8 pm sharp he eagerly agreed.

When he arrived Sonia had changed into a skin-tight leather mini-skirt and a clinging wool sweater over an uplift bra. She'd piled her hair on the top of her head in a severe way and wore knee-length kinky boots. Although she looked the part of a domi-nant mistress she certainly didn't feel it. She was nervous, and prayed she could carry it off. She hoped the fact that she disliked the man might swing it for her.

Exactly what Claude expected to find at The Billings, or why he'd accepted so eagerly, was hard to understand. Maybe it was Sonia's new attitude towards him, for since she'd treated him coldly he'd warmed to her. She lost no time in setting the scene so he knew what she had in mind. She'd soon find out whether the man was a submissive. If he wasn't, he'd either turn on his heel and walk out, or tan her arse. She began as she meant to go on.

'I've found your attitude towards me less than respectful.'

'I'm sorry,' he murmured.

'I thought you'd be sufficiently intelligent to

realise my encounter with the Prince was completely out of character for me.'

'I see that now.'

'I've asked you here to clear up any misunderstanding between us, and to impress on you the sort of respect I expect a snivelling fool like you.'

His eyebrows shot up, but his expression was one of anticipation. She could tell he liked the new woman who was prepared to dominate him. She slowly and deliberately unfastened the leather thong which was knotted around her waist as a belt and saw a flicker of depraved longing in his eyes.

'Put your hands out in front of you,' she ordered icily.

He obeyed instantly and she swiftly wound the thong around his wrists until they were fastened together with no more than six inches play between them.

'Now drop your trousers,' she barked.

He didn't move. For a terrible moment she thought she'd overacted, but that lewd look of yearning was still in his eyes. She took a chance.

'Do as I say, you miserable man. If I have to take them down for you, I'll tie your testicles in a knot!'

He dropped his trousers quickly and as they fell in a heap at his feet Jilly and Mandy walked into the room. They paid no attention to Claude. It was as if they were used to seeing men being dominated by their stepmother.

'What do you want?' she snapped fiercely.

'You told us we must report here at 8.30 pm sharp for our punishment.'

'You are both to be caned. Go upstairs and I'll be there to see to it in a minute.'

'Yes, stepmother,' they both murmured respectfully.

'You will bare your bottoms and stand facing the wall with your hands on your head until I arrive. Do you understand?'

'Yes, stepmother.'

'We'll decide how many strokes you deserve later.'

They turned to go. 'Yes, stepmother.'

The little pantomime seemed to convince Claude that Sonia really was a mistress of discipline. He followed her into the adjoining room where a single bed stood and, after being ordered to strip, was made to lie on it. She swiftly secured his wrists to the bed rail above his head and, grabbing his ankles, swung his legs way above his head to tie them to the bedrail either side of his wrists. Thus she had rudely exposed him as men loved to expose women. He was doubled over with his buttocks spread and his crotch at the mercy of the wide world. Already his cock was beginning to swell. She cuffed it with her open palm. He gasped and pulled in his breath.

'We'll have none of that until I've finished disciplining you. If you take your punishment sufficiently well to excite me, I may, perhaps, reward you.'

'Yes, mistress,' he murmured contentedly, 'thank you, mistress.'

'I shall now punish my wayward daughters, but

while I'm away I'll give you something to occupy your mind.'

So saying she produced a large vibrator, held it between his lips to be moistened, and with one force- ful thrust drove it crudely up his arse. He squealed and squirmed, but she drove it unmercifully up into his rectum until only the end was visible. Grinning sadistically at her handiwork she switched the machine on and left him.

Upstairs the two girls sat giggling. 'How's it going?' they gurgled.

'All right, I suppose.'

'What are you doing to him?' asked Mandy inquisitively.

'Nothing that little girls should know about.'

'Come on. Give us a thrill!'

Sonia ignored her. 'Let's have a few screams, girls. Put him in the mood.'

The two girls obliged, squealing sufficiently loudly for the willing captive to hear them. Sonia picked up a long swishy bamboo cane with a sigh.

'Ah, well, here I go.'

Jilly chuckled. 'Lay it on the bastard real hard, mum!'

On the Friday morning the two girls both received a parcel which stopped them joking about the caning Claude had received from their stepmother. Soon it would be their turn. They'd seen a lot of the Ladd brothers during the Royal Meeting, but as nothing had been said about their Niagara trip they thought it had been forgotten. They realised they were wrong. The twins now made it clear that they meant to collect the raincheck they'd taken that last night. Each parcel contained a white T-shirt and ankle socks and a short pleated kilt skirt. It was a style of dress favoured by many young American teenage girls. Enclosed in Mandy's parcel was a handwritten note. 'Our hotel tonight 6.30 pm. Wear these.' In the second parcel was a longer typewritten note: 'What is a whipping girl? She's a young female who receives discipline on another's behalf. You have been chosen as whipping girls for our two sassy nieces whose derrieres we'd love to warm, but sadly never will.'

They spoke to Sonia. 'Well, what do you think?'

'It's your bums on the line. You must do as you think fit.'

'They've been pretty good to us and have promised a great deal more, haven't they?'

'Yes.'

Mandy grinned. 'I'm willing. A spanking never hurt anybody.'

Jilly pulled a face. 'I ran away from Finishing School to avoid the cane.'

Mandy whacked her rump playfully. 'Go on, you'll enjoy it.'

Jilly looked sorrowful. 'Wanna bet?'

The King's Stand stakes is one of the half-dozen

really big sprints of the season. Run over five furlongs at breakneck speed, it usually brings together
some of the top sprinters in Europe but rarely is
an American horse seen. Crazy Face was more of a
curiosity than a live contender to the Ascot crowds.
He was offered at 20–1 on the bookies' boards, but
after the Ladd twins admitted in a TV interview
that the horse had been under a cloud it drifted to
25–1. Peggy-Sue allowed the colt to run its own race.
It broke from the stalls like a bat out of hell and
blazed a lone trail for two furlongs. Peggy-Sue could
feel the amazing power and strength of the big black
colt beneath her, but in spite of his obvious natural
ability the horse ran on without quickening to finish
seventh of twelve. As she galloped past the post
Peggy-Sue had a premonition that all was not well
with the animal. She was positive something was
amiss, but what? She suggested as much to Sonia,
who said she'd get the vet to give him a thorough
check.

After the races Jilly and Mandy changed on the
way to the hotel and raced across the lobby dressed
in their Yankee teenage gear. Their trainers made
no sound on the tiled floor and, to a casual onlooker,
they were just two high-spirited, effervescent youngsters skipping across to the lift. However, although
Mandy had left her mop of golden curls uncombed
and Jilly had tied her long tresses in a ponytail, they
both looked rather mature to be acting the part of
young adolescents. Several women looked at them

strangely in the lift, while their husbands stared at them for quite another reason. They fidgeted and giggled behind their hands like nervous youngsters, but fooled no one. By the time they arrived at the suite they were both light-headed and excited.

Hank let them in. 'Well, look who we have here?'

Joe looked up. 'Not those two sassy adolescent pups?'

'Who else?' growled Hank.

Mandy was in her element. 'Afraid so, Uncle Hank,' she giggled.

'You sent for us?' said Jilly flatly.

'You know exactly why you're here, young ladies.'

'We're here because we've played you up once too often,' gurgled Mandy merrily, 'and you're going to teach us a lesson.'

'Correct!' grinned Hank rubbing his hands together.

'So let's get on with it,' grinned Mandy saucily.

'You've been asking for this for a long time,' exclaimed Joe seriously.

'And now we're going to get it,' laughed Mandy.

Jilly looked nervous. 'What are you going to do to us, uncles?'

'You're gonna have your ass whipped, girlie.'

Mandy drew in her breath noisily. 'My, but you're a cruel old uncle!'

'Be that as it may,' grunted Hank grabbing her shoulder, 'but you're gonna get a dose of the strap, and your big sister's gonna be caned.'

Mandy glanced at Jilly. Her sister had gone quite

pale, she stood nervously biting her lip. Fate had dealt her the worst card. Mandy impulsively objected.

'I'm the naughty one. I'm the one who should be caned.'

Hank looked at her coolly. 'You want the cane, honey. You got it.'

'Thank you, Uncle Hank.'

'You like it, do you?'

'I've never had it. Boys get the cane, girls aren't allowed to.'

Joe laughed. 'Sex discrimination, is it?'

Mandy grinned. 'Yeah, if boys have it, so should we.'

Hank looked at her lecherously. 'Your wish is about to be granted, Cinderella!'

Jilly trembled as she saw Joe pick up the strap. It was short and wide, and made of leather. As he picked it up he swung it over to crack down into his palm with a vicious sound that set her teeth on edge. Jilly jumped. Very soon that nasty leather strap would be warming her rear. The sound was threatening. The thought of it brought butterflies to her tummy. She'd had her backside paddled by the old crone in France, surely it couldn't be worse that that? She watched tremulously as Joe put a low stool in the middle of the room and placed a cushion on the polished surface.

'Kneel on the cushion, Jilly, and bend forward so that your hands are flat on the floor.'

Instantly she conjured up the mental image of herself in that ignominious position. Her posterior would be raised high in the air. It was humiliating. They couldn't ask a grown woman to assume such a pose. And what was worse she knew she'd be expected to bare her fundament for all to see. She'd feel such a fool. She wouldn't do it. As she opened her mouth to object her reverie was rudely interrupted.

'Hurry up, girl. What are you dreaming about?'

'She's congratulating herself on getting away with the cane,' snapped Hank.

Mandy could see he was annoyed. He'd obviously wanted to cane Jilly. Her sister was the beautiful one with a bottom like a dream. She hoped the bastard wouldn't take it out on her when it was her turn to bend over. She knew Hank well enough to guess that he probably would. She came back to earth when Jilly stepped forward to kneel on the cushion.

Joe drew in his breath when the lovely Jilly knelt on the low stool. The short pleated kilt hung inches above her knees and her long bare legs, which seemed to go on forever, were doubled up beneath her. Although the T-shirt hid the fullness of her bosom, and the ponytail made her appear adolescent, the curves of her thighs revealed that she was a mature woman.

'Lean forward. Hands on the floor, please.'

She allowed her body to fall forward breaking her fall with her palms when they hit the floor, and as her upper body toppled forward so her bottom shot up. In that position the short kilt had risen to the line of her brief panties and the expanse of bare thigh she displayed was dazzling. Joe casually flipped the hem of her skirt up so that the kilt fell across the small of her back to reveal her beknickered seat. Her flimsy knickers were roughly jerked down to leave her rump bare and vulnerable. Jilly was aware of a tear welling up in the corner of her eye as this final humiliation was heaped upon her.

She gritted her teeth, but the strap was an anticlimax. In spite of his love of smacking female bottoms, Joe was a gentle man. The strap didn't sting her half as much as the paddle wielded by the old crone. She was pleasantly surprised, and even began to enjoy the stimulating whacks, but she had no intention of letting her audience know. She squealed and gasped, writhing beneath each stroke that walloped down across her ample butt. Her wriggling caused her pretty orbs to tremble and rotate, and each frenzied movement revealed more and more of the shimmering jewel between those twin moons. It was an erotic picture made sexier by her moving her knees further apart in an effort to convince her audience that the strap was setting her tail afire.

When it was finally over she was ordered to stand and watch her sister being caned. She saw Hank step forward cane in hand.

'Now, Mandy, you wanted a taste of the cane, didn't you?'

'Yes, please!' she answered saucily.

'Are you certain?'

'Yes. I've always wanted to be caned,' she murmured, adding cheekily, 'on my bare bottom.'

Hank pointed the cane towards the table. 'Happy to oblige, honey.'

Mandy walked to the table and stretched her body over the polished surface. 'I'm ready,' she giggled.

'No, you're not. Let's have that ass bared first.'

She stood up again and coquettishly raised the short kilt before pulling her knickers down to her knees. She was aware that half the eroticism was the baring of her pert buttocks so she took her time and afterwards posed for a long moment so the brothers could feast their eyes on her gorgeous arse. She stretched herself slowly and deliberately over the table until she could grip the far edge with her fingers.

Hank paused to drink in the beauty of her charming derriere, so sensually curved over the edge of the table, before measuring it for the cane. He raised his arm quietly, and Mandy was completely unprepared for the first stroke which sang down across her unprotected seat. A high-pitched squeak shot from her throat as the sting ignited her nates. A second, and a third, followed in quick succession.

'Are you enjoying it, young lady, as much as you thought you would?'

'No,' she lamented loudly, 'no, I'm not!'

Hank was a very different personality to Joe and

Mandy's squeals were for real. However, when the initial sting dulled and the fire became a smouldering ember she was surprised to find herself carnally stimulated. Hank was concentrating on the lower fleshy swell of her buttocks between which sheltered her sweet quim. She was conscious of a heat spreading through her loins which was stimulating a fervent lust for more. Such was her rapture that she knew she was approaching orgasm. She fought to control it. Oh Lord, what would they think of her? Then she heard Hank speak and the spell was broken.

'Come here, Jilly, and take your place beside your sister.'

'No,' shouted Mandy, 'you're not to cane her.'

'Steady down, Hank,' said Joe, 'she's had her share.'

Hank ignored them. 'Well, girl. Are you coming?'

Jilly had been watching Mandy's face closely and realised that something strange was happening to her. It was almost as if she was enjoying it. She wondered if that was possible. She had a sudden urge to find out for herself. She crossed to the table as if in a dream.

'Jilly, for heaven's sake,' muttered her sister, 'what do you think you're doing?'

After the first stroke Jilly was wondering what devil had persuaded her to bend across that table and offer her bare behind for the cane. The pink stripes she'd found so fascinating on Mandy's posterior would now be across her rump, too. Whatever bizarre feelings they'd stoked up in her sister they were just cane marks to her – and they stang. Jilly yelled in protest as the cane sang through the air to land squarely across her tormented backside. Meanwhile the presence of her sister next to her, freely offering her butt for skelping was deepening Mandy's dark emotion. She'd only the vaguest idea what a masochist was, but she was convinced she was one. She bawled ecstatically. Had Hank realised her feelings he would have doubled the dose, but as it was he laid aside the cane. The two sisters eased their panties up over their ravished seats.

Hank grinned. 'You better run along and change.'

'And be careful you're not seen crossing the lobby dressed like that, added Joe.

'Why? Who's going to see us?'

'Sonia and Barney and the stablegirl who does our two horses.'

'What?' hissed Jilly rubbing her tender rear above the short kilt.

'We've arranged a surprise party for you all before we fly home tomorrow.'

'I can't go to that,' lamented Mandy.

'Why not?'

'I shan't be able to sit down for days!'

Chapter 9

After the racing on Friday, Peggy-Sue helped her grandfather walk slowly back to the car park. Old Joe Rhyma was over eighty, but he'd been a top-class jockey in his time. He'd made his name in his native Ireland in the early thirties, and gone to England in 1937 to seek his fortune. His worth was just being recognised when war broke out. He'd joined up immediately but was so badly wounded in Burma that he never rode again. He'd returned to Ireland to work with his beloved horses and what he didn't know about them wasn't worth knowing. Now he hadn't long to live, he'd expressed a wish to attend one last race meeting in England. He hated hotels so Peggy-Sue was taking care of him at her bungalow.

'That big black thing you rode in the sprint,' he muttered.

'Crazy Face?'

'From America, you say?'

'That's right.'

'He's hurting.'

'What do you mean, Pops?'

'You were sitting on him. You should know.'

'He wasn't stretching right out. I'm certain he was holding something back.'

'Of course he was. The poor bloody animal's hurting.'

'How do you know that?'

'I've worked with horses all my life. I can tell when they feel pain.'

'Okay, Pops. I'll take you over to The Billings tomorrow. You can tell us where he hurts and we'll try and cure him.'

'Call in some vet who'll fill him full of drugs. Fat chance!'

The following day Tess walked the big colt around the yard for the old man. Peggy-Sue was afraid her grandfather would make a fool of himself but Sonia was open-minded.

'It's his off-hind that pains him. It'll stem from somewhere at the end of the spine.'

'He seems to be walking perfectly well to me,' murmured Sonia.

'Have it your own way. It's none of my business.'

'No, I'm sorry. Carry on with what you were saying, please.'

'It will niggle at him when he canters and as he goes faster it will become a stab. When the pain reaches a certain point he just won't go any faster.'

'Although he is capable of it?'

'Of course.'

'What can we do?'

'If I was twenty years younger I could find and pinpoint the trigger spot, but even if you knew it you couldn't cure him.'

'I can send him to a vet.'

'Bah!'

'What then?'

'There's a horse doctor in the west of Ireland who could cure him for you.'

'How?'

'Special care, manipulation, massage. She lays hands on horses.'

Peggy-Sue laughed. 'A faith-healer?'

'Call her what you like, girl. She cures horses.'

Sonia looked dubious. 'We could try, I suppose. What do you think, Peggy?'

Peggy-Sue looked at her grandfather. 'Are you sure about this, Pops?'

'Sure as my favourite granddaughter is the finest jockey in Great Britain!'

The month of July was a glorious one. The sun shone, the temperature soared into the high eighties and the west of Ireland was a wonderful place to be. Tess had been chosen to accompany the colt and been assigned to stay with him until his treatment was over. She found that the livery stables, where Crazy Face was to stay, were small and old-fashioned. Maybe they were not quite tumbling down but certainly they'd seen better days. The

female horse doctor was old and crotchety and rude
to anyone silly enough to talk to her, but although
she detested humans she adored animals, especially
horses. Her small farmyard was a sanctuary for cats,
dogs, goats and geese, but her life was horses and
their ills. Her methods were unorthodox and had no
place in veterinary books, yet she had had innumer-
able successes.

Now she was old she no longer had the strength to
treat her patients so her grandson, Sean, acted as
helper and assistant. He was a handsome young
man of nineteen who shared his grandmother's love
of animals, but he also had a healthy respect for
young women. And he, being a handsome lad, was
sought after by them. Thus when the comely Tess
arrived she was an immediate target. He set about
chasing her the moment her charge was safely stabled and she, seeing his good looks, didn't run too
fast.

Sean helped his grandmother in the mornings and
under her guidance the black colt appeared to
thrive. It was during the afternoons that Tess and he
were free and a secluded cove nearby became their
regular meeting place. Tess would strip off her bikini
top and her torn denim shorts to sunbathe naked on
the narrow strip of sandy beach beneath the rolling
cliffs, and Sean would eagerly run to join her when
his work was done.

She opened her eyes when she heard him shout
from the cliff top and watched him run helter skelter

down the rough track towards her. Once he hit the shore he threw off his clothes as he ran. She laughed merrily as he fell flat on his face while removing his shorts. He jumped to his feet covered in wet sand to shake his fist at her.

'Laugh at me, would you? I'll have you, my girl.'

She sprang to her feet with a little scream and ran hell for leather along the shoreline with water splashing about her ankles.

'You'd better stop,' he shouted hot in pursuit. 'It'll be the worse for you when I catch you.'

'You won't catch me,' she squealed happily as she ran further into the sea.

They looked like two happy children splashing wildly through the water, and when he caught up he tackled her around the legs. She was brought down flat on her face with an almighty splash. The water stung her breasts and belly as she crashed down full length and she squealed lustily as she found herself wallowing in six inches of seawater. He sank his teeth into the soft rounded flesh of her young rump.

'Aah,' she bawled, 'you bit my bum!'

He spluttered. 'Mmm, you taste sweet. And he bit her some more.

'Stop it, you pig. I'll have bites all over my bum.'

'That'll mean you'll have to keep your knickers on.'

'You won't like that,' she giggled.

'Not for me, for all the others.'

'What others?'

'I dunno, the public.'

'I'm not in the habit of taking my knickers off in public!'

He bit her tender seat again. 'I should think not.'

'Oww, stop it you fool. That hurt!'

As she spoke she hauled herself onto her hands and knees, only to find her body encircled by his arms in a great bear hug. The seawater flowed and ebbed around her calves and wrists as he held her motionless in the soft shifting sand, and she was bowed under his weight like a bitch under a dog. His upper torso was spread over her back and his arms were wound around her. His large, rough hands clasped her hanging white breasts, while his erect cock nudged amongst the pubic hair, seeking the entrance to her secret passage. If she took one hand from the sand to guide him to her waiting orifice she would collapse under his weight.

She bowed her head and arched her back so that her nether cheeks rose and parted, allowing the fat head of his swollen penis to nuzzle her pussy. Their genitals were by now soaked with seawater and when they met he slid smoothly between her cunt lips to disappear into her hole. She squirmed and wriggled under his weight as she was penetrated and, when he was hilted within her, clutched at his cock with her elastic vaginal walls. He lay spread over her like a dead weight, not attempting to move, her quim muscles squeezing and squeezing until she milked an emission from him. As he ejaculated, he kissed her hair and bit her shoulders and when she felt herself flooded she deliberately collapsed under him.

'Tess, my darling, you're wonderful. You're the best fuck in all Ireland.'

'Then get off me, you great ox, before I drown.'

He picked her up and swung her round like a small girl and placed her facing him. They sat inches apart in the lapping water, their legs intertwined, her pointed nipples brushing his chest, her lips kissing his.

'Do it again, Sean,' she whispered urgently, 'now, please.'

'Why hurry? We've all the time in the world.'

'I want you now, Sean. I want you to make me come.'

'You'll frighten the gulls away with your screaming!'

'I won't.'

'Sure you will.'

'I won't make a sound. I'll be as quiet as a mouse.'

'You won't. You'll howl and bawl until the fish come up to see what all the noise is about.'

'Okay, whatever you want I'll do. I'll scream obscenities to the four winds if you want.'

He laughed. 'There's no need for that.'

He lifted her like a doll and sat her on his lap so that his resurgent penis was in her crotch. She reached down with her fingers to guide him into her satin sheath and as he drove into her so she forced her hot little tongue into his mouth. They sat arms and legs entwined, two bodies welded into one, and for several sublime moments she pumped up and down deliriously on his iron-hard tool while her tongue scoured his mouth. And when she brought herself to orgasm she was filled with a tingling, amazing pain that made her scream ecstatically into his throat.

Her climax over she kissed him with eager lips in great slow, wet, warm kisses willing herself to another orgasm while she held his shoulders and moved her saturated vagina the length of his sticky pole. She knew he would soon ejaculate and flood her once more with the warm cream she so loved. She knew that only lack of time would rob her of a third ejaculation, for at nineteen Sean was at the zenith of his sexual prowess.

During the first fortnight the big colt was only allowed an exercise walk after his intensive treatment, but at the beginning of the third week the horse doctor announced he could be cantered and that he must swim. As there was no luxury stable nearby with a pool they had to use a freshwater lake. Tess and Sean took the colt swimming every afternoon. Tess would lead him from the bank while Sean swam lazily at his side . . .

'Tether the horse and come into the water,' he shouted.

'I'm not a great swimmer.'

'No matter.'

'You won't push me under, will you?'

'No, I want to fuck you.'

'In the lake?'

'Yes, in the lake, under the water.'

She frowned. 'Is that possible?'

'You've done it in the bath, haven't you?'

She giggled. 'That's not the same though.'

'You mean the water's got to be hot?'

'Don't be silly.'

'And you've got to have a bar of soap?'

She didn't bother to answer. The horse had arrived at the point where they usually took him out. He enjoyed swimming so there was no difficulty getting him into the water. She watched his big nostrils snuffle and snort as he drove forward in the still waters. Her eyes moved to Sean. He was swimming lazily beside the big horse. She knew he was naked, and could picture his dick floating large and loose under him and suddenly she wanted him. In spite of the hot sunshine on her back a little shiver ran through her. She stopped walking and urged the colt out of the water.

'Tether him and come on in,' he called.

'Yes, okay.'

The horse stumbled out of the lake. His smooth coat was awash with water and it gushed down his body and legs in small torrents. She led him to a fallen tree.

'That was lovely, wasn't it, Crazy? Did you enjoy that, fella?' she burbled as she tethered him to the trunk.

Already the hot sun and the warmth of the animal's body was turning the water to steam. She stooped to take off her trainers and swiftly yanked her T-shirt over her tousled black hair. On the bank she looked at Sean impatiently treading water.

'Hurry up, Tess. I'll have to be getting back soon.'

She didn't move. Standing there amidst the beauty of the Irish countryside with the sun hot on her back and breasts she felt serenely peaceful.

'Come on. Get those shorts off and jump in.'

Jerking down the brief denim shorts she padded to the edge of the bank. She was a much better swimmer than she'd made out and knew the water was deep enough for her to dive. She pretended to hesitate.

'Is it cold?' she asked.

'No, it's lovely.'

'All right, here I come.'

She made a quick shallow dive beneath the surface and, disappearing below the water, glided towards him. When his legs came into view she swam around them and surfaced close behind him. As she cleared the surface she grabbed at him. Her right arm wound around his neck as she snuggled her body up to his back, while her left hand searched in front of him for his testicles.

'Shake, friend,' she giggled as she grabbed a handful of his prick.

'Christ, you're like an octopus!'

'Am I?'

'I thought you couldn't swim.'

'I was kiddin'.'

Her sharp teeth bit into his shoulder in a series of little butterfly bites, while her fingers explored his genitals as if she'd found something strange and exciting.

'Wank me,' he said quietly.

'No, my pussy wants you in her.'

'It will be difficult.'

'I thought you said you wanted to screw me?'

'That was to get you into the water.'

She prepared to duck under the water. 'I'll see if I can suck you.'

'Not a chance. You'll swallow half the lake.'

But she'd already plunged below the surface and was moving down towards his crotch. She held onto his hips with her hands and pulled her face down his flat stomach to search for his cock with her mouth. She almost burst out laughing when she saw it waving gently like a long stiff sea plant in the still water. She wound her fingers around the root of the sea monster and guided it to her lips. Having placed the smooth tip against her closed lips she slowly parted them as she accepted the thing into her mouth. It didn't work. More water than prick filled her mouth and she was forced to the surface spluttering wildly.

'What did I tell you?' he laughed.

Without warning she reached up and ducked his head under the water. When he surfaced, shouted threats, she was gone. He dived under in search of her and for several minutes they chased and fought like two children at the seaside. Finally she swam to him and wrapped her legs around his thighs and her arms around his neck. Try as they might they couldn't couple satisfactorily under the water. She could feel he was becoming frustrated.

'Let's swim to the bank and do it there,' he suggested impatiently.

'No.'

'It's impossible under water. I keep slipping out of you.'

'Lie still, and I'll masturbate you. That's what you wanted, wasn't it?'

She signalled him to float on the water with his legs apart, and she swam under him to finish with her head between his legs and her feet under his shoulders. She quietly paddled with her feet to keep her position, while her small hand reached up between his thighs to grab at his rampant penis. Holding him enclosed in her fist, she began to toss him off. Slowly she worked the loose foreskin backwards and forwards with long positive strokes until she felt his muscles contract. One final quick rub supplied the necessary friction for him to achieve ejaculation. She watched the creamy spunk shoot heavenwards like spray before splashing down on the surface of the water. They swam slowly to the bank and slept in each other's arms.

They were rudely awakened by a thunderous voice that seemed to be calling the wrath of heaven down upon them.

'What the hell are you doing here? Is this your horse?'

Tess woke with a start, trying to hide her nakedness.

'It's mine,' she stammered.

The man continued to look thunderous. 'I know it's not his. I know Sean only too well. Him and his cranky grandmother.'

'It's a thoroughbred. I'm his stablegirl. Sean's gran is curing him.'

The man snorted. 'I can tell it's a thoroughbred, young woman, and a valuable one, which makes me curious why it's wandering about loose.'

'Loose? It can't have been. I tethered him.'

'If you did you didn't do it very well, my girl.'

She was certain the man hadn't found Crazy Face loose, but why should he pretend he had? She looked at him. He was dressed for riding. His britches and jacket were expensively cut and his boots shone like silver. She guessed he was in his late forties: probably an old-fashioned landowner who thought it was still the nineteenth century. He had a large moustache and muttonchops, and his eyes shone like red-hot coals through an angry scowl.

'Take this animal home, Sean,' he commanded.

Sean hesitated.

'Immediately, boy.'

Sean grabbed the bridle the man was holding and led the big colt away.

'And you will come with me, young lady. We'll talk about your behaviour and whether I should report you to your employer.'

Tess climbed back into her shorts and T-shirt while hiding as much of herself as possible. 'Yes, sir.' she stuttered.

He remounted his own horse. 'Put on your shoes and get up behind me.'

She didn't want to go with him. She saw no reason why she should, but he was so aggressive and overpowering. The sort of man who either got his own way or threw a temper tantrum. She was a little afraid of him. She knew instantly that he had some sort of hold over Sean and he would be made to suffer if she didn't do as she was bid. She guessed the man was Sean's landlord, probably with the power to turn out his grandmother. She decided to do what he wished within reason and swung up behind him. Even in the open air she could smell the stale tobacco on his clothing and as she rode behind him she could tell he was a very competent horseman.

He took her to a beach house nearly a mile away. It had probably been built in the last century by his family for use in the summer months. A retreat for the older folk or a holiday spot for the children. Either way, it was large enough to house an ordinary working family. It appeared deserted. He dismounted by the door and bid her stable the horse. She was left speechless, but had little option other than to do what she was told. The man was rude and overbearing, she thought. Inside she found him sitting in an upright window seat, awaiting her. She approached with some trepidation. He beckoned her to stand before him and offered her one of two glasses standing on a nearby table. He raised one of the glasses to his lips and invited her to drink from the other. The liquid was cool and pleasant to the palate.

'You're a very pretty girl and no doubt good at your job, but I suggest you'd face the sack if I informed your employer of your carelessness.'

'Yes, sir. Probably, sir.'

He smiled cynically. 'Maybe I won't.'

'No, sir.'

'We'll see, shall we?'

'Yes, sir.'

He reached forward and, taking her hand, pulled her gently towards him. She'd guessed it would come to this. She found herself so close to him that she was standing between his knees. She trembled. The man was overpowering and, combined with his confident manner and handsome looks, she found him impossible to resist. She watched mesmerised, as his fingers moved to her T-shirt to peel it upwards until she automatically raised her arms for it to be pulled over her head. He threw the garment on the floor and sat motionless, drinking in the beauty of her perfectly shaped young breasts.

'You have exquisite breasts.'

'Thank you, sir.'

'So desirable and perfect to satisfy my whim.'

She didn't reply. She was too in awe of him to ask him his purpose.

'Don't you wish to know what I have in mind for your two sweet orbs?'

'Yes, sir. What must I do?'

'Pleasure me, pretty girl.'

Now it had finally come to this she was more confident. 'How?' she asked.

'Gratify me with your breasts.'

She looked puzzled and he became impatient. 'Rub me between your bubbies, wench. A tit fuck – isn't that what you people call it?'

She didn't, but she knew what he meant. She knelt down to unbutton his britches. It wasn't easy getting them off with him sitting like a statue in front of her, but finally she got them around his ankles. She saw his penis was already standing to attention in anticipation of her favours. She noticed it wasn't particularly big. She thought it would fit snugly between her plump boobs. She bent forward and provocatively nudged the upstanding rod with one breast, and then the other. She saw her cute pink nipples pulse and harden as she brushed them against his male protrusion. Swiftly, she plunged her body forward to cover his tool with her soft, warm melons and, when she had him nestled between those two pliable mounds, she was able to stimulate him with her rubbing.

He remained perfectly still as she worked to gratify him. He made no attempt to show her if she was doing right. She took her boobs between her hands and squeezed them against his rapacious prick and only then did he come to life. He grunted violently, pushed her away and, grabbing her head between his palms, urged her face down to his crotch. She'd expected him to ejaculate but instead he wanted her to fellate him.

She parted her lips as her face was forced down to accept his throbbing pestle deep into her wet mouth. She gagged as the broad tip hit the back of her throat, and pulled her head back hurriedly. Half choking, she allowed his pulsing cock to slip from her mouth and as she did so, he came. She felt the warm spunk splatter over her face, covering her cheeks and eyes and chin. She sat hunched on the floor at his feet as he dressed and suddenly she felt very, very sleepy.

When she awoke she was lying in the sun. She must have been carried out there. She wondered how long she'd been asleep. She guessed the wine had been drugged, but why? She sat up groggily. She was wearing her T-shirt, but nothing else. She saw the denim shorts by her side and, reaching out for them, glanced down at her crotch. She was shaven. Her pubic hair was gone. Her quim was as naked as her breasts. She hadn't been like that since she was a little girl.

'You perverted sod,' she shouted to the four winds, 'you kinky old bastard!'

She climbed into her shorts and a wide grin spread over her face. What bloody tricks to get up to. No wonder she'd been drugged. A mental picture of being shaved down there flashed before her eyes. She blushed. She saw the bungalow was deserted. He'd pissed off and left her. She started on the long walk home.

Sonia decided that what Misk Garnett needed was variety. Peggy-Sue rode her in all her fast work, and she was allowed to work away from the main string as she used to when she was with Mr Norster's stable. Sonia also made arrangements for the filly to swim in a neighbour's pool and to use his gallops once a week. The neighbour detested Bart and was the only big trainer who was friendly with The Billings. Thus Sonia ensured that the grey filly had changes of scenery and routine and, together with weekly trips to the seaside to gallop along the shore, she soon began to show signs of her old self. By the time Glorious Goodwood arrived, both Sonia and Peggy-Sue were confident the little grey rocking horse would run a big race in the Sussex Stakes. Unfortunately Mother Nature can upset the best-laid plans.

It had been raining heavily on the eastern sea-board of the USA for more than a week and parts of New England were flooded. When Hank and Joe Ladd arrived the day before Goodwood they brought the rain with them. It fell down all Monday night and drizzled all day Tuesday. By Wednesday, the day of the race, the going was bottomless. Early that morning Sonia rang the twins.

'I need your opinion,' she said.

'What about?'

'I'm seriously considering withdrawing the filly.'

'Not run her, you mean?'

'She hates soft ground and it'll be like a ploughed field.'

There was a pause. 'Will it hurt her to run?'

'No. Not if Peggy allows her to run her own race.'

'You mean she won't be ridden out to win?'

'That's right.'

'So she'll be there with no chance of winning?'

'I'm afraid so.'

There was another pause. 'Hold tight, we want to discuss it.'

Sonia waited. She hoped they wouldn't run the filly. Peggy was adamant she wouldn't go on the ground, but they were the owners and they'd come a long way to see the race.

'You still there, Sonia?'

'Yes.'

'We'd like her to run. It seems a long way to come without a runner, and with Crazy Face under treatment it only leaves the filly.'

'As you wish.'

'Look, we'll leave the final decision to you and Peggy-Sue. We'd like her to run, but not to come to any harm because of it.'

The two women decided to run the grey but only because of the owners. They agreed Misk Garnett should be allowed to stride out at her own pace and certainly wouldn't be pushed out in the ground.

The sun came out during the morning and took some of the moisture out of the ground to leave the going sticky. It wasn't a good sign for the grey. They both knew the filly would never get through it. However, the sunshine brought the crowds to the course and by early afternoon everything about Goodwood was glorious except the ground. Peggy-Sue rode one for Sonia in the first race and came back to say the ground was very holding, and the time for the race was well below average. In the paddock both brothers were jovial, having consumed a bottle of wine at lunch and numerous scotches since. They commented on the absence of Jilly and Mandy.

'Jilly's saddling one for the stable at Epsom tonight and Mandy's showing a potential owner and his wife around The Billings.'

'Pity, we'd liked to have seen them.'

And screwed them, thought Sonia, but she said. 'They're sorry to have missed you. Next time, perhaps.'

'Any chance of a surprise win?' Hank whispered to Peggy-Sue when she arrived in the ring.

'None whatsoever. If I make her race seriously in this she'll be put off the game forever.'

'Okay, we understand,' said Joe. 'We'll be happy just to see her run. It's a long journey to make for nothing.'

Peggy-Sue took the little grey to post very slowly and quietly, and although all the others dawdled, she was so far behind that the starter signalled her to get a move on. Only seven horses had been declared for the race, and two of those were withdrawn overnight, leaving five runners.

When the stalls flew open she took a tug meaning to settle the filly in behind, but all the other jocks had the same idea. Thus they all came out slowly and a game of cat and mouse ensued as each jockey waited for someone else to go on.

A couple of minutes passed with the horses jockeying for position and looking like five prancing circus horses. It was then Peggy-Sue felt Misk Garnett becoming fractious, she resented being held for so long on a tight rein. The last thing Peggy-Sue wanted was to upset the filly, so she let out a notch and felt the little grey bound forward. Instantly the other four fell in behind her and the rest of the race went as she'd expected. She allowed the filly to stride on in the lead, but when she found herself at sea in the ground she shortened her stride and slowed the pace. In spite of the slower pace the others stayed tucked in behind her until Misk Garnett was well into the final straight.

Peggy-Sue had taken the filly right across the course to the stand side in search of the better ground, but when the field accelerated past her she didn't attempt to go after them. It developed into a sprint finish and Misk Garnett trailed in plumb last. Later Peggy-Sue was called before the stewards who wanted to know why she hadn't ridden the horse out.

They accepted her explanation that the filly was all at sea in the going and had laboured throughout the race.

That evening Sonia received a call from Ireland. The old horse-doctor told her that Crazy Face was ready for fast work, to ensure the treatment had been successful. She said she'd got permission for the colt to work on Limerick racecourse. Sonia replied she wanted Peggy-Sue to ride and that she'd see she flew over the following day.

The next afternoon Peggy-Sue met the small party of Tess, the horse-doctor, and her grandson on the racecourse. Crazy-Face was full of himself and, once on his back, Peggy-Sue could feel he was a different animal. He galloped three furlongs at a fast pace and came back even faster. As Peggy-Sue dismounted the colt blew a bit but was obviously free of pain. The old horse-doctor had done the trick.

'He moved like a dream,' chuckled Peggy-Sue.

'He's cured,' announced the old girl, 'there's no pain now.'

'Is it likely to return?'

'Not unless you do something damned silly.'

'Such as?'

'Overstretch him so he pulls a muscle and don't give him the time to recover properly.'

'Is that what happened before?'

'I reckon so. Some damnfool trainer expecting too much too soon.'

'What happens now?'

'I'll keep him a couple of days to make certain before I send him back with young Tess.'

'When will he be ready to run?'

'Run him tomorrow if you wish.'

'Thanks. I'll tell Mrs Beechly.'

'Tell her I'll be sending the bill, too.'

Crazy Face and his rider had had an interested spectator when they worked. The handsome aristocrat who'd taken advantage of Tess so blatantly had been studying them and, as Peggy-Sue waved goodbye to the others, he approached her.

'Miss Peggy-Sue Rhyma?'

She turned quickly. 'Yes.'

'Joe Rhyma's grandaughter?'

She smiled at him. 'That's correct.'

He held out his hand. 'My name's Paul Pitt-Hollyer. I know your grandfather well.'

She took his hand. He was simply gorgeous. Strikingly handsome, self assured, immaculately dressed and with a wonderful smile. Peggy-Sue was rarely smitten with a man at first sight, but Paul Pitt-Hollyer was something else. He fascinated her. She thought he looked a cross between a stern Victorian gentleman and a matinee idol of the nineteen-thirties. She found his presence overpowering, as had Tess before her.

'I remember a Paul Pitt-Hollyer who used to ride amateur over the sticks. Is that you?'

He grinned. 'Guilty.'

'What happened?'

'I became too old.'

'Seriously?'

'Yes, seriously,' he smiled, 'ask your grandfather. He used to help me with my jumpers in those days.'

'Really? He's never mentioned you.'

'I wasn't that successful.'

'Now you're being modest. The Paul Pitt-Hollyer I remember was quite brilliant.'

He laughed. 'How long are you staying in Ireland?'

'Until tomorrow.'

'You must bring your grandfather and dine with me tonight.'

'I'm staying at a hotel.'

'Then I shall send cars to pick you both up.'

She liked the idea. 'Then I accept,' she smiled.

It was after dinner, when old Joe Rhyma had been sent home, that Peggy-Sue found herself the target of her host's easy charm. She'd had wines with the meal and liqueurs afterwards which, together with the heady atmosphere of a summer's night, made her feel amorous.

'You're a beautiful woman, Peggy-Sue.'

She laughed. 'Please. I know better!'

His tone didn't change. 'To me, Peggy-Sue, you are a beautiful young woman.'

'Thank you,' she replied, quietly subdued.

'Come here.'

It was said in a humorous way like an adult to a

child. Yet, strangely it seemed like a command. A command which irritated her but a command she wanted to obey. She stood up slowly and moved towards him. He sat on an upright chair and she moved so close that he could reach out and touch her. She knew intuitively that was what he wanted.

Peggy-Sue had few inhibitions and those that she had faded in proportion to her intake of alcohol. He stretched out his hands and began to unfasten her blouse at the neck. She stood motionless, looking like a small girl being undressed for bed by her parent. His fingers worked with gentle deliberation as he unbuttoned her to the waist. She remained perfectly still with her head bowed before him. It was as if she was mesmerised. He eased the blouse from the waistband of her skirt and pulled it loose. His fingers quickly moved to her skirt zip, and giving her skirt a little jerk slid it down over her hips. As it fell to the floor his thumbs hooked into the elastic of her bikini briefs, which followed her skirt to finish in a circle around her feet. Bidding her to step out of her skirt and knickers he gently urged her backwards into a large, comfortable armchair.

She found herself lying with her rump balanced on the edge of the seat and her head jammed against the back. He took her legs and swung them over the padded arms so that her thighs were spread wide apart and her genitals exposed. She looked on as if in a trance. What would be her fate? Would he suck her, or fuck her? Would he insert his fingers into her honeypot or tease her bare belly with his hot breath?

He did none of these things. Instead he rang a bell and a maid appeared to put a tray by his side. When she could see what was on it she recognised a man's shaving tackle. There was a shaving mug, and shaving soap, and hot water. She was startled and not a little curious.

'What all this for?' she asked.

'I'm going to shave you.'

'Shave me, why?'

'Have you never been shaved?'

The penny dropped. 'You mean down there,' she gurgled hastily, 'good heavens, no.'

'And would you like to be?'

'Not particularly. Why do you want to do it?'

'All women should be shaven. I dislike coarse hair hiding the gorgeous shining jewel between their thighs.'

'My pubes are not coarse!' she objected.

'To me they are.'

'All right, if you must. I don't suppose it will hurt me.'

'On the contrary you'll be as free of hair as you were before puberty.'

She grinned. The man was kinky, but then all men were bloody kinky. This one seemed harmless enough.

She watched, amused, as he soaped her by spreading the lather evenly between her legs, until her crotch was covered like a field after a deep fall of snow. She saw him pick up a razor. It was an old-fashioned cut-throat.

'Jesus, you're not using that thing!'

He laughed. 'I've never used anything else.'

She held her breath as she watched the blade slice away the thick lather to leave strips of white flesh until she was quite bare of pubic hair. Only the thick enfolded outer lips of her quim were visible. She grinned. She quite liked herself like that.

'Hey, that's not too bad. Maybe I'll keep myself like that.'

He rang the bell and the same maid appeared to take away the tray, but not before she'd attended to Peggy-Sue's shaven slit. The woman fastidiously patted her crotch dry before powdering and perfuming her, and when she was gone she noticed her host was now sitting trouserless before her.

'Bring that delectable shaven pussy over here to me,' he whispered.

She went to stand up. 'What do you intend doing to her?'

'I mean to try her out!'

She chuckled. 'She's not exactly a virgin, you know.'

'She's a virgin shaven pussy.'

She approached him. 'That's true, I suppose.'

'And I shall be the first in her now she's shaven!'

He leaned forward to clasp her around the waist and picking her up bodily lifted her above his totem pole. As she felt herself swung above his crotch she spread her legs wide so they hung either side of his thighs. With uncanny accuracy he lowered her body onto his waiting erection.

In one movement it penetrated between her shaven quim lips to be sucked deep into her dark tunnel of love. She was soaking wet and it was bliss when she felt herself impaled to his hilt. She flung her arms around his neck ready to slide her backside up his shaft in piston-like strokes, but he held her immobile. Apparently he was satisfied just to be inside her. Thwarted of movement she began to squeeze him with her vagina until, after what seemed an eternity, she milked him to climax. Her reward was a great spurt of spunk like warm cream inside her belly.

She overslept next morning and had just showered when Tess came bouncing into her hotel bedroom.

'Come on, we've got a plane to catch.'

'I know. I'm nearly ready.'

'I hear you were with the handsome squire last night.'

'Is that what he is?'

'He owns all the land around there. Sean says he's a tyrant.'

'He's a fascinating man.'

'So you found that, too?'

'An overpowering personality.'

'Do you know what the bastard did to me?'

Peggy-Sue stepped into her panties. 'No idea.'

'He shaved my twat.'

Peggy-Sue grinned. She turned quickly to face Tess and whipped her panties down to her knees. Tess put her hand over her mouth in girlish surprise.

'Crikey, you, too?'

'Me, too!'

'I don't mind. Sean loved it. He couldn't leave me alone. He said it was like sucking an orange!'

Chapter 10

Paul Pitt-Hollyer strode out of the Viking hotel and drove down Micklegate towards York racecourse. He was there to attend the three-day Ebor meeting. York racecourse is one of the top three in Britain: a large left-handed course which sweeps around the wide expanse of the Knavesmire, where racing has been held for more than two centuries.

Draped over his arm was an elegant black girl the sight of whom was enough to raise the blood pressure of every red-blooded man within fifty yards. Fiona Portius was a part-time model-cum-actress-cum-beauty queen from St Lucia and, like so many inhabitants from that island, had European, African and American Indian blood in her veins. Physically she was one of the lucky ones, blessed with the best features of each race. Her face was stunningly attractive and her ebony black skin as smooth as satin. Her long legs seemed to go on forever, and her buttocks and breasts were the envy of every young female who looked at her. She was indeed a queen of beauty and she walked with the grace of royalty.

However, for all Fiona's beauty, the real reason Paul was at York was to try to see Peggy-Sue. He'd been taken with the petite lady jockey and couldn't get her out of his mind. That the ravishing Fiona had attached herself to him in the meantime meant little. He was a man who'd attracted women all his life and his love life had always been a matter of easy come, easy go. He decided not to try to contact Peggy-Sue until after the big race.

The International Stakes over ten-and-a-half furlongs is classed amongst the top middle-distance prizes of the year. It was the race at which Sonia had aimed Iskmak after the filly's promising run at Royal Ascot. Peggy-Sue was adamant that the horse needed further than a mile, even though its sire was a sprinter. They'd discussed several options before deciding to run the filly in the International. Claude had frowned upon a lesser-class race, saying the Prince had a soft spot for the filly, and wanted her entered only in the highest class. Sonia's concern was that Iskmak was so light of frame and delicate of leg that she couldn't be raced very often and, together with Peggy-Sue's theory about distance, that didn't leave them much choice. When the International was finally chosen they agreed to wait until after that race to decide about her final race of the season. If it seemed best to bring her back to a mile she'd go for the Queen Elizabeth at Ascot; if she needed a full mile-and-a-half she might take her chance in the Arc de Triomphe at Longchamp.

Paul watched the twelve runners parade in front of the packed stands before they cantered across the centre of the Knavesmire on their way to the start. At the post he watched Peggy-Sue dismount to allow the starter's assistant to tighten the horse's girths. His binoculars were focused on the jockey rather than the horse. He hadn't bet on the race and his only interest was the dynamic little female jockey. At the Off he watched her tuck Iskmak into the middle of the pack and his powerful binoculars were focused on Peggy-Sue's cocked arse rather than the race.

He took little interest in the progress of the runners until the field turned into the long straight. The favourite, which was Fiona's fancy, had kicked for home and had quickly put two lengths of daylight between himself and the field. Peggy-Sue had sent Iskmak after him and appeared to be closing.

Paul was conscious of Fiona's fingernails digging into his arm as she urged her fancy on. Two furlongs out and the filly was beginning to cut back the leader, and by the furlong pole Iskmak was close on his heels. Fiona was screaming for the favourite to hang on but Paul began to feel excited. He realised Peggy-Sue could win the race. Iskmak was running the rail and suddenly the favourite rolled away leaving a gap for the filly. Peggy-Sue went for it, but as she did so the favourite rolled back. The two horses bumped badly and the filly, being smaller and lighter, got the worst of it. Peggy-Sue was forced to pull Iskmak out to try and go round the favourite, but Paul could see there just wasn't enough time for her to get her head in front. By concentrating his glasses on the two leaders he'd failed to see the second favourite racing up the middle of the track to take the race in the last few strides. Poor Peggy-Sue had to be satisfied with third place.

Paul had already left a message in the weighing room for the jockey, but now he assumed she wouldn't be in a particularly receptive mood. He heard that there would be a Steward's Inquiry announced over the tannoy.

Sonia was waiting in the winner's enclosure when Peggy-Sue brought Iskmak in. She looked at the filly anxiously. 'That was a nasty bump. Was the filly hurt?'

Peggy-Sue jumped down. 'I don't think so, but you'd better take a closer look.'

'Are you going to object?'

Peggy-Sue pulled off her saddle. 'Think I should?'

'Yes, I do.'

'The filly ran well. I could have won.'

'I thought that, too.'

'She was knocked almost to a standstill.'

'I know.'

Peggy-Sue walked towards the weighing room with Sonia at her side. 'She was full of running at the finish. She could go further.'

'A mile and a half?'

'I don't see why not.'

Sonia chuckled. 'I know what you're thinking, Peggy.'

'What's that?'

'The Arc?'

'Yep!'

'That is if Prince Khaneme can be persuaded.'

'That's the least of our worries.'

'Why?'

'You've got him eating out of your hand.'

'It's not my hand he eats out!'

After the inquiry the stewards reversed the placings and Iskmak was promoted to second. Peggy-Sue had no luck in the fourth race and, as she had no more rides she changed, ready to leave the course. She'd forgotten about Paul but he was waiting for her when she came out.

'You got my note?'

'Yes, I did. What are you doing here?'

'Watching the racing.'

'I thought you didn't like the Flat?'

'I prefer the jumps, but York is always a colourful meeting.'

'Yes, it is.'

'Although you didn't have a lot of luck today.'

'No, I didn't.'

Peggy-Sue had been looking at the girl on his arm. She was absolutely stunning. Paul motioned her forward to introduce them.

'Peggy-Sue, Fiona. Fiona's a model.'

They shook hands. She thought Fiona had a

pleasant smile. She guessed she was a genuine girl and took an immediate liking to her.

Fiona laughed lightly. 'Not a very well-known or well-paid model I'm sorry to say.'

Paul interrupted. 'We're staying at the Viking. Come and have dinner with us. We'd love that, wouldn't we, Fiona?'

'Oh yes, please say you will, Miss Rhyma.'

'Okay, thanks. I'm staying up here for the meeting, so why not?'

The meal was over and they were drinking liqueurs when Fiona excused herself. Peggy-Sue hadn't been able to resist seeing Paul again and had enjoyed herself. She'd eaten sparingly for, although she had no trouble staying at her racing weight of 7 st 10 lbs, she still couldn't afford to be greedy. She watched Fiona glide across the restaurant and wondered why Paul had invited her when he already had such an elegant woman in tow. At first she'd feared that Fiona would resent her and she'd be the gooseberry, but the St Lucian girl had made her very welcome.

'I nearly didn't come,' she said.

'Why?'

'I thought Fiona would resent me.'

Paul smiled. 'Fiona is very fond of girls.'

'What do you mean?'

'She has strong lesbian tendencies.'

Peggy-Sue didn't believe him. 'Then why is she with you?'

'She's bisexual.'

'How do you know that?'

'She told me!'

The idea fascinated her. She'd grown to like Fiona. A sudden flash of eroticism conjured a mental picture of Fiona making love to her. She flushed. She hadn't thought like that about another girl since she was old enough to chase boys. She saw the alluring black girl gliding seductively back towards them. Paul's voice cut through a sea of background chatter.

'Come upstairs and find out for yourself.'

'Find out what?' interrupted Fiona.

'That you're a raving dyke!'

She was unmoved. 'That's not quite right, darling. It's just that sometimes I get a yen for my own sex as a change from the fumbling and mauling of the male.'

Peggy-Sue laughed nervously. She wasn't quite certain whether these two were being serious or not.

Fiona turned to her. 'What's he been saying to you, sweetie?'

'He invited me to join you both upstairs.'

'Marvellous,' cried Fiona clapping her hands, 'I'd love a three-some. You'll say yes, won't you, darling?'

In the bedroom Paul sat watching the two women. He found something deeply erotic about two women making love, and the contrast of their ebony-black and snow-white skins made it all the more so. All three were naked, their clothes tossed carelessly on the floor. The petite girl stood by the bed looking demure and nervous, while the black girl's hands and lips were all over her.

Paul smiled – Fiona was indeed making a meal of Peggy-Sue. She fondled the pertly rounded titties and pinched the pink nipples, before covering them with her mouth to roll the soft, malleable flesh between her lips. He saw Peggy-Sue's nervousness die as she closed her eyes to the ecstatic thrill of Fiona's tongue caressing her flat belly.

Suddenly, slender black fingers reached up to squeeze milk-white breasts as Peggy-Sue was urged backwards onto the bed. With Fiona's teasing hands covering her tender boobs, and her hot lips buried into her stomach, Peggy-Sue was tumbled onto her back. Even as she fell she felt the woman release her tits to clasp her behind the knees and throw her legs upwards. Peggy-Sue lay passively on her back, her legs raised high, while Fiona gorged on her exposed pussy.

Paul found himself very aroused by the spectacle. His urge was to throw himself onto the two women, but he waited. He gave Fiona time to devour Peggy-Sue's juicy cunt with her agile tongue, while tantalising her tiny clitoris to pulsating erection. By that time, his cock was iron-hard for the want of Peggy-Sue's wet, warm quim.

'Come on, Fiona. Don't hog the goodies.'

'It's self-service,' she muttered, as her long tongue slid along Peggy-Sue's shaven vulva.

'I'd like the little lady on her hands and knees if you please.'

Peggy-Sue obeyed instantly. She was hot for Paul's cock. She rolled out from beneath Fiona and was soon kneeling across the bed. She couldn't deny she'd been aroused by Fiona's sexual antics but it was Paul she wanted.

From her position on her hands and knees she could see Paul standing before her. She leaned forward to suck his erection into her mouth. She could feel the thick shaft throbbing as she ran her tongue along the entire length and, while she fellated him, Fiona was raising her temperature to red-hot fever by licking her arse. Peggy-Sue loved the tongue-teasing at her derriere, but she was eager to be filled with prick.

'Hurry up, Paul. Do what you want with me. Stick it in me. Now.'

He moved behind her and, kneeling on the bed behind her, gently pushed his tool between the soft lips of her quim only to be sucked into her body as if her vagina were a hungry mouth. She sighed rapturously as she felt herself filled up.

When he was deep inside her, Fiona slid on her back, beneath their coupled genitals. She now lay between Peggy-Sue's open thighs, directly below her pretty saturated crack, where she could watch Paul's weapon shafting her with long hard strokes. She reached up to tease his swinging balls and, as he paused to savour her touch, Fiona raised her mouth to taste the dew which glazed Peggy-Sue's sweet fig.

As Paul's tool moved in and out like a huge piston, Fiona positioned her lips on Peggy-Sue's quim lips at the point where Paul's fat dick was fucking her. The feel of Peggy-Sue's velvety pussy and Fiona's skilful tongue rapidly brought Paul towards climax. Suddenly, Fiona doubled his enjoyment by removing his knob from Peggy-Sue's vagina and plunging it between her lips and back again. The very idea of alternating between one woman's cunt and another woman's mouth was sufficient to make him shoot off instantly. Fiona anticipated his need and slipped his pulsing rod back into Peggy-Sue so that she could milk the last drops of semen from his balls.

They slept like the dead, with bodies and limbs entwined. Peggy-Sue was the first to wake. The lights were blazing and the curtains drawn. She could just see the clock. It was three o'clock. She decided to dress and slip out of the hotel. She was due to canter a couple of Sonia's horses at 5 am. She tried to be quiet but the rustle of clothing aroused Paul. He opened one eye.

'You're not sneaking out on us?'

'I have to. Some people have to work for a living.'

'You're too beautiful to work. Come and live with me.'

She chuckled. 'And Fiona and the rest of the harem!'

He swung his legs off the bed. She could see he had a hell of a hard-on. His weapon stood up like a poker between his legs.

'Well, how about a fuck before you go?'

She slid her knickers back down her legs. 'Okay,

but it will have to be a quick one.'

He leaned forward and, grabbing Fiona's hips, dragged her to the edge of the bed.

'Sod off,' she mumbled full of sleep.

Peggy-Sue watched him manoeuvre Fiona's semi-sleeping body so that her legs were doubled beneath her belly and her backside was curved saucily over the edge of the bed. He signalled her to kneel on the bed beside Fiona. It seemed that he wanted to screw them both at once. She took her place beside the black girl, kneeling on the bed to present her pretty rear-end for his will. Standing beside them and finding them both wet and willing, he plunged into one, and then the other. Fiona wasn't fully awake until she was penetrated.

'Hey, what's going on?' she bawled. 'Whose idea is this?'

Peggy-Sue grinned. 'He caught me trying to sneak out.'

'And me asleep on duty, I suppose?'

She held Peggy-Sue's hand as he shagged them alternately, while Peggy-Sue mused that it had been a strange night. She wouldn't want to repeat it but she wouldn't have missed the experience. She squeezed Fiona's hand. It was as if they were sisters. Sisters in sex.

Joe and Hank Ladd flew over for the last day of the meeting. They'd had to interrupt a European business trip and fly from Frankfurt to watch Crazy

Face run. The colt was entered in the Nunthorpe Championship sprint over five furlongs. Tess had turned him out like a picture but Sonia was pessimistic about his chances.

'Is he going to win?' asked Joe eagerly.

Sonia frowned. 'He'll run a big race.'

'That's as maybe,' snapped Hank, 'but will he win?'

'Come off it, Hank,' replied Sonia, 'I don't know that. I can only tell you Peggy will be trying her arse off.'

'And a pretty arse it is, too!' smiled Joe.

Hank smiled. 'I'm sorry, Sonia. We're just anxious to know whether he's back to his brilliant best.'

'The treatment appears to have worked. He gallops freely now but he's not a hundred per cent. Remember, he's only been back in full training for a fortnight.'

Joe smiled wryly. 'We'll keep our fingers crossed.'

When Peggy-Sue came into the paddock they kept the conversation casual by kidding her about the rumours they'd heard that she was in love. They weren't so far from the truth, although after Tuesday night she'd decided to finish with Paul. She had come to see their relationship had little to do with love and everything to do with lust.

Peggy-Sue found the long parade in front of the stands a bit of a trial, for the big colt wasn't used to it, and without his American outrider he became restless. As he was Number One on the card, Crazy Face led the parade and the big black colt was the centre of attraction. Peggy-Sue and Sonia both knew he had only one way of running so there was no need of riding instructions. He would go flat out from the start so they prayed he would be fit enough to last home. All those connected with The Billings watched with bated breath as the big colt waited patiently in the stalls.

When the gates flew open Crazy Face came out like a rifle bullet and thundered hell for leather down the centre of the track. Peggy-Sue crouched motionless over his neck and allowed him to run his race. Such was his power-packed start that he was ten lengths clear by the end of the first furlong with the remainder of the field bunched behind, thinking he would tire.

At the two pole the black colt's pace still hadn't faltered and most of the others were off the bridle vainly chasing him. Inside the final furlong Crazy Face had had his lead cut to six lengths by the second horse when, half a furlong from the line, Peggy-Sue suddenly felt him change legs and falter. She balanced him, and began to ride hands and heels.

As the post approached she could feel the power of the dynamo beneath her weakening. She was tempted to use the whip but realised it was too late and would serve no purpose. She crouched lower, and pushed and pushed in rhythm with his stride. She was conscious of the noise of the crowd and could hear the sound of her pursuer's hoofs close on her heels. A big bay head appeared at Crazy Face's withers and crept up until they were neck and neck. The two horses flashed across the line locked together. The result would be on the nod and she firmly believed she'd got it.

As she rode in everybody asked the same question: '*Who's Won?*' Tess was as proud as punch and there were tears in her eyes as she fussed over the black colt. Neither jockey would ride into the spot reserved for the winner, and as Peggy-Sue dismounted she was surrounded by Joe and Hank and Mandy and Jilly all congratulating her while Sonia stood back nervously, awaiting the result of the photo. If Crazy Face had snatched the race it would be her first Group One winner and that meant a lot to a stable. She heard the click of the tannoy.

'Here is the result of the photo. First, Number One . . .'

Crazy Face's supporters went mad and Sonia realised she was crying. Not only had the big colt won, but he'd done it at 16–1 which meant that the twins had won a packet and the stable staff at The Billings had got their beer money for the weekend. The Ladd brothers accepted the presentation, followed by mementos for the trainer and jockey. Afterwards, Joe planted a whopper full on Sonia's lips to the delight of the crowd.

'Thanks, Sonia, it was a tonic. Now we must go.'

'Good heavens, so soon. What about the celebrations?'

'We'd love to stay but we're booked on the next flight.'

'We'll crack open a bottle for you,' shouted Jilly.

'Please do,' called Joe, 'it's been great. We loved every minute of it. Just remember to treat all the boys and girls tonight.'

Sonia laughed. 'We'll drink to you.'

'Put it on our bill, and thanks again.'

They left on a high. Joe waved as he moved towards the waiting taxi but Hank hung back. He had his arm around Mandy's shoulder.

'I'd like to bet my little girl's been misbehaving again, hasn't she?'

Mandy felt the skin at the back of her neck tingle. 'What if she has?' she replied tartly.

'Cos when her Uncle Hank comes next she's gonna get her pretty ass tanned.'

'No chance,' she retorted sharply.

'That's a promise, Mandy.'

She watched him go and thought she must be the colour of beetroot. She was dumbfounded that he'd spoken to her like that when stone-cold sober and in the midst of a crowd, but even more startled that it had evoked a thrill of anticipation within her. He knew that she couldn't wait to have her bare bottom slapped again. She'd worried over it for some time, but now he'd spoken of it openly she didn't care. She had no sexual inhibitions and was quite able to face up to the fact that she enjoyed being spanked.

Sonia had been walking away from the presentation when a hand fell on her shoulder. It had a strangely familiar touch. She looked around quickly. It was Bart.

'Congratulations on your first Group One winner,' he smiled.

'I thought we weren't talking?' she replied sharply.

He grinned sheepishly. 'I'm sorry. It was spiteful and small-minded of me.'

'That's true.'

He apologised again. 'I'm really sorry.'

'So you should be. You did everything you could to stop me being a success.'

'I know and I'm ashamed of myself. Can't we kiss and make up?'

'We could make up, but there'll be no kissing!'

'Anyway, you made it on your own. You're a successful trainer now.'

'No thanks to you.'

'Well, you must admit you were a trifle devious.'

She giggled. 'I suppose I was, but I didn't think you'd be that annoyed.'

He laughed. 'I did go over the top a bit.'

She held out her hand. 'Truce?'

He accepted it solemnly. 'Let bygones be bygones.'

They both laughed self-consciously. Their feud had melted away as quickly as it had begun.

'Are you going to the dinner tonight, Sonia?'

'Which one is that?'

'The celebrity charity affair in aid of various racing funds.'

'No, I haven't been invited.'

'You must come with me.'

'I was going home after racing.'

'Surely you can stay one more night?'

'I suppose I could.'

'Everybody will be there, and it will be an opportunity to show we've buried the hatchet.'

The meal was excellent and the after-dinner speakers amusing. Initially, Sonia had been nervous but Bart had fed her champagne and she was quickly at ease. He knew of old that a little champagne relaxed her. He also knew the more she drank the more amorous she became. He made it his business to keep her glass topped up.

Everybody was surprised to see them together and most were pleased their feud was over. Many came over to offer their good wishes but several remained aloof, unable to change their attitudes that quickly. By the end of the evening Sonia was stoned and the fresh air caused her to stagger. In the taxi, Bart held her hand and tried to steal a kiss but she pushed him away, giggling like a teenager with her first boyfriend. At the hotel they shared a lift with another couple, but when it stopped at the third floor he tumbled her out.

'Where are we going? This isn't the fifth floor.'

'I thought we'd walk the rest.'

'Why?'

'It might help you sober up.'

301

She giggled. 'I'm not tipsy.'

He guided her to the back stairs. 'Of course you're not.'

He'd deliberately ignored the plushly carpeted stairway to open a fire exit door which led to deserted stone steps. Taking her arm he pushed her up half a dozen steps.

'What the hell,' she gurgled, 'where are we going?'

He spun her round to face him. She was standing on a step higher than him and their faces were on a level. He kissed her.

'Steady on, mister,' she gasped, 'we're not supposed to be doing this.'

He held her close. 'Why not?'

'Cos we're not very friendly.'

He kissed her again. 'Oh, but we are.'

'Are we?' she breathed softly.

They didn't speak again. Their lips were sealed together, their tongues entwined: and soon they were drinking each other; they'd been too long apart. Both were thirsty for sex. Sonia had nothing against taking up where they'd left off. She thought a great deal of Bart, even loved him in her own way. Bart buried his face in her neck. She could feel his hot breath on her throat and his erection against her thigh.

'I want you, Sonia. I want you now.'

'Couldn't we go to my room?'

'I want you here,' he whispered urgently, 'this very minute.'

'Bart, please. It would be nicer in bed. I don't like a quick tuppenny standing!'

But his hands were already fumbling beneath her dress and her panties had been hauled down to her knees. She knew he had his cock out as she could feel the warmth of it against her thigh. She couldn't object further: the champagne served to heighten her carnal desire.

She parted her legs wide as she felt him insert two fingers into her slit to find she was already moist for him. She wound her arms tightly around his neck as he thrust lewdly up into her hot, inviting channel. She groaned as he jabbed into her, hurting her and meaning to: and she gasped at the deepness of his penetration as he ground her like a lascivious tomcat. In the intensity of their desire, they failed to hear the young couple climb the stairs towards them.

'Excuse us,' giggled the girl.

They continued in their coupling, oblivious to the world around them.

The young man laughed. 'We don't want to break anything up, but can we pass?'

Sonia and Bart were on the verge of a world-shattering mutual orgasm. They were as likely to stop as a runaway train. The young couple stood watching for a moment until the girl's embarrassment overtook her. She grabbed the boy's hand and pulled him back.

'Come on, let's leave them to it.'

The boy chuckled. 'Let's watch. We could learn something.'

She pulled him away. 'You know too much already.'

'Do I?' he drawled smugly.

After a win and a second in Group One races, life began to look up at The Billings. They say nothing breeds success like success, and although the winners had been coming in a trickle since Epsom now they came in a torrent. During the following fortnight they turned out winners as far apart as Chester and Sandown, Yarmouth and Brighton, Salisbury and Ripon. Barney strode around the yard, his face wreathed in smiles, playfully punching the lads' shoulders and slapping the lasses' bottoms. He even laughed it off when he was caught giving Tess one in an empty stall, although Sonia wasn't too pleased. All in all The Billings was a good place to work those last two weeks in August.

It was early September that Crazy Face was to attempt his second Group One win in a five-furlong race at Haydock Park. It was the last Championship sprint of the season in Britain. Sonia had a call from Buffalo to say only one of the twins would be coming over to watch the race. They were very busy and had tossed a coin for it. Hank had won. When Mandy heard the news she pestered Sonia to allow her to go to Haydock with her, while Jilly was left at home to saddle a couple at Kempton Park. Sonia had arranged to meet Bart at Haydock and was pleased Mandy would be there to entertain Hank. She knew

Hank liked Mandy, although if she'd guessed what the two had going she wouldn't have been so happy.

Hank flew into Manchester on the morning of the race. He booked into a suite at a hotel in the city hoping to persuade Mandy to join him after the races. The weather turned nasty at the last minute and it poured all afternoon. The rain changed the going from Good, to Good to Soft, but the big black colt ploughed through it to win with ease.

Peggy-Sue never had a moment's anxiety. The horse shot out of the stalls, made all the running, and won doing handsprings. Bart said he'd never seen such a powerful sprinter and the press crowded round wanting to know where it was running next. Sonia explained that her target was the Breeder's sprint cup at Santa Anita in Los Angeles in November, but the horse might possibly go for the Prix Abbay at Longchamp on the way. Hank and Mandy disappeared into the bar to sup brandy and champagne until after the last race, when Hank had ordered a limo to take them back to Manchester.

They were speeding down the motorway when Hank reached forward and pulled down the screen behind the driver.

'Now, my pretty, what's all this I've heard about you while I've been away?'

'I've been a naughty girl,' she giggled.

'And what should we do about that?'

'Smack my bottom?' she gurgled in her little girl's voice.

'Is that what you want?'

She changed to her ordinary voice and manner. 'Yes, Hank. I want to be spanked. I'd like you to tan my backside, please.'

He looked puzzled. Why had she changed her demeanour? She was no longer the little girl of the game they played. It put him at a loss. He wasn't used to grown women asking for CP so blatantly. He preferred to play games.

She saw him hesitate. 'Hank I don't want to play games any more. I enjoy being spanked. I'm not ashamed of it. I want you to whack my bum good and hard, and no more make-believe.'

'Okay, if that's what you want, honey.'

'No more games?'

'No.'

'No more dressing me up like a schoolgirl?'

'No.'

'Right,' she grinned, 'let's do it!'

He didn't hesitate this time. If he'd been thrown off balance by her outburst he didn't show it. He whipped a length of leather thong from his pocket and secured her wrists.

'Okay, honey, so you're a big girl now. Let's treat you as one.'

He pushed her roughly back onto the seat and jerked her skirt up.

'For heaven's sake, Hank. Stop it, not here.'

In spite of her struggles he continued to yank her skirt upwards until the bare flesh above her stocking tops was visible.

'Hank, there are cars going by. They'll see us.'

But she realised he wasn't going to stop. He wriggled the skirt up over her backside until it was bunched around her waist and when she relaxed, thinking he'd achieved his objective, he jerked her knickers down and off. She beat at him vainly with her tied hands.

'You pig,' she squealed, 'you're beastly to me!'

'You wanted your butt tanned. That's what you're going to get.'

'Not here. Not with all these cars passing. I'll die if they see my face.'

He pulled her towards him. 'It's not your face they'll be seeing!'

'Hank, you bastard. Stop it.'

He dragged her across his lap. She struggled wildly to free herself, but she was helpless with her wrists tied. She suddenly relaxed. It was pointless wriggling and writhing across his knees. It probably only excited him and therefore make him the more determined to give her that sound spanking. Anyway that was what she wanted. She was very conscious of her raised skirt and she could see her flimsy knickers lying on the floor of the car. She realised her bare buttocks must be jutting up naked for the world to see. Anyone driving up the motorway, who glanced into the big limo, would see her lying ignominiously across his knees. She hung her head until her short curls touched the floor. At least they wouldn't see who she was.

It was when the spanking began that she began to kick and struggle. His palm whacked down across her tender twin moons until she could feel the plump flesh trembling and shaking like jelly beneath the sting of his hand. She began to bawl like a child until the tears flowed from her eyes. Only then did it strike her that the driver would be listening. She panicked, and gasped in embarrassment.

'Oh, my God. Stop it, Hank. You must stop it.'

Her tone was so urgent that he stopped momentarily. 'Why?' he asked.

'You must stop it, please. Immediately.'

'Oh, come on,' he said realistically, 'it can't be hurting. You've taken a lot more and enjoyed it.'

She lowered her voice. 'It's the driver. He'll be able to hear.'

He chortled and whacked her tingling rump heartily. 'So what?'

She clamped her lips tight determined not to make another sound. She'd been acting like a silly schoolgirl blubbering like that just because she was being spanked. Soon the sting of each smack spread the heat across the whole surface of her delectable derriere and the fire began to eat into her loins. She became very aware that the slapping was beginning to arouse her sexually. She was becoming like a bitch on heat and every smarting thwack was heightening her lust. She felt him slide a finger between her thighs.

'You're soaking wet, girl,' he whispered.

For what seemed an eternity he alternated sharp smacks with the fingering of he salacious twat. She lay passively over his lap accepting and enjoying this harsh treatment – and hoping it would never end.

At the hotel she stood by his side as he registered and felt weirdly stimulated, standing there with a sore arse. She wondered what the other guests would think if they knew her wrists were tied, her bum was burning and her knickers were in his pocket. In the apartment they ordered from room service and, while they waited for their meal, he made her kneel on a stool so he could admire her poor abused seat. He leaned forward and kissed the lightly bruised flesh and then, as if to make up for the punishment he'd given her, he commenced to lick every inch of her rounded fundament. She closed her eyes to enjoy the sensual feeling of his tongue worshipping her superb arse. Finally he gently covered her tender buttocks with a soothing ointment.

They ate naked, facing each other, gorging greedily upon the food and washing it down with wine. Soon she was eager to wallow in another session of masochistic pleasure. He showed her a selection of straps and paddles that made her eyes light up. She wondered what the Customs would have said had they opened his case. She was made to stretch face down over a table with her ankles secured to its legs. He found a wide leather strap which he passed over her body and under the table so that she was secured helplessly to the tabletop. Her wrists had been tied again so she was unable to struggle. She watched him select a tawse and measure it across her pert backside which had been placed so prettily for discipline. An electrifying thrill of sexual anticipation made her tremble as the tawse whistled down towards its target.

When Mandy arrived back at The Billings Sonia was angry that she'd stayed overnight in Manchester without telling her. She said that she wasn't yet old enough to wander off as she pleased. Mandy wondered what she'd have said if she knew how she'd spent the night, or saw her ravished posterior. She confided in Jilly, who listened but did not understand.

Hank had departed saying that he and Joe would be back to see Misk Garnett run at Ascot, and to attend the Sales with Sonia. Mandy determined to bring Lumberboy in from holiday and to begin his training for the National Hunt season. She didn't fancy another session with Hank too soon after her last encounter. She'd enjoyed the pain but she'd got it out of her system for the moment. However, she knew deep down that it was something she'd have to live with.

When Sonia decided to hire someone with special responsibility for the yearlings, Mandy suggested Sam and, when he was contacted, he jumped at the job. Yearlings had to be broken. They had to be taught to walk on a long rein and accept a saddle on their back before they could be mounted. It's a long skilful task which requires patience and care and love, and Sam had worked with horses all his life. Because of their recent success, the numbers stabled at The Billings were rising. Several new owners had brought their horses to Sonia and the Ladd twins were increasing their string to twelve. In addition, Claude had hinted that Prince Khaneme might increase his numbers with her. Thus, by the end of the season she hoped to have all fifty stalls occupied and amongst them would be several top-class animals. It was those top-class thoroughbreds which won the kind of races that made a stables' reputation.

Joe and Hank came over for the whole three-day Ascot meeting, but their real interest was on the Saturday when Misk Garnett would run in the Queen Elizabeth stakes. The race was over the old mile and was usually considered the race which would crown the champion miler of the season. Eight horses were declared and Sonia knew the grey filly would have to be at her best to be in the shake-up.

The twins preferred the quieter atmosphere of the September meeting to the royal meeting. It was all about racing, without the distractions of fashion, snobbery and posing. For the first two days they escorted Sonia and Jilly, as Mandy had occupied herself with Lumberboy. After racing on the Friday Peggy-Sue introduced them to Fiona, who had left Paul and was using her friendship with Peggy-Sue to find a sugar daddy amongst the racing fraternity. She struck lucky with Hank who invited her to the Saturday's racing.

The Queen Elizabeth stakes is the centrepiece of the Festival of Racing, which is what the Saturday card is called. The stands were packed, the sun was shining, and each and every race was both valuable and well-contested. Jilly, Joe, Fiona and Hank settled down for an afternoon's entertainment. A table had been booked at the Savoy, where the twins were staying, for the evening so whatever the outcome of the race they intended to have a good time. For Sonia and Peggy-Sue it was very different. A win for Misk Garnett would give them the kudos of another Group One win, but more importantly it would show the world that they could bring a horse back to its best after it had lost its form.

When asked afterwards, Peggy-Sue always put the race down as one of the best she'd ever ridden. After the grey filly had fought for her head at the start, Peggy-Sue managed to settle her. She switched the filly off at the back of the field until they were racing into the short straight. The main players were fighting it out down the rail, and Peggy-Sue was faced with a wall of three horses in front of her.

She found herself sitting with a double handful

and nowhere to go. She was completely boxed on the rail and forced to sit in behind a labouring colt which was going nowhere. She waited patiently, but the jockey in front wouldn't give up until finally the tired horse beneath him swung off the rail to give Misk Garnett a peep of daylight. Peggy-Sue slapped her behind the saddle and urged her through the narrow gap. The little rocking horse bravely bounded forward to shoot through the gap like a scalded cat and win by a short head.

That final half furlong would live with Sonia forever as she went through the gap to finish like a runaway train. It was the grey filly back to her brilliant best and put Peggy-Sue amongst the best jocks in the country.

'My God, that was brilliant,' cried Joe, 'how about if I rode a finish like that on you, Jilly?'

She grinned. 'It would be the death of you, Mr Ladd!'

'Jeeze, what a way to go. Can we try it tonight?'

She laughed. 'If you promise not to die on top of me!'

'How about you, honey?' Hank drawled in Fiona's ear.

Fiona chuckled. 'What about me?'

'Would a crack across your butt get you going like that?'

She smiled. She knew all the angles. 'I'm not into CP, I'm afraid.'

'But you've still got a power-packed finish I bet?'

313

She squeezed his arm. 'You'll find I don't need the whip, darling!'

At the Savoy, Joe suggested they went straight up to their suite to change for dinner, but Hank took Fiona to the bar. He'd watched his brother and Jilly crawl all over each other in the car from Ascot and knew they both had a bad case of the hots. If he took Fiona for a quick drink it would give them time to jump into bed. The lift that took them up was crowded, but they were oblivious to the disapproval as they smooched like two lovesick teenagers. On their floor they walked along the corridor entwined in each other's arms. At the door they paused while Joe fumbled for the key.

'I could eat you, Jilly.'

'You have. My neck will be covered in love bites.'

'I can't wait, Jilly. I could die for the want of fucking you.'

She stuck her tongue into his open mouth. 'And I'm dying to be fucked.'

'Are you, Jilly? Really dying for it?'

'Mmm, hurry and get that door open.'

'Once we're inside I'm going to strip you naked.'

'Mmm, please. I want to be naked for you.'

The door swung open. 'Are you ready?'

'Yes.'

'*Now!*'

They both jumped like joyful children, giggling wildly, and slammed the door shut behind them.

Instantly they were at each other's clothes. She dug her hands inside his jacket pushing it back from his shoulders until it slid from him, and immediately her agile fingers were unknotting his tie and unbuttoning his shirt. Those flying female fingers made him look clumsy as he struggled to unfasten her clinging dress only to become hopelessly entangled with buttons and zips.

She laughed. 'You're a clumsy old man, haven't you ever undressed a girl before?'

'No, never.'

'Fibber.'

He managed to inveigle her dress from her shoulders. 'I'm really an innocent soul.'

'You tell great big porkies, Joe Ladd.'

His trousers fell to the floor and her hands were inside his vest. He laughed as he pulled her dress down, as if he were peeling a banana.

'What's that mean?'

His shorts were down around his ankles as she yanked his vest upwards.

'Pork pies – lies,' she explained.

She made him raise his arms and when his vest came off he was naked. He stood covering himself modestly. 'You minx, you've taken all my clothes off'

She swiftly slipped from her lingerie. 'You're an old slowcoach.'

He watched her pose stark naked and it took his breath away. 'Lord, what can I say? Except that the lady's beautiful!'

'The lady wants fucking,' she purred.

'And so she shall be!'

He took her in his arms and pushed her against the wall. She could feel his erection hard against her stomach and when she invitingly parted her legs he bent his knees so as to position his rampant tool at the mouth of her pussy. When she felt the smooth head nudge against her warm nest of pubic fur she almost swooned.

'Put it in, quickly. I'm dying for a fat dick inside me.'

He thrust into her. 'Like this?'

'Aah, mmm, yes. Right in, push it right in. I want every inch inside me. I want to gobble it all up.'

He impaled her to the hilt and continued thrusting as if he was trying to reach the very centre of her.

'Oh God, that's lovely. Now carry me to the bedroom.'

She swung her legs up and wrapped them around his thighs so he had to carry her around his neck. His prick was still deep inside her, forcing him to support her under her buttocks with his hands. He staggered into the bedroom and fell forward onto the bed.

Immediately, she rolled over on top of him to take the initiative. She sat astride him, her big tits quivering as, consumed with lust, she forced herself down onto his stiffened rod until she was well and truly corked. His hands moved to her breasts, cupping those delightful orbs until, under the stimulus of his caressing, she reached the brink of climax. Allowing her passion full reign, she exploded into orgasm and her wanton fucking took him over the brink, his penis spurting a stream of warm seed deep inside her pulsing quim.

In the midst of their mutual orgasm they failed to hear the door slam as Fiona and Hank tumbled into the apartment. They were both well the worse for wear. The two double scotches they'd swallowed on top of the afternoon's alcoholic mix had put the hat on it. Both were as tight as fiddler's bitches. Yet in spite of, or because of, the alcohol they were both hellishly randy.

Without further ado Hank tossed Fiona over the back of a chair and, lifting her skirt, jerked down her knickers. Now her posterior was bare he could marvel at the beauty of it. The cleft of her arse was parted sufficiently for him to spy her succulent fig peeping from between the fleshy cheeks of her bum, and to gaze upon the small round hole in the centre of her bottom twinkling like a little star. He drew in his breath. She had the most divine derriere, but unfortunately she'd already made it clear she wasn't into spanking.

'Fiona, honey, you've got the sweetest buns.'

'Really?'

'How about taking a length up your ass? What do you say to that?'

'Have you done it to many girls?'

'I have, my sweet.'

317

'I mean posh girls like the Beechly sisters?'

'Jilly and Mandy? Yes, both of them.'

'And did they enjoy it?'

'I think so. They didn't give it to me in writing!'

'Okay, if it's good enough for them I guess it's okay by me.'

He had a beat on up to his eyebrows just talking about it. He dropped his trousers and moved lecherously behind her. Instantly she reached back and her fingers closed around the shaft of his lascivious pego.

'Steady up,' she cried, 'if you're going up there let's take it nice and easy.'

He stood back and gently inserted two fingers into the moistness of her tender vulva and, moving an inch upwards, smeared the juice from her quim around the puckered rosette of her tiny anus. He felt her draw in her breath as the tip of his knob prodded against her back entrance and gasp as he penetrated her sphincter. As he speared into her, Fiona yelped like a surprised puppy. She found it a brutal, intimate act. Her vision of it was a blur of pain and pleasure. She felt utterly humiliated, yet acutely aroused. She arched her back and thrust her butt back onto him. She was being despoiled and she was enjoying it! She flicked her head from side to side, sobbing quietly. This shouldn't happen to a nice girl. She felt the pleasure stir and build inside her. Evidently, she wasn't a nice girl.

While Jilly and Fiona were in the midst of their

sexual antics in London, and Mandy was entertaining Sam in a quiet corner of The Billings, Sonia and Peggy-Sue were sharing a meal in Newbury.

'That win means we get the whole weekend at Longchamp,' smiled Sonia.

'You mean Misk Garnett will be entered there, too?'

'The Ladd brothers want to run her on the Saturday so we've decided to go for the Prix Dollar.'

'But that's over a mile and a furlong, isn't it?'

'Yes, but it's only a Group Two race so she should have sufficient class to last the final furlong.'

'You're probably right.'

'And on the Sunday the twins have Crazy Face in the Prix Abbay.'

'He'll gobble up the opposition over that fast five furlongs.'

'You sound confident,' chuckled Sonia, 'but now for a lovely surprise.'

Peggy-Sue loved a surprise. She was like a little girl. 'Come on, hurry up and tell me or I shall wet myself!'

'I've spoken to Prince Khaneme on the phone. He's definitely going to run Iskmak in the Arc de Triomphe.'

'My God, that's brilliant.'

'It could be unforgettable, Peggy-Sue. Three runners in two days and all there with a chance.'

Chapter 11

Sonia decided to fly her horses over to Paris on the Friday. It was only a week since Ascot and she hoped the race wouldn't come too soon for Misk Garnett. On the Tuesday she gave Iskmak and Crazy Face their last bit of searching fast work, but the grey filly was only cantered to keep her joints loose. Crazy Face was his usual strident self and he careered up the gallops as if his life depended on it. It seemed the colt had two speeds: stop and flat-out. Iskmak was easier to assess for she was a temperamental filly. Both Sonia and Peggy-Sue thought they'd never seen her on better terms with herself.

Sonia had kept one surprise up her sleeve, but unfortunately it didn't come off. Unknown to the others she'd entered Man Samson for Longchamp. It was more for sentimental reasons than any hope of victory, but she'd decided the old fellow deserved his moment in the limelight. However, he broke down on the gallops doing his last bit of fast work, and Sonia guessed from the heat in his leg that it was serious.

The vet confirmed her fears and it was decided to retire the gelding. Sonia thought she'd use him as her hack once he was fit enough.

On the Saturday morning Jilly and Mandy met the twins at Charles de Gaulle airport when they flew in from New York. The four of them took a taxi into Paris where they booked into a luxurious hotel just a stone's throw from the Eiffel Tower. Sonia had travelled straight to the racecourse in the company of Bart, who had two runners at the meeting. They all intended that the two days would be a grand holiday and celebration as well as a working weekend.

Although the racing on the Saturday was valuable, and of a high class, Longchamp was almost deserted. It spite of the poor atmosphere the little party settled down to enjoy themselves. Misk Garnett looked a picture in the parade ring and it was a thrill for the twins to have a runner. After watching the grey filly walk onto the course they climbed up into the vast stands which would be packed the next day for the Arc de Triomphe, but were now almost deserted. Through their binoculars they could see the horses circling at the start which was almost opposite the stands, on the far side of the large right-handed course. Below them a few dozen people wandered around aimlessly. They all missed the colourful variety of the British racecourses, where rows of bookies and bustling punters enlivened the scene. The Pari-mutual, France's equivalent of the

Tote, showed Misk Garnett was a fairly warm favourite.

At the start Peggy-Sue tucked the grey filly in behind and as there was little pace the race was being run to suit her horse. She was the sole British representative in the field, and the French jockeys were riding their usual waiting race until just after the final bend, when they all went hell for leather for the line. This played into Misk Garnett's strong suit for at her best she had a devastating turn of foot. Sonia watched with bated breath as Peggy held up the filly until inside the final furlong. She worried whether the horse would answer her jockey when she was asked to go. She watched Peggy-Sue change her hands, give the filly a little more rein and suddenly she was flying. Such was her burst of acceleration that she'd passed the field in a couple of dozen strides and won by four lengths slowing up.

There was no throng of bustling spectators to welcome and cheer her in. Just a little polite clapping from the thin crowd. However, the Ladd brothers didn't let that spoil their fun. They kissed Sonia and Peggy-Sue and Tess and the horse. The French press loved the extrovert Americans, and when Hank surreptitiously goosed Tess her surprised squeak got the loudest applause of the afternoon. Sonia stood back from the celebrations and was surprised to find Claude at her elbow. She hadn't realised he was on the course.

'Hello, Mrs Beechly.'

'What are you doing here, Claude? The Prince hasn't got a runner this afternoon.'

'I came to see you.'

'You want to play your little game with me?'

He blushed. 'No.'

'What then?'

'The Prince has decided to come racing tomorrow.'

Sonia was surprised. 'Good heavens, I thought he was a recluse.'

'In his own country he appears regularly in public.'

'But not in Europe?'

'No, only at official functions.'

'And never at racecourses?'

'No, never. He's never seen one of his horses run.'

'So why now?'

'He says he's taken a special interest in the filly you are running tomorrow.'

'Iskmak?'

'Yes.'

'Why?'

'I really don't know. He doesn't confide in me.'

'Come on. It's more than that, isn't it?'

Claude looked flustered. 'He's decided he'd like to move amongst the French people and following his thoroughbreds will give him that opportunity.'

'To ogle the women and proposition the ones he fancies, I bet.'

He looked uncomfortable. 'You're nearer the truth than you realise.'

Sonia laughed. 'It's you who'll be expected to proposition them for him, you'll see.'

Claude inspected the toecaps of his shoes for some time before answering.

'That's exactly the task I've been given!'

'What is he prepared to pay?' she smiled.

'Really, that's none of your business, Mrs Beechly.'

Sonia grinned. 'Shall I see the Prince here tomorrow?'

'More than that. He's chosen you to be his escort. You'll be picked up at your hotel at noon and stay with him all afternoon.'

Sonia looked aghast. 'You're joking?'

'No, I'm not.'

'The only women in his company walk ten paces behind. I'm not doing that for any man.'

Claude shrugged his shoulders. 'I don't think he'll expect that of you.'

That evening Jilly and Mandy accompanied the Ladd twins to a restaurant on the Champs Elysées. The atmosphere was convivial and, as wines flowed freely throughout, the celebrations were soon under way. It was towards the end of the meal that Jilly began to feel that the evening should have a wilder side.

'Where're we going after?' she asked.

Joe looked upset. 'Don't you like it here?'

She quickly covered his hand with hers. 'It's been a lovely meal but to really celebrate we need to up the tempo a bit, don't we?'

Hank laughed. 'Spoken like a true partygoer.'

'We could go somewhere to dance?' suggested Mandy.

Hank turned to Joe. 'Have you still got that address?'

Joe hesitated. 'Isn't that a bit hot for an evening like this?'

'Hot!' shrieked Jilly. 'Come on, what's hot?'

Hank grinned. 'It's a club we were told about last time we were in Las Vegas.'

'A gambling club?'

'No, a sex club.'

'Really? Is it in the red-light district?'

'I'm not certain where it is. We've never been there.'

'Well, let's go.'

Joe turned to his brother. 'What do you think, shall we give it a try?'

'Hell, why not?'

'Good for you,' laughed Jilly, 'only I'm not sure it's the place for a little sister!'

Mandy bridled. 'I doubt whether you three licentious bastards will be allowed in. You'll need me to enhance the tone of the party!'

Jilly grinned. 'If you're going to act the lady, little sister, you'd best put on a pair of knickers!'

In the club they sat around a small circular table drinking cheap champagne. It was a compact room made to look like an intimate theatre. The tiny raised stage was complete with a catwalk and the auditorium was packed with small circular tables. There was a bar at one end but drinks were served by waitresses. As in all such clubs the booze was inferior and expensive and the waitresses blowsy and near naked. Without warning, the lights went out to the accompaniment of squeals from the smattering of young females in the audience. They heard the curtains swish apart. The show had begun.

The stage was in darkness but for the light of two candles. All eyes were drawn to the flickering flames which began to move slowly up and down as if held by invisible hands. Only when the eyes became used to the darkness could shapes be made out.

Jilly was beginning to guess at them when floodlights illuminated the stage. Two attractive young women, one black and one white, were lying on their backs on padded benches which sloped at an angle of forty-five degrees. The girls' heads were at the lowest points, and thus their posteriors were raised high in the air. Each had allowed her legs to drop onto her chest so that the full sensual curve of her bum was displayed, and each had a lighted candle thrust into her vagina, so they looked like a pair of human candle sticks. Both were simulating masturbation with their candles, so the two flickering flames appeared to cavort to some erotic dance. It certainly seemed to excite Hank.

'Hey, that's dead sexy,' he cried.

'It's bloody crude,' snapped Mandy.

'It's not a bad opening to a sex show,' said Joe.

327

Jilly giggled. 'Bring on the men, say I.'

She got her wish. The first act began with a handsome young Lothario shimmering to centre stage, where he stood swaying to an old-fashioned rumba in what he believed was a sexually arousing way. He was short and slim, wearing flared leather trousers, a leather waistcoat and a fancy studded belt. His bare arms were beautifully muscled and swinging amongst the rug of chest hair was the inevitable gold medallion. As he swayed he posed and smiled, sensually confident of his masculine appeal to the ladies in the audience. His partner was a pretty brunette, as tall as a boy, with luxuriant waved hair and the body curves of a Page Three girl. She was attired in calf-length kinky boots and a leather mini skirt . . . and a bolero jacket which did nothing to hide her bulging breasts.

Jilly found her mind wandering away from the movements of the couple as they stimulated some sort of strange courtship. She would have preferred something wilder, more passionate. She was so wrapped up in her own thoughts that she paid little heed to the show. She noticed both figures had forsaken their leather gear and were displaying their bodies to the audience. They both swayed with exactly the same movements. It was like watching two slabs of meat hanging in a market stall. There was no eroticism, no passion, no warmth. They moved towards each other as if in a dream. It was only when they kissed they came to life.

Jilly's interest was now kindled. She realised the boy and girl were lovers, that they were in love. The kiss said it all. They held it for a long moment and buried themselves in each other. Jilly suddenly liked them and felt sorry for them.

The tender moment passed and they returned to work. The boy supported the girl's body as he lowered her to the thin mattress on the floor. As he knelt at her feet she spread her long legs, swung them upwards and, while she clasped her ankles high above her head, the young man sank between her thighs. The music quickened. The girl moaned as the boy's mouth closed over her exposed labia. He pleasured her with long exaggerated licks of his tongue. Jilly realised he wasn't doing it to thrill the girl but to entertain the audience. It was too obvious. He wasn't much of a showman.

It was when the girl knelt up to face her partner that the show began to hot up. As she leaned forward to gently massage the limp penis before taking it into her mouth she had the audience watching spellbound; and when her full red lips closed around the aroused prick it was very obvious they were seeing a female well-practised in her art. She enacted a slow, amorous act of fellatio and it was magic. She oozed salacious sex.

Then the positions were reversed and the girl lay supine as the boy entered her. From the corner of her eye Jilly noticed a young woman at the next table shove her hand inside her partner's fly as if digging for gold. She watched curiously as the busy fingers caused a flurry inside the trousers. When she looked back at the stage the girl was on her hands and knees and the boy was taking her from the rear. He was shafting her with fierce, penetrating strokes and grunting like a pig to the echoing slaps of his bare belly against her rump. Jilly turned back to the next table where the woman wanking the man now had the tip of his cock peeping from his fly. She had half a mind to dive inside Joe's pants, but the act finished and the lights went up. The girl at the next table hurriedly removed her hand. Jilly deliberately caught her eye and the girl looked away quickly.

'Go on, darling. We don't mind. Give him a good old wank!'

'Do it yourself if you're that keen,' snapped the girl.

Jilly laughed aloud. 'You want me to jerk off your bloke? What are you, a dyke?'

The girl blushed. 'If I was I wouldn't touch you with a barge pole.'

Jilly looked at her coldly. 'I wouldn't have you inside my knickers if I was full of Spanish Fly and had both hands tied behind my back.'

'Hey, what's to do with you girls?' interrupted Joe.

'It's your girlfriend,' snapped the girl, 'she's jealous.'

'What's she got to be jealous about?' enquired Joe.

'You're damned right,' smiled Jilly wryly.

At that moment the auditorium lights went out

and the curtains parted again. On stage were two attractive women dressed in fancy bras and shorts. They were stroking themselves to the music. In appearance they were poles apart. One was blonde and cuddly, a throwback to the days of burlesque when showgirls had abundant curves in all the right places. Her partner could have been deliberately chosen to be the complete opposite. A slim, sinewy girl with long straight red hair who looked more like the present-day image of a diet-conscious model. If the blonde could be described as a blowsy chorus girl, the redhead had the muscled build of a fitness fanatic.

Having stroked their own bodies they moved closer, to commence fondling each other. Busy fingers were soon unfastening bras to expose soft white breasts, but their boobs were as different as their appearance. The blonde had a bosom like two ripe melons set off by lush pink nipples that seemed to harden by the second. The redhead had a small youthful bust which paled to insignificance beside the forty-two inch trophies of her voluptuous partner.

When the redhead moved behind the blonde the fun began. The audience could see her long manicured fingers tear the velcro fastening of the blonde's shorts and, as they fell apart, they revealed a dark swathe of short curly hair between plump feminine thighs. The redhead's fingers slid down into the other girl's fur. The cuddly blonde spread her legs wide and forced out her belly to attract the audience's attention while she groaned and rolled her eyes as if she was being felt up by some young stud from Hollywood.

Without warning, they changed places and the blonde whipped the redhead's shorts down to her ankles. Mandy, who'd been watching the act without much enthusiasm, gasped aloud. Jilly's eyes nearly popped out of her head and the girl at the next table squealed with surprise. Hanging down between the redhead's legs were a pair of testicles and a fat dick.

'My God,' cried Mandy, 'it's a man!'

Jilly giggled. 'Or a woman with a prick.'

'A man in drag. Who would have guessed?'

'It's more than that. Look at his breasts.'

'How'd he get like that?'

'I dunno. Hormones or silicone, I suppose.'

The girl at the next table leaned across. 'For the sake of you innocents, he's a She-male.'

The blonde was fondling the sleeping cock with her plump fingers, coaxing it upright for the audience and finally applying the finishing touch with her mouth. Soon it was standing proudly erect like some heathen totem pole. The blonde stood aside so that an inquisitive audience could see the slim, girlish She-male with the rampant dick. All the women and many of the men were strangely aroused as they gawked at the female figure displaying a great upstanding cock. Most were too occupied staring at this curiosity to see the blonde strapping on a huge rubber dildo.

Now the audience was treated to the sight of two female figures with male appendages, but while one was genuine the other looked ridiculous. The blonde moved very deliberately behind the redhead and as he bent forward she manoeuvred the top of the dildo between the cheeks of his arse. Then, with a clumsy thrust, the dildo penetrated the She-male's back passage. The audience watched transfixed as the weird scene unfolded before them. A woman was shafting a man who looked like a girl, with a dildo strapped on like a penis.

It went on until the audience became restless with this strange perversion being acted out for their entertainment. Then the blonde went over on her back, with the dildo stripped from her, and the She-male began poking her with all the aggression of a male. When the lights came up the audience grinned at each other sheepishly.

'What did you think of that?' asked a puzzled Mandy.

'I dunno. Was it some sort of lesbian show?' replied Jilly.

'It can't be lesbian when one of the women had a cock,' interrupted the girl at the next table.

'I bet you wish you had one,' said Mandy rudely, 'you'd never have your hands off it!'

'You silly little girl, you wouldn't know what to do with one if it was put in your hand.'

They were interrupted by the MC who had seen them bickering. 'Here's your chance to settle your argument, girls.'

'What is?' asked the girl at the next table.

'We now come to amateur hour, when couples are invited to come on stage and perform.'

'So now's your chance to do it in public instead of under the table,' grinned Jilly at the girl.

'I dare you!' replied the girl aggressively.

The MC saw he'd landed a fish, maybe two. They'd only need a word more of encouragement.

'Come on up, girls. We supply masks to hide your blushes!'

'It's not their faces we'll be looking at!' shouted a loud voice.

The audience laughed and clapped the two women onto the stage. The girl at the next table grabbed her man's hand and dragged him with her.

Jilly turned to Joe. 'How about it? I could do with a quickie after watching all that.'

Joe knew Jilly was a blatant exhibitionist and wasn't surprised she'd taken up the challenge. He was doubtful about performing in public but she urged him on. It was the mask that clinched it. He wasn't worried about not getting it up. Jilly was a dabhand at that. The crowd applauded as the two couples climbed onto stage.

Two minutes later Jilly was stark naked at the front of the stage, posing boldly for her audience. She stood in wild abandon with her long legs parted, her stomach drawn in, and her luscious, perfectly shaped boobs thrust out towards an appreciative audience. By forcing her shoulders back she'd made certain that those delectable orbs were shown to their best advantage and she'd surreptitiously pinched her nipples to bring them up stiff and proud. She completed her wild pose by raising her arms and stroking her long golden hair behind her head. She was Cleopatra stepping from the bath, Salome after her dance, Aphrodite rising from the sea. The other girl stood beside her showing her wares more openly and she was beautiful: but Jilly was truly magnificent.

The two men were lying on comfortable, padded benches and both were glad to be staring at the ceiling. When Jilly approached to jerk off his trousers and shorts Joe knew she was lost to the crowd. Her innate exhibitionism had taken control. She was there to satisfy her own sexual wants and that there was an audience watching her every movement only served to make her behaviour even more brazen.

She mounted him as she might mount a horse and, standing astride his thighs facing her audience, lowered herself until she had impaled her body on his ramrod. Joe glanced towards the other couple who were already copulating as if their lives depended on it. The girl had her back to the audience so her buttocks rose and fell to reveal the ring of her quim wrapped around the man's thick penis.

Jilly was facing her audience, preferring to show off her exquisite body, and Joe could tell by the way she was urgently plunging up and down on his charger that her performance was more than an act.

The applause of the crowd had turned Jilly into a frenzied whore. Her exhibitionist streak was so strong that she was giving him the fuck of all time. He could hold back no longer and, reaching up, he squeezed her sumptuous breasts as he ejaculated inside her. And as she bemoaned the passing of her pleasure the audience sighed with her.

Hank bent towards Mandy and whispered in her ear. 'How'd you fancy having your bottom smacked on stage?'

Mandy blushed. For a second a little devil danced inside her. It told her how much she'd enjoy sharing her little kink with others, but she ignored it.

'No,' she replied, 'I don't think so. Let's leave it until later. In private.'

Prince Khaneme's limo arrived at Sonia's hotel just after noon and she was surprised to see him in western dress. He appeared to have lost weight: either that or the expensive Savile Row suit had been cleverly cut to conceal his huge bulk. He looked presentable, even handsome. He was accompanied by his beautiful Ethiopian wife, dressed in an expensive creation from a top Parisian couturier. That he had her with him was surprise enough yet, even when surrounded by an inquisitive press, they looked and acted as if it was usual for them to be out in public together. It was the first time the Prince had been to a racecourse and he insisted Sonia stay with him once he stepped outside his luxurious box. Iskmak was his only representative of the afternoon and by the time the Arc was due to be run, he was confident of his surroundings.

In the parade ring he stood with his wife and Sonia and one extra-large bodyguard, waiting for Peggy-Sue to join them. She was the first jockey to walk into the paddock and looked stunning in the Prince's bright silks and a pair of extra-tight riding britches. She seemed so petite and feminine and, after her win on Misty Garnett the previous afternoon, she was already the darling of the French racing press.

Crowds of enthusiastic spectators lined the paddock to get a glimpse of the famous owners and jockeys, jostling for places with professional punters who were there to see the thoroughbreds. Longchamp was vibrant and almost bursting at the seams. The Bois de Boulogne had been one vast traffic jam before the races, and would be worse afterwards when thousands of vehicles fought their way back into the city centre.

'Is my horse going to win, Peggy-Sue?' asked the Prince.

'You aren't alone in wanting to know the answer to that, sir.'

'And so what's your opinion?'

'I shall be trying my best, sir.'

'Your best will be expected, Miss Rhyma.'

'Be assured I shall give it, sir.'

He smiled. 'You're a diplomatic young woman. I must see more of you.'

Both Peggy-Sue and Sonia knew what that meant.

His smile was pleasant, but the look that accompanied it stripped the clothes from her back. Peggy-Sue shivered. She felt as if she was standing naked before him, and she realised that if she was to continue to be his jockey she'd have to grant him the same favours as Sonia and Jilly already had. She pondered idly on what it would be like to have this giant of a man spread over her. She pulled herself together quickly, as the time for the jockeys to mount arrived. Sonia gave her a leg up and patted the horse's rump fondly.

'Just remember to stay up with the pace. I want you in the first half dozen when you come off that penultimate bend.'

Peggy-Sue grinned. 'We've been over the race and how I'm going to ride it a hundred times.'

'I know, Peggy, but I'm nervous. Nothing must go wrong.'

'Okay, Sonia. I'll be up there.'

'Good luck.'

Sonia walked the temperamental filly out onto the course, and smiled at Tess when they released the horse to send her on the way to the start.

'Oh Lord, I hope she gives a good account of herself, Tess.'

'She will, Mrs Beechly. She's as fit as a flea.'

Peggy-Sue cantered the filly past the vast grandstands to the mile-and-a-half start where she went over the coming race in her mind. After the race at York she was absolutely certain Iskmak would stay further. She was convinced the filly needed a mile and a half to bring out her best, and it was her conviction that had led to the filly being entered in the Arc. She had been drawn unfavourably on the outside but the plan was to stay up with the pace the whole way. The Arc was usually a rough race, with a host of hard luck stories afterwards about horses that had been bumped or boxed or struck into – and Iskmak was too temperamental to be in the thick of it.

There were twenty runners, and Peggy-Sue was familiar with all the jocks' faces, although she didn't know several of the Frenchmen very well. Surprisingly, she found some of them even more chauvinistic than the British and Australians. Of the twenty runners, six were from Britain, two from Ireland, one from Germany and one from Italy.

All the horses went in quietly for the French handlers, and when the stalls flew open Peggy-Sue kicked Iskmak into action. The filly didn't like the stalls and came out like a greyhound. Peggy-Sue allowed her to spring into the lead before taking a hold on her head to settle her into fourth place.

Throughout the race the filly had no trouble holding her place and Peggy-Sue sat quietly, letting the horse lob along within herself. It gave her a warm confident feeling that the filly was going so easily and seemed happy to be up with the leaders. As the race hotted up around the penultimate bend she heard the shouts and curses of jocks who had found themselves buried in the pack as they jostled for position. She smiled. She was glad to be out of it. She allowed the filly to run wide around the final bend and, balancing her, let out a notch so she would go up to the leaders.

All the horses left in contention were now racing seriously. The Italian horse had crept up on her inside, but was already under pressure and going nowhere. In the centre of the field she saw Bart's horse take the lead with two French horses in pursuit. She could feel her filly was still full of running and suddenly she realised she could win this race. There would be no truck with riding for a place: she was going to win or bust.

From the corner of her eye she saw the furlong pole flash by. Ahead of her were three horses but they were labouring. She knew she could take them when she pleased. The danger would be from behind. She glanced towards the rail to see a big chestnut head breathing fire and finishing like a train. There was her danger. She changed her hands and pushed the button. She was brim-full of a confidence that told her Iskmak would last home. The filly put her head down and ran as straight as a gunbarrel to the line to win by three parts of a length. Afterwards Peggy-Sue knew nothing would have lived with Iskmak that afternoon. The filly had run like the proverbial wind.

The Brits in the crowd went mad. Jilly and Mandy and the Ladd twins had shouted themselves hoarse, and Sonia had tears rolling down her cheeks. Only the Prince had watched dispassionately but he was wreathed in smiles. The press had a field day. Prince Khaneme, a racing recluse, was there to accept the prize and be photographed. A female jockey had ridden the winner for the first time and the trainer was the first British woman to train the winner. It was all marvellous fare and guaranteed to sell newspapers. They took photos of everything that moved and a lot that didn't. Sonia and Peggy-Sue had both made their names. They had two winners at Longchamp, one of which was the Arc de Triomphe, and the afternoon wasn't yet over. Crazy Face was yet to run.

Everybody agreed that the Prix Abbay over five furlongs was a three-horse race. Only the British winner of the July Cup, the Irish winner of the King's Stand, and Crazy Face were considered likely winners. After her win in the Arc, Peggy-Sue was full of confidence, and Crazy Face was at his arrogant best. He came out of the stalls like a runaway train: Peggy-Sue just sat on him and went along for the ride. It was a steering job. The big colt took ten lengths out of the field in the first furlong and nothing got any closer as he shot across the line. The Ladd twins hugged each other and kissed any female who got within arm's length, and many did. Sonia and Peggy-Sue were photographed time and time again. Three winners during the Arc meeting. It was the stuff that dreams are made of.

Next day the racing papers pictured Sonia and

Peggy-Sue kissing Iskmak's big brown nose with the heading 'Heroine three'. Another had Iskmak and Misk Garnett and Crazy Face under a similar banner, while the popular tabloids conjured up wilder and more fanciful headlines about British heroines capturing Paris. Sonia knew her reputation had been made. The hullabaloo would die down, but her name would remain in the record books. She'd proved she could train thoroughbreds to win the most prestigious races. On that Sunday in Paris in early October she'd arrived as a trainer of racehorses.

Chapter 12

That eventful night when Sonia finally returned to her hotel after the celebrations, a note awaited her. It was from Prince Khaneme, who requested her presence at his hotel the following morning.

She got there just after noon, having first supervised the loading of her three superstars onto the plane home. She knew there would be a party that evening at The Billings and wanted to be with her stable staff, so she hoped the Prince wouldn't keep her too long. She noticed all his luggage had been packed as she was shown into his room by his Ethiopian wife. He indicated that they should both sit.

'This trip to Paris was the idea of my advisers. I can't say I cared for their idea.'

'You haven't enjoyed yourself, sir?' said Sonia incredulously.

'I didn't say that. I said I didn't want to come.'

'But Iskmak changed your mind?'

He smiled. 'She's a lovely filly. I enjoyed the race. Thank you.'

Sonia smiled back. 'It's always great to win, sir.'

He laughed. 'I didn't realise it could be so enjoyable.'

Sonia became a trifle impatient with small talk. 'Why do you want to see me, sir?' she asked.

'I was much taken with Longchamp and the racing scene. I have decided that I shall attend more often.'

'Will you come to England?'

'That, Mrs Beechly, is why I sent for you. It would be pleasant to attend the Derby next year. Have I a horse capable of winning?'

'I'm afraid not, sir. The two-year olds you sent me are not up to that standard.'

'Could you get me one?'

'I could possibly buy one entered in the race, but if it had a realistic chance it wouldn't be for sale.'

'Buy me one, Sonia, I'd like to be represented. And look around for a colt good enough to win the following year's race.'

She laughed. 'I'll try, sir.'

'Of course you will, and as money's no object you might succeed.'

'I hope so, sir.'

She couldn't help but notice that his wife's slender fingers were creeping towards the Prince's crotch. She tried to keep her eyes away but the erotic fluttering of those sensual black fingers as they fished out his slumbering penis was spellbinding. Nor was it sleeping for long for those busy fingers soon had it as stiff as an iron bar. The Prince continued in a tone of voice that denied anything was happening.

'Furthermore, I have a mind to increase the number of horses I have in training with you.'

'Thank you, sir.'

'How many more shall we say?'

'It's really up to you, sir.'

His wife was at his feet teasing his trousers down his legs, and when he was free of them she stood watching Sonia.

'Perhaps you should strike a bargain, Mrs Beechly?' she said quietly.

'How?'

'Over the table, perhaps?'

Sonia immediately saw what was wanted. After her success at the weekend she had promised herself the days of granting sexual favours to further her career were over. Now here she was, the very next day, considering taking off her knickers for the first owner who promised her a couple more horses. It was wrong. She'd get a reputation if she wasn't careful.

Oh, what the hell, she thought, as she unzipped her skirt and walked towards the table . . .

A selection of Erotica from Headline

SCANDAL IN PARADISE	Anonymous	£4.99	☐
UNDER ORDERS	Nick Aymes	£4.99	☐
RECKLESS LIAISONS	Anonymous	£4.99	☐
GROUPIES II	Johnny Angelo	£4.99	☐
TOTAL ABANDON	Anonymous	£4.99	☐
AMOUR ENCORE	Marie-Claire Villefranche	£4.99	☐
COMPULSION	Maria Caprio	£4.99	☐
INDECENT	Felice Ash	£4.99	☐
AMATEUR DAYS	Becky Bell	£4.99	☐
EROS IN SPRINGTIME	Anonymous	£4.99	☐
GOOD VIBRATIONS	Jeff Charles	£4.99	☐
CITIZEN JULIETTE	Louise Aragon	£4.99	☐

All Headline books are available at your local bookshop or newsagent, or can be ordered direct from the publisher. Just tick the titles you want and fill in the form below. Prices and availability subject to change without notice.

Headline Book Publishing, Cash Sales Department, Bookpoint, 39 Milton Park, Abingdon, OXON, OX14 4TD, UK. If you have a credit card you may order by telephone – 0235 400400.

Please enclose a cheque or postal order made payable to Bookpoint Ltd to the value of the cover price and allow the following for postage and packing:
UK & BFPO: £1.00 for the first book, 50p for the second book and 30p for each additional book ordered up to a maximum charge of £3.00.
OVERSEAS & EIRE: £2.00 for the first book, £1.00 for the second book and 50p for each additional book.

Name ....

Address ....

....

....

If you would prefer to pay by credit card, please complete:
Please debit my Visa/Access/Diner's Card/American Express (delete as applicable) card no:

Signature .... Expiry Date ....